49

Keith Ablow received his degree from Johns Hopkins and completed his psychiatry residency at New England Medical Centre. A practising psychiatrist with a specialty in forensics, he has written several works of non-fiction. He lives in Boston, USA. *Denial* is his first novel.

DENIAL

A NOVEL

KEITH ABLOW

PIATKUS

Copyright © 1997 by Keith Ablow

First published in Great Britain in 1998 by
Judy Piatkus (Publishers) Ltd of
5 Windmill Street, London W1

This edition published 1998

**The moral right of the author
has been asserted**

A catalogue record for this book
is available from the British Library

ISBN 0 7499 3070 5

Book design by Fearn Cutler

Printed and bound in Great Britain by
Mackays of Chatham PLC

For Pat Hass, my friend and editor

ACKNOWLEDGMENTS

Whatever a reader might take from the pages that follow is due in large measure to the guidance and enouragement given me by Dan Frank, Pat Hass, Claudine O'Hearn and Beth Vesel.

One

I shot up, sweat dripping down my face. I searched the darkness for my father and panicked at a glint of light off his silver belt buckle. I turned to flee, but felt his fingers wrap around my forearm, dragging me back where I was desperate not to go. I struggled, but weakly, knowing I would lose, until the ringing of my bedside telephone pulled me awake.

Kathy was tugging on my arm. "C'mon, get it."

I fumbled for the receiver. "Clevenger," I gasped.

"Frank, Emma Hancock. Sorry I woke you up."

"Don't be." I collapsed back on the mattress. I was breathing in gusts. The pillow was soaked with sweat. It felt cold against my neck. "Less running."

"Less what?"

I ground the heel of my hand into my eyes. "I was getting up to go out for a jog."

"A little six A.M. workout, huh? Good for the soul."

"Right. You didn't call this early to discuss my soul."

"I'm afraid not. We have another case for you—a homeless man who killed a young woman in the woods behind Stonehill Hospital."

"And?"

"And what?"

"You're calling me, Emma. What's the crazy part?"

"He cut off her breasts. Deep, down to the ribs. Butchered her. He called us from a pay phone screaming like a maniac that he'd killed a virgin, then waited with the body until we met him. When we got there, he was covered with her blood."

Part of me wanted to hang up before I heard any more. It hadn't been a month since my last murder, and that one had been bad enough to end six months of sobriety for me. I'd given some thought to quitting forensics and reopening my psychotherapy practice, but I knew I was in no condition to heal anyone. Maybe I never had been. "What do you know about him?" I asked.

"I know he's a loon. That's all. We found a full, two-year-old bottle of Thorazine on him when we picked him up. And he says his name is—get this—William Westmoreland. The general. Another advertisement for head-shrinking, huh Frank?"

I let that go. Homicide detectives like Hancock have to keep their distance from psychiatry. Otherwise they might start wondering why they hang around killers. They might start fantasizing about crossing the line. "So what's the rush?"

"The rush is I need your stamp of approval that he's sane—at least sane enough to give us a statement. He says he wants to confess; I don't need him thinking it over too long."

"Confess to what?"

"Huh?"

"He wants to confess to what?"

"Are you awake? I just told you I have a woman in the morgue with craters where her breasts are supposed to be."

"Who was she?"

"She didn't have ID on her, Frank. She was naked. OK? When can you make it down here?"

"Give me two hours." I hung up the phone, switched on the lamp on the nightstand and lay back down on my sweaty pillow, waiting for inspiration to get up.

"Leaving me for a dead person again?" Kathy whispered. She rolled flush to me, still half-asleep, and rested her head on my chest.

"I said a couple of hours."

"Good," she smiled. She brushed the sheet off of her so I could see her naked body, tan everywhere except the creamy skin of her bottom.

"Another goddamn murder. I don't know if I can—"

"Shhh." She held a finger to her lips, then slithered down the mattress and drew her tongue along the shaft of my penis.

"I—"

She took the head in her mouth and bit down playfully.

Usually, we'd get woken up by the Stonehill Hospital obstetrical service calling for Kathy in the middle of the night, and I'd try to get off before *she* left. I'd get hard picturing Kathy in the delivery suite with a patient spread-eagled in front of her crying out in pain. But the idea of having sex just before going to see a corpse was getting me stiff, too. I grabbed a fistful of Kathy's long blond hair and thrust myself deeper, into her throat.

•   •   •

Just as I had on thousands of mornings, I watched the whole world change in the ten-minute drive to Lynn from my Victorian perched over Marblehead's Preston Beach. The houses along the water slowly shed awnings and brass numbers, then fresh paint, then windows. My tires stopped gliding along the road and started dropping into potholes. Crossing the Lynn line, I knew in advance to press the Rover's air-recirculation button to keep out the stench wafting from a leaky sewer pipe that had spawned a mile of tenacious, foul algae. I slipped the B-52's into the CD player, snorted a blast of cocaine from the vial I keep in the glove compartment and turned up the volume.

I took the first exit off Lynn Shore Drive, heading away from the water and onto Union Street, ten blocks of boarded-up storefronts, graffitied walls and abandoned cars. The tension melted out of my neck and shoulders. My breathing slowed. For as long as I can remember, I have been soothed by squalor, one symptom of having grown up in Lynn as it decayed.

Almost at the end of Union I pulled over in front of the morgue. Paulson Levitsky, the city pathologist, had graduated Tufts Medical School with me in 1981. I wasn't buddy-buddy with him while we were there, but the whole class had known how skilled he was at dissecting his cadaver, which he had named U. B. Dead. The muscles had been meticulously separated from one another, with pristine red and green and violet tags labeling each point of origin and insertion. The organs looked exactly like their pictures in *Gray's Anatomy*. My stiff, Abra Cadaver, had looked like hash by the time I'd gotten done with her.

"Ha, ho, look who's here," Levitsky shouted when I walked into the autopsy suite. "I knew I'd see *you* when I saw *her*." He pointed down at a gray body lying on a gleaming stainless steel table. Kevin Malloy, a Lynn cop I'd once reported for brutality, was observing the autopsy.

"It's a job," I said. "A strange job, but a job." I smiled when I noticed Levitsky's lab coat was spotless despite the work he was doing. Not a hair on his head was out of place. I walked over to the table. The smell of death—a combination of feces, urine and pooled blood—blanketed me.

"She was hot, don't you think?" Malloy winked.

I just stared at her.

"I mean, when she had tits," Malloy said.

Levitsky put a hand on my shoulder. "It's one of the worst wounds I've seen, Frank. And I've been at this a long time."

"Frankenstein's going soft on us," Malloy said. His dry, cracked lips smiled around his yellowed teeth. "You know, he feels for people—people who can fork over a hundred bucks an hour."

"Why don't you have some respect?" Levitsky seethed.

I felt light-headed.

"She ain't gonna tell you her problems, Doc, no matter how long you wait." Malloy laughed, his fat body jiggling.

"Shut the fuck up!" Levitsky said.

I grabbed the side of the dissecting table to steady myself. "I know her," I said. All I could hear for a while was the hum of fluorescent bulbs.

"You *know* her?" Malloy asked finally.

I was still staring at the haphazard holes on either side of her chest. Then, although I tried not to, I let my eyes drift to her crotch. It was shaved clean. "Sarah Johnston. She's a psychiatric nurse at Stonehill Hospital. The locked unit."

Malloy slammed his fist into his open palm. "That's pay dirt. Ten to one, our General Westmoreland was treated there."

"She's a friend of Kathy's," I said.

"I'm sorry you walked into it," Levitsky said. "Why don't we have somebody call Chuck Sloan? I hear he's taking forensic cases now."

"No. I want it."

"Are you sure?" Levitsky asked.

I dragged my eyes away from Sarah and turned to him. "I'm staying on this case."

"You'll tell me if you change your mind . . ."

I nodded.

"OK, then. Let me get you caught up." Levitsky produced a telescoping stainless steel pointer from his lab coat pocket, pulled it crisply to its full length and began speaking loudly for the microphone hanging over the table. "Surface inspection of the wounds shows they were caused by a sharp, straight edge, most likely of a pocket knife, or even of a razor blade. There are many short lacerations at multiple levels, indicating the blade was not long enough to penetrate deeply. But each laceration is straight and clean, not jagged." He aimed the pointer at me. "You know we don't have the breasts. They're missing."

"Westmoreland must have hidden them," Malloy said. "Or eaten them."

"Eaten them?" I said. "Either you're going to bad movies or you're still enraged about being bottle-fed."

"Give it a rest," Malloy said. "I don't have time for your psychobabble."

"How about the murder weapon? Did you have time to find that?"

"Not yet. He probably buried that, too."

"Maybe he ate it."

Levitsky sliced the pointer through the air between us. His face screamed we were violating the sanctity of his workplace. "You are guests in this laboratory, at my discretion," he said. He waited a few seconds, then pointed to the crown of Sarah's head. "There is a single depressed skull fracture, of the kind made by a blunt object, which is the likely cause of death." He began to walk slowly around the table. "Multiple skin contusions are present on the dorsal surfaces of the forearms, which may indicate the victim had attempted to ward off blows. There are parallel spotty surface bruises on the arms and shoulders of the type caused by a powerful grip." He stopped at the foot of the table and put the tip of the pointer between Sarah's legs. "The genitals had already been shaved when the body was presented for autopsy. There is evidence of recent sexual intercourse, with semen recovered from the vaginal orifice and vault," he said. He paused. "But there is not evidence of forced vaginal entry." He walked to the instrument tray at the side of the table and picked up an oversized iron scissors. "It gets a little messy from here, gentlemen," he said. "You can stay or you can go. I'm not sure how much more we're going to learn on the inside, but everything will be in my report."

"I've seen enough," I said. I didn't care to see Sarah filleted, and I needed another blast from my vial. "I'm headed over to see Westmoreland."

"I'll stay," Malloy said.

Levitsky squinted at him. "You have a special interest in pathology?"

"In *evidence*."

"Right." Levitsky looked at me and rolled his eyes. "Please tell Kathy I'm sorry about her friend."

"I'll do that." I walked to the door, but stopped and turned around. "By the way, Kevin, it's one-eighty," I said.

"What's one-eighty? What are you talking about?"

"My time. One-eighty an hour. I don't want to get the reputation of giving it away cheap, you know?" Then I walked out.

• • •

I grabbed the vial out of my glove compartment, sprinkled some coke onto a Visa Gold card and snorted it. Then I took another little pinch and spread it over my gums. They went numb a few seconds later, and my anxiety died down a minute after that. I looked into the mirror, tied my hair back in a ponytail and started for the station.

I dreaded breaking the news to Kathy. She had met Sarah a year earlier, when a new mother on Stonehill's obstetrical service had become severely depressed and had to be transferred to the psychiatry unit. The two of them had hit it off immediately. They were both bright and attractive, thirty, and moving in with older men who had sworn off marriage. I was Kathy's problem. Sarah's was Ben Carlson, Stonehill's chief of cardiothoracic surgery. The four of us had begun to spend most of our free time together, until, just a few months later, Carlson abruptly moved on—alone—to a teaching position at the University of Texas.

There was another reason I feared Kathy would take the news especially hard: She had lost her baby sister in a house fire. The memory of that childhood tragedy had never really left her and seemed to intensify with any loss she suffered as an adult.

I pressed the car phone's AUTODIAL button.

"Hello," Kathy answered.

"It's me."

"Too bad you aren't here. I just jumped out of the shower."

I pictured her all wet, sitting on the side of the bed. "Kathy, I have bad news. Very bad news."

"You're going to try to make dinner again tonight."

"I'm serious." I took a deep breath. "It's about the murder."

"Isn't murder always bad news?"

I didn't respond.

"Are you there?"

I pulled the car over to the side of the road. "It's worse when you know the victim," I said.

Silence. "You know the victim?"

"We both do." I didn't know how else to play it. "The woman who was killed was Sarah Johnston," I said.

"No. . . . No, that can't be."

Denial, even fleeting denial, is a remarkable thing. "It was Sarah," I assured her. "I saw her. Sarah's gone."

"My God," she gasped. "What happened?"

"We don't know exactly. I'm on my way to the station now to find out more." I could hear her sobbing. "Will you be OK?"

"I just can't believe it."

"There are bound to be rumors at work. I wanted to tell you first."

"When will I see you?"

"I'll stop by the hospital after the station."

"Promise."

"I promise."

I hung up and watched the cars speeding by. What would it be like, I wondered, to get a call that Kathy had been murdered? I closed my eyes and pictured her with her breasts hacked out of her. But I shook that image quickly out of my mind and pushed the accelerator to the floor.

◆   ◆   ◆

By the time I got to the police station around 10 A.M., Emma Hancock had phoned Sarah's father in San Francisco. "I'll never get used to telling the family, no matter how many times I do it," she said. She was sitting at her metal desk, clicking the long red nails of her thumb and forefinger against one another. "Here's a man who lost his wife two years ago and now his only child's dead. He's crying to me how he was about to come visit because they hadn't seen each other for a year and how maybe she'd still be alive if he'd come sooner. What do you say to someone who's lost most of what he cares about in the world? What do I know about that?"

That was a tough question. Hancock had dedicated herself

wholly to her job, becoming the first female police captain in the state. Rumor had it she was about to be named commissioner. Past fifty, her short brown hair going gray, she had no husband, no children and no apparent interests other than fund-raising for her church. "You know that you don't know," I said. "It's hard to go wrong from there."

"Yes, well . . . you're a big help, Dr. Freud. I feel so much better now." She shook her head. "Here's something else I can't figure: The monster locked up back there is all set to confess to murder any time we're ready, but he won't indulge me with his real name. He's still General William C. Westmoreland."

"Maybe he'd rather be known for genocide than be known for who he is," I said.

"Profound. You've got a one-liner for everything." Hancock stood up and started to walk toward the cell block, then turned and looked me directly in the eyes. She is a meaty, powerful woman who stands five feet six, but seems to occupy more than her physical space. When she grabbed my shoulder, it hurt. "Nobody around here has forgotten the Prescott case. I keep calling you in because I don't think you were entirely to blame. And because you've been reasonable since then. But I'm out on a limb every single time I use you."

Marcus Prescott was one of my first forensic cases, a thirty-two-year-old attorney who had raped a Lynn Classical High cheerleader. When Prescott had pled insanity, claiming he had no memory of the attack, I had testified that his symptoms were consistent with multiple personality disorder. He had been found innocent and committed to Bridgewater State Hospital. After four years of treatment the Bridgewater team released him, and he tracked the girl down at Brown University, raped her again and strangled her.

"That was a long time ago," I said.

"A young woman died."

My jaws tightened. "So what's the real reason you keep calling me in, Emma? You enjoy having me on the hook?"

"I think everyone deserves a second chance. We're all sinners, after all."

I shook my head. "Let's not bullshit one another. Prescott has nothing to do with this case. The truth is, you don't need a bleeding-heart liberal shrink like me getting you the wrong headlines. Not when you're a few months from the commissioner's job."

"Your mouth to God's ears."

"You know, for my part, I'd like to see you get that promotion. I really would. I think it could be good for both of us. Even the city. But I don't think God gives a flying fuck either way."

Hancock tightened her grip. "Do not curse." She paused for emphasis, then smiled. "One hand washes the other," she said. "I've always made sure your invoices are paid right on time. And nobody watches the clock."

"*I* watch the clock."

"Time flies." She winked and let go of my shoulder. "I'll have Zangota let you in to visit the general."

Angel Zangota, a Lynn cop new to the job, took me to Westmoreland's cell. I smelled him before I saw him. He was sitting cross-legged in front of his cot, wearing too many layers of soiled clothing. When the door was unlocked, he struggled to his feet and shuffled to the back wall. He looked about forty-five, starvation thin, with matted salt-and-pepper hair and deeply set steel blue eyes.

Zangota put his hand on his gun as he opened the door. "You want me in there with you?" he asked.

I doubted I'd get anything out of Westmoreland in front of a uniformed officer. "Down the hall is alright," I said. Zangota left, and I walked in and stood against one of the side walls; my first rule is to never be the barrier between a prisoner and an exit. Westmoreland glanced at me, then muttered something. I noticed his eyes dart to an empty corner of the room a few times. "You see something over there that bothers you?" I asked.

He looked me over head to toe.

I crouched down and sat against the wall to let him know I intended to stay a while. "The police tell me your name is Westmore-land."

"William C. Westmoreland, born 1914," he announced.

"You were in Vietnam?"

He stayed silent for a while, then chuckled to himself. "I killed there."

I nodded.

"Priest?"

I was wearing a black turtleneck jersey. "No. Psychiatrist."

"Same thing," he said evenly. He sat slowly down. His eyes flicked back to the corner of the room and lingered there. "I confess, Father. I failed."

"Failed?"

"God's test. I violated his design."

"How?"

"By design."

Schizophrenics use words as shields against meaning. I wanted to get past the defense. "What did you do that violated God's design?"

"I violated her."

"In what way?"

He picked at his sleeve as if something was stuck to it. "In way. Out way. Every way."

I decided to try another approach. "Where is the knife?" I asked.

Westmoreland looked me directly in the eyes for the first time. "There is no knife," he said. "Yet there is no life."

Rhyming is another way schizophrenics block communication. "Did you hide the knife?" I persisted.

His eyes darted away, this time to the ceiling over my head, then focused on mine again. He struggled to his feet and took a few halting steps toward me. I was ready to get up myself when he stopped. "She could have been my wife!" he screamed. "But I took her life with this knife!" He started to unbutton his military-style pants.

I jumped up, worried the police hadn't searched him thoroughly for weapons.

Westmoreland dropped his pants and grabbed his penis. "I killed her with my cock!" he yelled. "My cock is a rock!" Then he threw himself at me, his hands outstretched toward my neck.

I took the full impact of his body with one shoulder, managed to get hold of his hair, and brought him down face first into the concrete floor. Blood poured out of his nose and lip. I heard Zangota running down the hall. I put my mouth close to Westmoreland's ear. "I'm sorry," I whispered. "You scared me." Seconds later Zangota had cuffed him, and I was on my way to Emma Hancock's office.

She was cleaning her revolver when I walked in the door. "Tell me you and I aren't going to have a problem," she said without looking up. "He's rational enough to confess, right?"

"You know I wouldn't disagree just to disagree," I said.

"Then don't."

"He exposed himself and attacked me."

She squinted into one chamber, then blew into it. "Well, you aren't exactly my cup of tea, but I can see why he might take a liking to you."

"He's hallucinating."

Hancock looked up from the gun and shook her head slowly. "Come now, Francis. We're talking open-and-shut. He was covered with her blood." She snapped the barrel shut and tossed the gun in her desk drawer. "Give me a break."

"If it was close, I would. You know that. But this guy isn't making any sense."

"You're really gonna soak me?" She threw up her hands. "Why should I care? Put in for five hours." She shrugged. "I don't really mind if you bill for ten, provided you remember the favor come fund-raising time."

I thought about taking her up on the ten hours. I'd had a run of bad luck at the track and that, combined with coke at a hundred a gram, had me scrambling for my mortgage payment. But something Levitsky said at the morgue had stuck in my mind. "I can't do it," I said. "Not yet."

"I'm sorry to hear that. I did want to use you for this case. But I see that I can't."

"You wouldn't change your expert after one interview with the accused. The defense will have a field day with it in court."

"Listen to me. This savage may see visions or hear voices or both. I don't deny that. But he knew he was doing wrong when he sliced that girl up. He knew he was breaking the law. He even knew enough to call the authorities afterwards. He felt guilty because he *is* guilty."

"Some people feel guilty because of what they think, not what they do. You should know that; the Catholic Church is full of them."

She stiffened. "I've warned you before: Do not denigrate the Lord in this office." Then she relaxed. "Malloy tells me you knew the victim."

"She was a friend of Kathy's."

"So I have the right to remove you. You're personally involved."

"Look, all I'm asking is that you let me put him back on some Thorazine and interview him again tomorrow. Maybe he'll be more rational."

"No thank you."

"Who you gonna get, Chuck Sloan? He's slightly to the left of Lenin. George Schwartz would send this guy to the hospital because he's dressed funny."

"I can only keep him seventy-two hours on suspected murder without either a confession or the court's permission. And you know Judge Katzenstein will just direct-deposit our hacker to Bridgewater State Hospital. I'm not going to let that happen."

"Give me two days."

"Why should I?"

"Because," I said, "you know there are things you don't know."

The furrows in Hancock's brow deepened. She started clicking her nails again. I imagined her struggling in vain to turn back the moral residue of the twelve years she'd spent at Lynn's Sacred Heart School for Girls. She shook her head, then finally looked at me. "You've got thirty-six hours."

Two

I made it to the hospital just after 1 P.M. I took the stairs to Kathy's office in the Ob-Gyn Department, but she had left to start a delivery. That gave me about an hour free, and I wanted to use it. I headed to medical records.

The whole department was really a long room that looked like an overstuffed filing-cabinet drawer. Ray, a tiny black man who had run the place for thirty years or so, was sorting through the mound of loose papers that always covered his desk. I interrupted to ask if he would check for any record of Westmoreland being treated at Stonehill.

He inspected me over his half-glasses. "What did that man do?"

"Who said he did anything?"

"An Officer Malloy called so I'd hold that chart for him. He's coming here with a subpoena."

"So Westmoreland *was* treated here."

"It would be mighty unusual to have a chart without ever being a patient, even with me doing the filing," he said dryly.

"Can I have it?"

He went back to searching through his papers. "Tell me why he's so special."

"He may have killed somebody."

He peeked over his glasses again. "That's not special. Not these days. Not in Lynn."

I felt like blurting out that he had cut Sarah Johnston's breasts off. But I settled myself down. "Ray," I said, "I need that chart."

"I already told you: The police are coming for it."

"Well they haven't picked it up yet, have they?"

"No, but . . ."

"I only need fifteen minutes with it."

He looked at me doubtfully. "You've got a reputation with me, Doc. Late records. Lost records. Coffee spilled all over records. Cigarette burns through records."

"I'll read it right here. You can watch me."

"You really think I got nothing more important to do? Those nurses chasing after you finally gone straight to your head. I hear 'em in the cafeteria. 'Hair like a rock star.' 'Shoulders like a football player.' To listen to them, ain't no part of you looks like a psychiatrist." He pulled the chart out from under his desk and handed it over. "Don't go far with it," he warned.

"You're a ray of sunshine."

"Don't press your luck."

I took the chart to a sitting area just across from his office and began to read through it. The admitting psychiatrist's initial note was dated December 11, 1992:

IDENTIFYING DATA: *The patient is a middle-aged male with no known address who was brought to the emergency room by the police and then admitted to the locked psychiatric unit. He gave his name as General William C. Westmoreland.*

HISTORY OF PRESENT ILLNESS: *According to police, Mr. "Westmoreland" stole a marble bust of the Madonna from the altar of the Church of Angels during Sunday services today. He was found by officers at the Lynn Common seated on a park bench embracing it. On direct questioning he informed them that he was in love with the statue, intended to bring it to life and planned to marry it.*

On admission, the patient repeated his belief that he has the power to "breathe life into" the Madonna. He was extremely upset that the carving had been taken from him. His affect alternated between rage and despondency. At several points during our interview he broke into tears.

Mr. Westmoreland did not respond to questions about his perceptions, but seemed preoccupied with internal stimuli. It is likely that he is experiencing both auditory and visual hallucinations.

The patient denied homicidal ideation but remained mute when questioned about suicidal thoughts.

Blood and urine toxic screens for alcohol and illicit drugs were negative.

The fact that the patient has adopted the name of a well-known general would suggest that he is a veteran of the conflict in Vietnam, but he does not confirm this. Nor does he respond to questions about his Social Security number, last address or actual family name.

PAST PSYCHIATRIC HISTORY: *Unknown. The patient does, however, have a series of horizontal scars on his left wrist suggesting a past suicide attempt.*

PAST MEDICAL HISTORY: *Unknown.*

ASSESSMENT AND PLAN: *The patient clearly suffers from a psychotic condition that may prove to be chronic paranoid schizophrenia or a delusional depression. In either case the use of antipsychotic medications is indicated and will be initiated. Antidepressant medication will be considered. We will continue to monitor Mr. Westmoreland's safety carefully, given his refusal to answer questions related to suicidality.*

> *Tom Klein, M.D.*
> *Attending Psychiatrist*
> *Stonehill 3*

According to the daily progress notes on the chart, Westmoreland had refused to take any of the medications prescribed for him. Dr. Klein had filed a substituted judgment motion with the Lynn District Court and gotten permission to inject him three times a day with an intramuscular preparation of Thorazine.

Westmoreland had fought against the injections for days, spending as long as six hours at a stretch in a seclusion room, tied down in four-point restraints. But within a week Klein's notes described him as "greatly improved"; first he willingly accepted the shots, then he agreed to take his medicine by mouth. Ten days after being admitted, he assured the treatment team he had no feelings whatsoever for the statue. He was discharged to the Lynn Shelter with a supply of Thorazine and an outpatient appointment at a local clinic. The unused, two-year-old bottle of Thorazine found on him at the crime scene probably meant he'd never followed up.

I smirked, thinking about the "dramatic ten-day recovery" from a "paranoid schizophrenic reaction" that Klein had documented in Westmoreland's discharge summary. There was a serious flaw in his reasoning: Thorazine takes about three weeks to stop psychotic thinking.

I was suddenly aware of someone standing over me. I looked up and saw Kevin Malloy.

"The pieces do seem to fit together, don't they?" he taunted. "Her blood all over him. Him being a patient where she worked. And—this just in from your buddy Levitsky: Sperm from someone with Westmoreland's blood type was inside her. But, you know, you can never be too careful with a killer's rights. Maybe we should wait to take a confession until someone can show us a fucking videotape of him cutting her up."

I got to my feet, moved within a foot of him and looked straight into his black eyes. "You'd like to watch a snuff film like that, wouldn't you? I can tell. You'd enjoy the panic in a woman's face the moment she realizes her life is about to be drained, that she's looking into the last face she'll ever see. You dream about crossing the line."

He stared at me for a few seconds. "You don't know jack shit about me," he said.

I handed him the chart. "You can only hope," I said, then walked past him.

•   •   •

I found Kathy in the oversized closet that passes for the doctor's on-call room. She was wearing scrubs, sitting on the bed writing out her obstetrical note. "Seven pounds ten ounces," she said, glancing at me. "I swear I saw him smile at his mother when she held him."

I sat next to her but said nothing. I was born shy of five pounds to a mother so mortified by the look of pregnancy that she starved to keep her girth in check. Images of maternal bliss have never moved me. "I'm sorry about Sarah," I said.

She slipped her pen into her shirt pocket and let her head fall into her hands. "Who did it?" she asked.

"A man with schizophrenia turned himself in."

She gazed up at the ceiling. "Was she shot?"

"He used a knife."

A tear started down her face. "Did he, you know . . . Did he . . . do anything else?"

"Yes. He did. He raped her."

"He *raped* her?" She stared at me, and her expression changed gradually from sad to confused. She leaned so close to me I could feel her breath, then, suddenly, drew back like she had smelled something rancid. "You're doing coke!"

The call room is just off the main hospital corridor. "Quiet down, damn it," I said.

"Don't talk to me like a fucking child!" She stood up. "I can't believe you'd go back to it. You're not even five months out of detox."

I got up and looked in the mirror. There was white powder just under my nose. I wiped it away and turned to her. "You should be a cop."

"You fucking bastard," she sputtered, shaking her head. "Don't you think I've lost enough? Do I have to wake up and find you stroked out next to me in bed?"

"I'm not going to die on you, Kathy."

She tried to push past me.

I backed up against the door. "I'll get off it as soon as this case is over. I promise."

"Don't waste your breath. I don't care what you have to say."

"You never do."

"Oh, you poor, misunderstood boy. Let me see if I have it right: You have to get high because I'm not sensitive enough to your needs." Her lip curled. "What bullshit."

I took a step toward her and laid my hands gently on her shoulders. "Let's talk about this at home."

"I'm not coming home. I had more than my fill five months ago."

I lost it. "You had more than your fill of me—or Trevor Lucas? Half the goddamn hospital still talks about you shacking up with that egomaniac while I was sweating my balls trying to get clean."

"Funny—before you got sober I would have sworn you cared more about scoring drugs than you did about how often I was getting laid."

"So you decided a plastic surgeon could pinch-hit for a while. That's loyalty, Kathy. Real character. You have another specialty in mind now? A urologist might be kind of interesting for you."

Her face turned to pure defiance. "At least Trevor wasn't too wired to get it up."

I felt like smacking her, but I figured that was what she was looking for—to trade one kind of pain for another. I took a deep breath. "You and I going at one another isn't going to bring Sarah back."

"I don't need a shrink to tell me my friend isn't coming back from the grave. OK? And if you knew anything, you'd know that you're the only one I've ever wanted to bring back. But you're too coked up to think." She moved toward me and reached for the door handle.

I slipped in front of it. "We're not finished."

She took two steps back and grabbed the pen out of her pocket, clutching it like a dagger. She was trembling. "Get out of my way. Now."

I knew enough about Kathy's temper to know I could end up with anything from a dry-cleaning bill to eye surgery. I eased over toward the bed.

She hurled the pen at me but missed. It bounced off the wall. "Don't call me or page me or come looking for me," she said through clenched teeth. "We're through." She stormed out.

Part of me wanted to follow her. But I figured her anger would flip back into grief on its own. I looked in the mirror to make sure there was no powder left on my lip, smoothed my turtleneck into my pants and walked out.

•   •   •

Gut feelings are not random events. They are crystallizations of subtleties—things seen but not seen, heard but not heard. So I listened to myself with my "third ear" when I still couldn't get my mind off one thing Levitsky mentioned at the autopsy. Sarah had suffered no vaginal trauma. I drove back to the morgue and let myself into his lab.

He didn't hear me come in. He was hunched over a microscope examining slides of tissue he had taken—as he always put it, *harvested*—from Sarah's chest. "She had serious fibrotic changes at the margins of the wound," he said for the microphone.

"Could be a smudge," I whispered.

He looked up at me and rolled his chair to one side. "See for yourself."

I peered through the scope's eyepieces but had no idea what I was supposed to see. I'd been happy to forget pathology after nearly failing the course in medical school. "Terrible. What is it caused by?"

"A bad case of fibrocystic disease, I'd have to say at this point. The damage is serious enough to wonder about a pervasive connective tissue disorder—something like scleroderma that can really turn membranes to leather—but I don't find evidence for it in any other part of the body. Her esophagus, for example, was soft and pink."

"I'm sure she'd be relieved to hear you speak of it that way, Paulson. Did you determine time of death?"

"Midnight, give or take an hour."

"Westmoreland called the police just after three A.M. That leaves plenty of time for him to have gotten rid of the knife—and the breasts."

"Cooked them up into a nice stew," Levitsky laughed. "Is that Malloy a piece of work, or what?"

"He's a piece of crap. But I've got something else on my mind."

"What's that?"

"You said you'd found no evidence of forced intercourse."

"Correct."

"No tears. No hematoma. No bruises. No nothing."

"Right."

"And . . ."

"And what?"

"Westmoreland didn't tell me much, but he seemed clear on one thing: He had sex with her. And I hear you've found that his blood type matches whoever came inside her. Do you see perfectly normal genital anatomy often in cases of rape? Rape and murder?"

"Not often." Levitsky hated loose ends more than anyone I knew. He let out a sigh.

"So tell me: How come there's no vaginal damage?"

"Maybe she got too scared to keep fighting and just let it happen. Maybe she had a thing for bums, and he killed her after they went to the moon together."

"Sure."

"Hey, I don't put anything past people."

"That's your answer?"

He shrugged.

"She wanted it?"

"What are you pushing for? You're the maven on human behavior. I just report what I see."

"So it's over, as far as you're concerned. Case closed."

Levitsky smoothed a wrinkle from his lab coat. "You forget who you're dealing with here? Since when have you known me to *give up*? I'm a compulsive, Frank. A drill bit. Sometimes the answer comes to me in my sleep. I've literally had dreams about the aorta. And the appendix. I once dreamed I was a bacterium—*Clostridium difficile* to be exact—and I was eroding my cadaver's ulcerated colon. I stained for Clostridium in the morning and, sure enough, found it." He was getting overly excited. "I've been a fucking cytomegalovirus during a five-minute nap on my couch between sitcoms, my friend. And these things don't just visit me in my sleep. I might be eating rigatoni—"

I held up a hand. "I get the picture. You're not signing off."

"No. But our friends at the police station would like me to. Malloy's already called me three times to ask when my final—accent, *final*—report will be in."

"Emma Hancock doesn't want any loose ends interfering with her nailing the commissioner's job. She gave me a day and a half to come up with any reason Westmoreland shouldn't be fast-tracked for trial. And that was hours ago."

"You didn't find him competent?"

"Taking a confession from him now would be like taking one from a child having a nightmare. He doesn't even know what's happening to him. He's lost in a psychotic fog of voices and visions."

"Opinions like that aren't going to make you the darling of law enforcement."

"No," I allowed. "Hancock was pretty steamed. I can't even say for sure that she'll stick to our bargain."

"You've got a lot to lose here. People at the station are starting to trust you again. You're getting regular work. It's been a while since I've heard anyone talking about—"

"I know. I know. I need the work. Believe me. And I want them to trust me, Paulson. I really do. I can't tell you how much I want that." I paused. "But it's even more important that my patients be able to trust me. Even a patient accused of murder."

He frowned and nodded. "Emma Hancock may not appreciate that," he said. "But I do."

•   •   •

It was getting dark when I left Levitsky's lab. I phoned the lockup from the Rover with instructions that Westmoreland be given his dose of Thorazine, even though I knew it wouldn't do much more than sedate him. He'd end up slurring his confession instead of stating it clearly. Like it or not, though, letting him down easy for the night was all I could do for him before seeing him again in the morning.

I was out of energy and money, which are very closely linked when you're chasing coke. I inhaled the last of my supply and started over to my mother's apartment at Heritage Park. We had made dinner plans days before, and I'd left her a message that I was strapped for cash.

Heritage Park is actually a cluster of five-story glass-and-steel buildings on Lynn's pier that was supposed to spark gentrification and save the city. Instead, the development was itself consumed by urban blight and spit back out as subsidized housing for the elderly, disabled and poor. My mother qualified on the first count: She was seventy. As to her health, despite the ravages of fifteen years of diabetes, she insisted she had been sick not a day in her life. And she was far from poor; my father's life insurance policy had netted her about half a million dollars.

I leaned to kiss her at the front door. Her thin, cool lips brushed my cheek. She retreated a few steps and squinted up at me. "You look sick."

I have always looked weak or ill to my mother. As a boy, I trusted her impressions of me, which ultimately made me feel disabled. No doubt she had the same corrosive effect on my father. "I feel great," I said. I walked past her into the living room. "Eyes bothering you again?"

She stayed at the door and inspected me as I sat down on the couch. Her eyes had narrowed to slits. Deep crow's feet fanned across her temples. At five feet two and about a hundred pounds she reminded me of a deeply rooted weed.

"Dr. Fine told me he suggested laser treatment for your retinas."

"He'd like to make a little money, that friend of yours." She readjusted a strand of pearls that had drifted to one side and captured her little breast, then limped into the kitchen. The diabetes had destroyed most of the nerves in her left foot. "Nothing's wrong with my eyes. I see everything I want to."

I smiled at that truth, remembering her habit of locking herself in the bedroom and blaring the television whenever my father flew into one of his rages. "You got my message?" I yelled to the kitchen.

"No . . ."

"I left a message on your answering machine."

"Oh?"

I picked up a piece of blown glass twisted to look like candy. It was just one of the fake things in the room. The decor—including oversized, never-opened coffee-table books, antique spectacles perched on the side table, a silk flower arrangement on the mantel of the false fireplace—only resembled that of a home. I felt like I was in a Levitz furniture showroom. "The message was about my mortgage," I yelled again.

"That? Oh, yes, I got it." She brought our plates to the dining room table. "I hope you still like tuna. I found a beautiful piece at Star Market."

I have always disliked fish, and I was certain that my mother, if only unconsciously, remembered this. "Tuna sounds perfect," I said.

"Come. Sit down."

I sat at the dining room table with her, tried to ignore the odor of fish mixed with her perfume and picked around the tomatoes in my salad (which cause me an allergic skin reaction).

"How's your Kathy?" my mother asked, slicing her fish into a checkerboard.

"Wonderful."

"I never got a thank-you note for the bracelet I sent for her birthday. It's been a month." She stared at me as she chewed one of her fish squares. "So I wondered maybe something was wrong."

"She's been busy at the hospital."

"Everybody's having babies. Probably you would have been happier as an obstetrician yourself. You wouldn't have to think so much." She added two heaping sugars to her tea and took a sip.

"If you don't watch your sugar, your foot will get worse."

"My sugar's fine."

I swallowed a forkful of tuna without chewing or breathing. "Excellent fish," I nodded. "So what do you think about the mortgage?"

"What mortgage is that?"

"The message I left . . ."

"Oh, of course. The loan."

"Right. The loan. A few thousand would tide me over. I'd have it back to you in a month."

"You're not eating. You don't have an appetite?"

I swallowed another forkful of tuna.

She glanced at the tomatoes pushed to one side of my salad. "Why it was so important for you to live in Marblehead escapes me. I have to tell you: Two thousand a month sounds like you're paying for an address. Who needs the aggravation? Extra stress." She patted her mouth with her napkin.

My mortgage was close to five thousand a month. "No way out of it now," I said.

"Thank God, Kathy helps out. You couldn't live the way you do on what you make."

My mother had never worked. I smirked, thinking again about the insurance money she'd inherited from my father. "Those days are gone, huh?"

She stopped chewing. "Meaning?"

"Meaning you're exactly right. Kathy and I both have to pitch in."

"So, anyhow, since I hadn't heard from her, I called her today."

"You called Kathy?"

She nodded. "She told me you're using that cocaine again."

"She's lying."

"Why would she lie?"

"I don't know. Ask her."

"So I put two and two together: the loan and the drugs."

Without really intending to, I raked the teeth of my fork against the mahogany beside my plate.

My mother's eyelids fluttered a bit as she watched the fork scratch the high-gloss finish.

"If you don't want to give me the money, just tell me," I said quietly. "I'll have to find it somewhere else." Fast.

"Your father and I worked hard for our money."

"It's his life insurance money. He didn't work for it at all. He just died."

She reached over and took the fork out of my hand, then dipped her white cloth napkin in water and tried to polish away the scratches I had made. Her fingers moved very quickly. Her cheeks flushed. "He did the best he could while he was alive." She stopped, laid my fork on my plate and used a dry corner of her napkin to buff the table to a shine. The scratches were barely visible. She took a deep breath and ate another fish square. "I can give you a few hundred dollars, if that would help."

I had the desire to drive my fork deep into the mahogany, but I needed all the money I could get. "Every little bit helps," I smiled.

"You'll stay for dessert, then?"

"Of course."

"I know you love rice pudding."

I detest rice pudding. "Sounds great," I said.

She seemed to relax. "Maybe I could manage three hundred."

◆　　◆　　◆

Later that night, standing on my deck with a tumbler of scotch, the ocean crashing against the sea wall, I felt more and more uneasy. Kathy had threatened to leave at least a dozen times during the ten months we'd been living together—over my drugs or my women or my gambling—but it was eleven o'clock, and my gut told me she might stay away this time.

I had to admit, if she finally called it quits, it would be partly my fault. You can't expect a woman to stand by you when she doesn't know you. I'd tried to tell Kathy how different Lynn had been when I was a boy, when the beach was clean, and the leather factories boomed, and people drove ten miles north from Boston to spend the day shopping on Union Street. But I hadn't told her how watching the city fade into a gray, hobbled shadow of itself had darkened something in me. I hadn't told her about seeing my father, who wholesaled leather for the J. L. Hanbury Tanning Company, working more and more, making less and less. I hadn't told her that the most attention the man had ever paid me were clumsy, drunken beatings that twisted pain and pleasure forever in my mind.

Not that she would have listened for very long. She had always been quick to dismiss my pain as a lousy excuse for my lifestyle.

I carried my scotch inside and wandered through the hallways, staring into rooms filled with overstuffed couches, worn leather wing chairs, antique wooden chests, oil paintings of the ocean, vases of cut flowers—all of it selected and arranged by Kathy. She seemed to be gone from the house and everywhere in the house at the same time, which reminded me of something painful I couldn't quite put my finger on. My throat tightened, but I held back the tears and reminded myself that withdrawing from a woman is no different than kicking a drug; you feel shaky and you want it, but eventually the need passes, and you feel restored.

Mine was run-of-the-mill loneliness anyhow. A man like Westmoreland was truly cut off, hearing voices no other soul could hear and seeing visions no one else could see. Some unspeakable horror had driven him into a fortress of terrifying private thoughts, and only an extraordinary therapist would stand a chance of helping him find the door. Luckily, my only job was to say whether he knew what it meant to confess to murder.

I walked into the master bedroom and lay down on the tall pine four-poster bed. Kathy had ordered it from Ethan Allen, then outfitted it with white lace pillowcases and a duvet cover of white-on-white-striped, polished cotton she'd found at Pierre Deux on

Newbury Street in Boston. An undertow of despair pulled at me. I felt utterly alone.

I got up and paged my dealer, but he didn't call me back, probably because I already owed him a thousand dollars. I tried two more times with no luck.

I wasn't about to go through the night feeling so low. I drove down the road to the Surf Lounge, but couldn't find anybody selling. Then, lying to myself that I'd turn around before I got there, I drove all the way back to Union Street in Lynn and parked in front of the Emerson Hotel, a forty-five-dollar-a-night fleabag. Hookers from fifteen to fifty paraded about. Pimps and scam artists lurked around public phones. Within a minute, a teenager wearing a purple velour sweatsuit and a half-dozen gold rope chains slunk up to my window. He peered into the car. "Serious coin for a rig like this," he nodded.

"Fifty-two grand." I reached between the front seats for the hunting knife I kept there. The handle had been made from the foot of a deer, and the blade was six inches long. I kept it out of sight on my lap.

He shuffled around. "Them's wheels."

My heart raced. "I'm not here to talk about cars," I said. I ran my thumb back and forth along the blade.

"I got me a sister in the hotel. Thirteen years old. She be just a tight little girl down there, but she be *stacked*. Forty bucks for anything you want."

"I don't care about your fucking relatives, either."

"She'll go for thirty bucks."

"*Fucking relatives*, get it?"

"Huh?"

"Never mind."

"Twenty-five, but that's rock bottom."

"For anything?"

"Right on. She do what you say, or I beat her ass myself."

My breathing quickened. I held the knife up so he could see it. "I want to watch her while she cuts your throat."

He danced back a couple steps and grinned nervously. "Put that away, man, you scarin' me."

I lowered the knife. "Do you have anything to sell me besides little girls?"

He looked right and left as he ran through his other products. "Joint, three bucks. Junk, ten-a-bag. Tootie, hundred-a-gram. Needle, five bucks."

"One-sixty for two grams."

"I'm talkin' good shit."

I touched the gas pedal and shot forward.

"Wait up!" he shouted. He jogged over, but stayed a few feet back from the window. He reached into his pocket and showed me two little cellophane packets of white powder.

I took eight twenties from my pocket. "One-sixty."

"You said one-eighty."

I threw the door open. "You calling me a *liar*?" I yelled.

He backed further away. "I ain't calling you nothin', man. One-sixty, like you said."

I held out the money, and he came just close enough for just long enough to make the exchange.

I drove a hundred yards and pulled over. My whole body felt energized. I took slow, deep breaths. When my heart stopped pounding, I snorted a big blast off the blade of my knife. It *was* good stuff and it chased Kathy out of my head.

I got back on the Lynnway and followed it away from Marblehead to Route 1, so I could stop at the Lynx Club strip joint.

When I walked in, Sade's "Smooth Operator" was blaring through four-foot speakers. The air smelled like a mixture of beer, sweat and smoke. I took a seat at the runway—perverts' row, they call it—folded a dollar bill in half and stood it up like a tent on the countertop in front of me. The dancer, a pretty redhead with the kind of lithe body I get lost in, sauntered over and squatted in front of me. She smiled and brushed the dollar onto the floor with her toe. Then she turned around and bent over so I could look between her legs. I nodded, for no particular reason, and smiled involuntarily—

a boyish reflex which has sickened me when I've seen it in men at bachelor parties. I folded a five and propped it up. "Spank yourself," I told the upside-down face between the legs. She stood up and slapped herself hard three times, then winked at me and brushed my five off the countertop with her foot. I watched as she danced to each man in turn, performing for a dollar or two. When I saw her smile and wink at a three-hundred-pound drunk in precisely the way she had smiled and winked at me, I went to the men's room, did a little blast, then went to the bar and ordered a scotch.

Before I had finished my drink, she was at my side in a skimpy satin robe. I figured the five-dollar bill had bought me a little special attention after all.

"I'm thirsty," she smiled.

"Be my guest." I gestured toward the stool next to mine. Without the benefit of the runway's red lights, her skin was pale, and her freckles showed. But her lips were full, and her eyes a true golden brown. She looked about twenty-five. "What's your name."

"Tiffany."

"That your real name?"

She laughed and tossed her auburn hair. "I don't use my real name here. It's safer."

"For you, or the customers?"

Before she could answer, the bartender, a bulldog of a man, came by. "How about a nice bottle of champagne for the lady?" he coaxed.

"Ginger ale is fine," Tiffany said.

"Tiffany, you love the bubbly. How about a little Frexenet?" he nodded.

"Thanks anyhow, Max," she said.

"The gentleman here wants to treat you like a lady. So order like a lady."

"Max, you're way off," I interrupted. "Not ten minutes ago I paid her to bend over and spank herself. Ginger ale sounds fine to me."

He glared at me. "You some kind of big shot? Maybe I should have your ass—"

"Look," Tiffany broke in. "I earned out at the bar an hour ago. So pour me a fucking ginger ale."

"Fuck you, too." He grabbed the soft drink nozzle. "Nice ass and you think you own the world. Maybe *I* could use a couple extra bucks in *my* pocket. Ever think of that?" He slid the ginger ale in front of her and waddled away.

"He gets five percent," she said.

"Seems like he earns it."

She shrugged her shoulders, took out a pack of Marlboros and lighted one. Her fingers were long and graceful. "How about you? What do you do?"

"I'm a psychiatrist."

"You don't look like a psychiatrist—or act like one."

"I'll take that as a compliment." I put my hand on her knee.

She swept my hand off of her. "You can't touch me," she said. "The manager watches from upstairs." She pointed across the way at a line of mirrored glass panels high on the wall. "He'll have you thrown out."

"Your guardian angel?"

"Something like that."

"I guess better late than never."

"What's that supposed to mean?"

"Maybe you could have used one sooner."

"Want to do me a favor? Don't get shrinky on me. OK?"

"No problem." I downed the last of my scotch. "Sometimes I lose myself and start to give a shit about people." I got up and took my seat back at the runway.

A blonde who couldn't have been eighteen yet was lying on her back with her legs spread, moving her hips like she was having sex to the rhythm of "Addicted to Love." I rolled up a dollar bill and threw it at her. She smiled at me and licked her lips. She looked a little bit like Kathy, the same hazel eyes and perfect white Chiclet teeth. I pictured Trevor on top of her and imagined her coming with that bastard inside her. I threw another dollar at her, then got up to leave. As I was passing the bar, Max called me over and handed me a folded-up napkin. "From Tiffany," he barked. I handed him my last ten-dollar bill and walked out.

I unfolded the napkin in the Rover. She had written the name Rachel and her beeper number. You just never know with people. I stuffed it in my pocket and started the car. As I was leaving the parking lot, I looked in the rearview mirror and saw Trevor Lucas' red Ferrari pulling in—or thought I saw it. But tootie combined with booze can play tricks with your mind.

I drove home and swallowed three Valium before heading for bed. One used to keep the nightmares at bay, but no longer. I lay there stiff, unwilling to let go the reins of my mind. It seemed an hour passed before the competition between sedatives and stimulants for my brain's chemical receptors finally wrenched me into a realm midway between sleep and wakefulness. In that purgatory, praying that I would be saved, I heard myself wonder again how a man violent enough to butcher a woman could force himself on her so gently as to not bruise a tissue nor tear a membrane of her softest part.

Three

I sat bolt upright, my arms crossed over my face to repel the next blow. My legs pedaled against the mattress until I was crouched against the headboard, rocking like a child. My eyes scoured the dark room, knowing the dream was over, but still smelling the mixture of alcohol and tobacco on my father's breath. My nose burned, and my jaw ached from grinding my teeth. My mouth was painfully dry.

I turned on the lamp. I hadn't changed for bed and was still wearing my boots. The odor of scotch and smoke I had smelled was wafting off me, no one else. I struggled to my feet, stripped and went for a drink from the bathroom faucet. The cold water made my teeth ache, but soothed my mouth and throat. I lighted a Marlboro from the package in the medicine cabinet and sat down in the wing-back chair by the bed. I felt anxious and empty. Raw.

How much more stable was I, really, than a man like Westmoreland? On the surface, as a physician, driving my Rover, living in Marblehead with another physician, I had nothing in common with a psychotic drifter. But in my heart I knew I wasn't entirely different from him. He was homeless; I was uncomfortable in my own home, even in my own skin. He was plagued by voices and visions; I was tortured by memories that chased me out of sleep and into the haze of drugs. How much and what kind of pain, I wondered, would it take to push me over the edge of sanity?

More than a third of the thirty-six hours Emma Hancock had given me had passed, and I didn't know a whole lot more about Westmoreland than when I'd started.

I was about to pour myself a scotch when the phone rang. I figured it was Kathy and I wasn't sure whether to pick it up or let her wonder where the hell I was. There is a scene at the end of *The Verdict* where Paul Newman lets the phone ring and ring, sensing his deceitful ex-lover is calling, and I tried to do the same. But I'm no Paul Newman and I really wanted to talk to her. "Clevenger," I answered.

"Got it!" the voice at the other end said.

"Hello?"

"I got it."

"Paulson, do you know it's three o'clock in the morning?"

"Didn't you hear me? I said, 'I got it.' "

He sounded like a manic patient. "Calm down. What the hell have you got?"

"Ready?"

"I've got nothing else on my agenda right now."

"OK. Here goes. You listening?"

"Paulson . . ."

He was chuckling. "It was simple, that's why it was complex. Like anything worth a damn in science. It was hard to see because it was right in front of my face. Until I had this dream. I can tell you because you're a shrink, so I know there's not a lot you haven't heard before. Remember how Malloy, that prick, said Sarah was hot, even though she was dead?"

"Sure."

"Well, I must have filed that away somewhere. And I guess he was right because I . . . well . . . I took advantage of her in the lab. I made love to her after the autopsy."

"In your dream?"

"Of course, *in my dream*. What do you think I'm crazy?"

"Go on."

"That's it. I made love to her after she was dead. Just like Westmoreland. He didn't rape her, then kill her. He killed her and then raped her. That's why she didn't put up a fight, didn't even tighten up down there. She couldn't because she was dead."

That seemed believable. I took a drag off my cigarette.

"You there?" he asked.

"Is there a test that can prove it?"

"Nothing definitive, but I've got something that fits. Normally, involuntary smooth muscle contractions sweep semen up beyond the cervix, even in cases of rape. In Sarah there was no sperm beyond the vagina. I figure by the time Westmoreland violated her, her muscles weren't doing much more than twitching."

"Not bad, my friend. Not bad at all."

"I just don't know why I didn't think of it right away. I mean, screwing corpses isn't exactly unheard of. I've had at least one other case myself."

"You couldn't think it, only dream it."

"Huh?"

"You couldn't entertain Westmoreland having sex with her after she was dead because you wanted her yourself. Right there on the dissecting table. Just like Malloy did. You had to suppress the whole idea. But the id is a tenacious bastard, Paulson. Take it from me."

"You're talking to a pathologist, Frank. With all the brains I've dissected, I've never found an id. If I can't see it, you're gonna have trouble convincing me it's there."

"We all rely on your concrete thinking."

"What did you think about her being shaved?"

"She looked good—a lot better than the slides you made of her fibrotic breasts."

"Well, I'm glad you said it." He cleared his throat. "The trouble is, I doubt all this is going to change anything for Westmoreland."

"Maybe. Maybe not."

"Last time I checked, the sentence for raping, then murdering, was the same as for murdering, then raping."

I wiped my nose and noticed a streak of blood across my fingers. "Why are you so sure he's the one who killed her?"

"I'm not. I'm not sure at all. But I'm a realist. The way Malloy and Hancock are moving on this, it might not matter—especially now, with Sam Fitzgerald involved."

Sam Fitzgerald was a forensic psychiatrist whose expert opinions varied predictably with who was paying his fee.

"What do you mean, *with Fitzgerald involved?*" I asked.

"I thought you knew. Hancock hired him on. I went down to hand over my preliminary report last night, and Fitz was just heading in to see Westmoreland. He said he'd be calling you right after he finished up."

"So much for the Sacred Heart School for Girls."

"Sacred what?"

"Nothing." I blew a smoke ring and watched it float away. "I should know by now that the straight path will only take you where somebody else wants you to go."

◆   ◆   ◆

I needed more sleep but didn't have time for it. Luckily, I hadn't killed my supply. I grabbed my jeans off the floor, fished one of the little cellophane packets out of the pocket and sucked up what was left. Then I headed for the shower.

The warm water running over my back relaxed me. I leaned into the corner and let my face rest between the cool marble walls. Rachel came into my mind, seated on that barstool in her satin robe, open nearly to her crotch. I started to touch myself. I imagined she had let my hand linger on her leg. I separated her knees and traced the inside of one thigh with my finger. With my other hand I yanked her stool closer to mine. I could reach everything, but I was careful to stop without touching what she needed me to touch. She took hold of my wrist and urged it toward her. I let my finger brush the dampness of her cotton panties. "Please . . ." she whispered. I took a pinch of cotton in my fingers and pulled up on it. She gasped. I stroked the skin surrounding the cloth. I pictured her biting her lower lip and started to work myself faster. She was pleading with me. "Please, please, please . . ." My rhythm faltered. I pressed against the wall and closed my eyes as my body went on autopilot, expelling Rachel from my mind.

I turned into the shower stream and washed the hair back off my face. The coke was kicking in, and my thoughts were coming clearer and faster. I needed to get inside Westmoreland's head. I didn't have five years to psychoanalyze him in order to unearth the roots of his psychosis. I didn't even have the couple of weeks it would take for Thorazine to quiet his voices. Emma Hancock would never go for it, but I knew that Amytal was the only answer.

Amytal dissolves the mind's defenses and frees up traumatic memories. I'd first used it as a psychiatry resident at the Boston V.A. Medical Center. We were one of three national referral centers for the worst of the posttraumatic-stress-disorder patients, "treatment failures" left over from Vietnam who'd witnessed atrocities so abominable they still couldn't remember them, let alone speak of them. The starkest evidence of what they had been through was their suicide attempts. Every other day someone was trying to off himself with whatever could be had—a plastic fork, an exposed wire, a pair of pants looped like a noose over a bathroom stall. Like surgeons lancing boils, we injected patient after patient with Amytal and listened as their suppressed horror seeped out. At least then the camouflage was stripped away; we knew the ghosts we were battling.

Giving Westmoreland an injection of Amytal wouldn't cure him of schizophrenia, but it might overcome his resistance to describing what had happened in the Lynn woods.

I turned off the hot water and held my breath. Whenever Kathy and I showered together, we'd make a contest of who could stand the cold spray longer. She almost always won because her pain threshold was much higher than mine—higher, really, than anyone I'd ever met. I'd never seen her use so much as an aspirin, even the time she'd smacked the wall after one of my indiscretions and broken two fingers. I leaned back against the marble and tried to imagine her naked in front of me, snickering like an imp while

I shivered. Where, I wondered, would she be showering this morning?

◆   ◆   ◆

I got to the station at six-fifteen. Tobias Lucey, another recruit to the force, was on duty in the little teller's booth at the door to the lockup. He was reading the *Boston Herald*. "I'm Dr. Clevenger," I interrupted, "Mr. Westmoreland's psychiatrist."

He glanced at me, then went back to reading. "I'd need a clearance from Captain Hancock to let you in." He was wispy for a cop, and his voice had arrogance in it.

"I know you just started," I smiled. "I visit suspects all the time."

"I got no notification," he said. He turned a page.

"You think I'd come down here this early just to bust your balls?"

He finally looked me in the eyes. "Westmoreland gets no visitors. He's on special precautions. He attacked someone yesterday."

"I know that. Do you know how I know?"

He didn't respond.

"Because I'm the one he attacked. And he could go off again if I don't get in there with his medication." I held up a vial of Amytal.

"I can't let you visit anyone until Captain Hancock gets here. No exceptions." He glanced at his watch, then went back to reading the paper. "She'll be in by seven-thirty."

"Well, then. I'll just leave this with you," I said. I slid the Amytal under the glass window. "You tell your Auntie Em I came by to give the injection at six-thirty, just like we planned. If Westmoreland loses it and busts his head against the wall, I'm not taking the heat. I was here, trying to do the right thing." I started to walk away.

"Uh, Doctor . . ."

I stopped and turned around. "Clevenger. Frank Clevenger."

"One hour really matters?"

I made a great display of calming myself. "Well, Officer Lucey, it's hard to say. Westmoreland might do just fine until seven o'clock. He might be able to go until seven-thirty. Possibly even eight. Then again, he might chew off a finger or pluck out an eye in twenty minutes."

"I didn't know," he shrugged.

"That's the first step."

"Excuse me?"

"The first step toward enlightenment. You know that you don't know."

"Sure . . ." He looked at me as if I might be crazy myself. "Let's get his medicine into him."

Westmoreland hadn't gotten his Thorazine until after midnight and was curled up on the floor of his cell in a deep, fitful sleep, wearing only a T-shirt and soiled boxer shorts. The rest of his clothes were laid out in the shape of a person on his cot. The sun was coming up, and the bars on his window cast long shadows across him. Of a sudden, one or another of his limbs would jump.

"He stinks like garbage," Lucey said. He grabbed a ring of keys off his belt and jammed one into the lock on the cell door.

I caught his wrist and pressed my thumb into the soft place between the bones. "Quietly," I said.

He winced and tried to pull away.

"Quietly," I repeated. I let go and held a finger to my lips.

He glared at me, but then eased the door open.

I walked in alone and knelt at Westmoreland's side. His eyes whipped back and forth under his lids. His breathing was a series of gasps. I drew the Amytal into a syringe and carefully tied a tourniquet around his arm. A vein ballooned up. I buried the tip of the needle. Westmoreland grimaced but didn't wake up. I slowly pushed the plunger down.

Amytal burns as it flows in, and just as I was finishing the injection, Westmoreland's eyes snapped open. He stared for a few seconds at the little drop of blood gathering on his skin, then at the syringe in my hand. His face twisted with terror. Without a word, he punched himself in the face.

"Grab him!" I called out to Lucey.

Westmoreland started swinging wildly at himself. I could only pin down one of his hands. He landed a blow to his nose.

Lucey was standing over us, looking scared.

I reached up, grabbed his belt and pulled him toward the floor.

Together we wrestled control of Westmoreland's arms, but not before he had split his lip and opened a cut over one eye. He was still struggling against us—or against himself—with everything he had.

"What the hell is happening to him?" Lucey demanded. "What is that crap you gave him?"

"The crap is sap!" Westmoreland yelled. "The tree is me!"

"It'll be over soon," I said evenly.

Westmoreland struggled free of Lucey's grip and landed a solid blow to his own ear.

"He's crazed," Lucey said.

"Shut up and hold him."

"Jesus Fucking Christ." Lucey lunged for Westmoreland's arm, caught it and held it to the ground.

"Mother Mary came, came, came to me," Westmoreland spewed. He arched his back in a last attempt to overcome us, then collapsed to the floor.

"If he's dead, it's your ass," Lucey said.

"He's not dead."

He looked at me doubtfully. "I'm calling this in to Captain Hancock immediately."

"I could use you here."

"Don't do anything else to him," he warned. He got up and walked to the door.

"What did you have in mind?"

The cell door clanged shut. "Crazy sonofabitch," he muttered.

Even with blood trickling down his face Westmoreland seemed more at peace. He was lying still with his eyes closed. I stayed silent about a minute, then took his hand in mine. His skin was dry and thick with calluses. "Mr. Westmoreland," I said, "I'm a psychiatrist.

My name is Frank Clevenger. Do you remember speaking with me yesterday?"

He didn't respond.

"The medicine I gave you will make it easier for you to talk with me," I suggested. "It's like truth serum."

He moved his lips silently.

"It makes it OK to speak."

"OK," he whispered.

I wanted to start with simple facts. "Do you know where we are?"

"Yes."

"Where is that?"

"Hell, Father. The bowels of the universe. I am the excrement of humanity."

"And what is your name?"

Westmoreland grimaced and stayed silent.

I didn't want to lose him by pushing for something he wouldn't yield. "Why are you here, my son?" I asked.

"God gave her to me," he said, beginning to weep. "Purest of pure."

"You received a gift from God?"

"Thus was the Virgin Mary delivered unto me in a wood." He opened his eyes and looked through me. "I destroyed her. No son of God shall ever walk the earth again."

I remembered Westmoreland's delusion about the statue of the Madonna he had stolen from the Church of Angels. "How did you destroy the virgin?" I asked him.

He was silent for a while. "The serpent," he said finally. "I put the serpent in her mother part."

"Did she struggle against you?"

"She has never been against me."

"Did she cry out?"

"She never awakened. My angel slept in a cloud of leaves."

"In a cloud of leaves . . ."

"Only her hand reached out to me. But I was not content with a hand, Father. No. No. Not even that holiest of holy hands. I uncovered her legs and her mother part. I am a sinner worthy of His wrath. I am the most vile demon to ever visit the earth. I must be judged."

"How did you know the Madonna was dead?"

Westmoreland started to hyperventilate. "I lifted her in my arms. . . . God had left His terrible mark. . . . Blood . . . sticky . . . wet . . . everywhere."

"What mark did God leave?"

"He took . . . He took back her milk."

I heard the cell door being opened.

"End of discussion, Frankenstein," a voice said. "You've overstayed your welcome."

I looked up and saw Malloy standing there, feet apart, hands on hips. Lucey was with him.

"You've really outdone yourself this time," Malloy sneered. "Captain Hancock's gonna hand you your head on a fucking platter. She said to wait for her in her office."

"Someone has to watch him," I said, nodding toward Westmoreland. "The Amytal won't wear off for at least twenty minutes."

"You know what? I've told you before: I'm tired of your bullshit psychobabble. Come on out of there."

"Who's going to watch him?"

He wrapped his chubby fingers around his baton. "Maybe you'd like for me to come in and get you."

I stood up. "Come get me," I said, staring at him. "Or is it true you only like to mix it up when the other guy's already cuffed?"

He stared back for a second or two, but then his eyes drifted. "I said, 'Get out of there.' "

I walked slowly out of the cell and right up to him. "Now listen to me, Malloy. You or Officer Lucey had better stay with Mr. Westmoreland. If he starts feeling like somebody just stole his thoughts from him, we could have pure panic on our hands. Understand?"

He turned to the cell. "Hey, General," he called out, "you missing anything?"

Westmoreland didn't stir.

I could easily have put Malloy down with a knee to his soft belly, but Lucey was standing a few feet away, and there's no telling what a new cop will do with a gun. I took a deep breath and shook my head. "I don't know what happened to fuck you up so badly, but you'd better figure it out before I stop giving a shit."

"I'm so scared I'm shakin' inside."

"There you go. That's a start," I said, walking past him. "Now you can take me to Emma."

He pushed past me to lead the way.

"A couple more sessions, and you might not need the shiny boots and badge," I said.

◆   ◆   ◆

Three hours of sleep wasn't carrying me. I wanted to dip into my second gram, but thought better of using at the station. I paced Hancock's office, looking at the photos of her with local noteworthies that covered her walls. There were pictures of her with Mayor McGinnis, Representative DeTuleo, Superintendent of Schools Coughlin, City Councilor Caldwell, Commissioner Rollins. Each photo seemed mostly Hancock, partly because she was so bulky and partly because she was the only woman in the shot. I chuckled, but grimly. Waiting for her reminded me a little of the times as a boy when I'd sat in my claustrophobic room on Shepherd Street, trying to distract myself with a Spider-Man comic book from the fact that my father was deep into a fifth of bourbon, pacing the living room and barking orders left over from the front lines of Korea, a place he never spoke of sober. I'd hear him start up the steps, and my mind would run down a list of lousy options. I could hide under my bed or in my closet, but the beating would be even worse once he found me. I could make a break for my window and the fire escape, but I was convinced he could outrun me. I could yell for my mother, but I knew she was probably hiding already herself. So I'd wait in silence, listening for my father's deliberate footsteps on the hardwood staircase. Closer and closer. For moments I could almost convince myself that Spider-Man was clinging to the wall outside my window, ready to shoot me a web to swing to freedom on. But like clockwork, when my father reached the fourteenth step, I could just make out the clink of a buckle coming loose, followed by the awful thwacking of leather being pulled through belt loops. The worst part was the expression on my father's face when he came through my door. He didn't look angry. He looked tired and put upon, like he had to take out the garbage. I didn't understand his detachment then and was terrified by it. Now I know he wasn't after me, didn't even know where his violence was coming from, which probably explains why it always went on so damn long.

I was just finishing a lap around Hancock's walls of respect when she walked in. She was winded. Her ruddy face had gone red. "Morning, Frank," she said without looking at me.

"Sorry to complicate your day."

She went over to her desk and started to unpack her briefcase. "I rushed over as fast as I could when Malloy called. But I'm glad you had a little time to yourself in here." She dropped a sheaf of papers on her blotter, then pulled out a stack of folders and started slipping them into her file cabinet. "It's not much of an office—nothing like a doctor's or lawyer's—but I'm kind of proud of it, just the same." She closed the file drawer, walked around to the front of her desk and sat on the edge. She nodded at the photos on the walls. "I like to think if you look around you get a sense that everybody working in a city, from a cop to a teacher, is connected to everybody else. It's very important that no one think of himself as a free agent. Because without teamwork this city—any city—would die."

I held up my hands. "I get where you're headed."

"I thought you did," she said, shaking her head, "but I'm not sure anymore. Unless I got the wrong report, you went behind my back and injected my prisoner with narcotics. If that's your idea of *teamwork* . . ."

"If you let me, I'll explain."

"Please." She worked her nails against one another. A chip of red paint flew into the air. "Explain."

"Look, I had to do something quick. Guys like Westmoreland, the real paranoid schizophrenics, believe they're constantly under siege. Everybody's trying to get inside them, listen to their thoughts, insert ideas in their minds. We'd have to fill him full of Thorazine for weeks to have any hope of breaking through his paranoia. And we need answers now."

"Maybe that's because you don't like the answers we've got. But you're not running this department. I am. And I only asked you one question—whether I could take a confession from my prisoner. Do you remember me asking you to start your own investigation?"

"Emma, I've got a lousy feeling about this case, and Amytal was the only way into Westmoreland's head. I figured if he was the one who killed Sarah, he'd be able to tell us where to find the murder weapon and"—Hancock was tapping her foot—"and the breasts. If he wasn't the killer, then maybe he'd seen him. What he told me adds up to him stumbling across Sarah in a pile of leaves. He had sex with her corpse."

"Disgusting. Are you finished?"

"She was already dead."

"She was already dead. Do you know how many killers have sworn to me that they *found* the body? What about the blood all over him?"

"He didn't see the wounds on Sarah at first. Not until after he'd violated her and picked her up in his arms. He thought she was the Madonna. When he called down here from that pay phone he wasn't screaming about *a* virgin; he was screaming about *the* virgin. The Virgin Mary. A gift from God."

"A gift from God. All I need is something like this hitting the *Item*. Maybe they'll run a sidebar about extraterrestrials." She shook her head. "Have you noticed how many psychopaths cloak themselves in the Lord? He is the devil's favorite disguise."

I would have liked to ask Hancock what her religion was helping *her* to hide. "Westmoreland's no devil," I said. "He's not even a common killer. He's just a crazy bum who turned up at the wrong place at the wrong time."

"He turned himself in at the scene. He's wanted to confess ever since. Now the two of you cook up another storyline while he's high on Amytal. I'm surprised at you. I thought after Prescott killed that cheerleader, you got real careful. This sounds like more of the same."

"Don't drag Prescott into this . . ." I felt myself losing control and took a second to settle myself down. "Amytal is a reliable technique to recover traumatic memories."

"*Reliable?* I thought they threw that shit on the garbage heap a decade ago. You could get anybody to say anything on it."

"Not when the interview is conducted—"

"By you. The master. I see. Well, the courts don't agree with you. Neither do I. Whatever Westmoreland said in there is irrelevant. And that's not even the thing that gets to me. What really disappoints me is you going behind my back."

That got my adrenaline flowing. "Behind *your* back? Why would I go behind your back? You've been up front with me. Right?"

"Don't talk to me in riddles. I know your friend Levitsky saw Dr. Fitzgerald here. So what? I have the right to get a second opinion whenever I want one. I told you you had thirty-six hours before the door closed on Westmoreland and I meant it. That doesn't mean I have to sit still while I wait." She pointed at me. "This is no small matter, Frank. I'm supposed to report you to the Board of Medicine. You didn't have a court order to inject Westmoreland, and you certainly didn't have his consent."

"How much are you paying Fitz?"

"Less than what I was paying you to stab me in the back. OK?"

"I'm not stabbing you in the back. I know a murderer on the loose makes for lousy headlines, but the damage is going to be much worse if you've got the wrong man locked up back there, and we end up with another body on our hands. Then you could really kiss the commissioner thing goodbye."

"Believe me when I tell you: I don't need a career counselor. I have things covered."

"I'm sure you do. Unless another body turns up. Then all hell could break loose."

"No question about it. But you know what? That isn't going to happen. I've been at this work a little while—and a lot longer than you. Westmoreland's going to trial for a murder he committed, and he'll be found guilty."

"The defense will call me, and I'll testify. It'll be me against Fitz. Westmoreland's not competent to confess. And I'll volunteer that I don't think he did it."

"You may not be a licensed professional in this state by the time he comes to trial."

My elevator was headed for the roof. I took a deep breath. "Stop threatening me, Emma. I don't respond well to being pushed around."

"Could be those late-night shopping sprees in front of the Emerson Hotel," she mocked. "If you don't sleep, you get edgy. Your judgment can be way off. That's something else I'm supposed to let the Board in on."

"What the hell are you—"

"Save it, Frank. We've had surveillance cameras in front of the Emerson for months. You really should be more discreet."

Just then Officer Lucey raced in. He looked panicked. "We need help in there. Westmoreland's going off again."

I ran to the cell with the two of them. Westmoreland was pressed against the far wall with Malloy facing him. He had stuck his tongue out and was biting into it. Blood was streaming down his chin and neck.

Malloy's hands patted the air. "Go easy," he said.

Westmoreland screamed. Blood sprayed into the air. He caught his tongue between his teeth again and bit down hard.

"Shit," Malloy said. He seemed to be wiping blood off his face.

"Can somebody bring me up to speed here?" Hancock demanded.

Malloy didn't turn around. "I asked him one simple question, and he went berserk."

I walked into the cell and stood next to Malloy. "What question?"

He shrugged. "His real name. That's it."

52 KEITH ABLOW

"Did he tell you?" Hancock asked.

"Not at first. I had to ask him half a dozen times before I got George La-something out of him. Then he went into his clam act."

Westmoreland clenched his jaws. The blood started flowing even faster.

"George, you're only hurting yourself," Hancock said.

It was a mindless thing for her to say and it made Westmoreland scream out, then bite even more fiercely into himself. But it also gave me an idea. I was starting to think that the *only* person Westmoreland was really willing to hurt was himself. I walked away from Malloy and stood against the wall about ten feet from Westmoreland. I took out a little silver pocket knife I carry to cut coke and clicked the blade into place.

"Put that thing away!" Hancock yelled.

I looked over at Westmoreland. His eyes met mine. I held my arm up where he could see it and pressed the blade against my wrist. "Your suffering is my suffering," I whispered. "Tell me when we can stop."

Westmoreland kept his jaws tight.

I ran the blade over my skin so that it scratched a white line across my wrist.

His eyes widened, but his jaw stayed set.

I gritted my teeth and dragged the blade across my wrist with just enough pressure to break skin. A clean line appeared, then turned bright red with blood.

"Oh, my God," Malloy whispered.

Westmoreland stared at my wrist, then glanced at his own.

I moved the blade to the beginning of the cut, closed my eyes and pressed hard enough for the tip to sink in about a quarter inch. I felt a sharp pain for a second, then a deep aching sensation spreading down my hand. I squirmed against the wall.

Westmoreland began to sob.

I looked over and saw he hadn't let go his tongue.

I pushed the blade in a little further.

He fell to his knees. His jaw finally relaxed. "Stop, Father," he pleaded. "My sins are great enough."

I lingered against the wall a few moments, then pulled the blade out of my wrist and walked over to him. I held out my hand. He took it and let me guide him to his cot.

"Make sure he gets seen at an emergency room," I told Hancock once I was out of the cell.

"That was quite a show, Frank," she said. "How did you know he'd stop?"

"Because he's not a killer."

She stiffened. "Your batting average on curve balls is already pretty low."

"I've never thought to keep score with people's lives," I said. I walked past her and out of the station.

Four

I trudged to the parking lot, pulled myself into the car, started the engine, then just sat there with my eyes closed. I was spent, and on the ropes. If Hancock went through with her threat to report me to the Board of Medicine, they might suspend my license. Then the house would be as good as gone, and probably the Rover, too—all at a time when my relationship with Kathy was falling apart. But I couldn't let any of that stop me. I was the only chance Westmoreland had, and I cannot stomach a helpless man under attack. There was no telling what horrors his mind would spin in captivity. To him the bars of his cell might be razors primed to shred him. The police could be aliens using him in bizarre experiments. I had seen a psychotic prisoner split his own skull by diving into the corner of a cell, convinced maggots had infested his brain. And Westmoreland's confinement was only half of the problem; if he was wrongly imprisoned, then the real killer was free to kill again.

I ripped open the second packet of coke and inhaled about a quarter gram. My wrist was throbbing, and blood was trickling down my hand. I grabbed a chamois cloth out of the back seat and put some pressure on the wound. The shallow part stopped oozing after about a minute, but the point where I had sunk the knife deeper kept flowing. Cocaine is a potent anesthetic and a decent vasoconstrictor, so I blotted my wrist clean and sprinkled some along the laceration. That took care of the burning and slowed the bleeding, but only for seconds. I needed a few stitches. I started the car and headed over to the Stonehill Hospital ER.

Nels Clarke, a family practitioner who could pass for a lumberjack, was on duty when I got there. I found him checking lab results on a computer terminal. He looked up and saw the bloody cloth I was carrying.

"What the hell happened to you?" he asked.

"It's nothing. Just a little cut. I don't think it's gonna close up on its own, though."

"Did you register out front?"

"Did I . . ."

"Register. You just expect me to drop everything and take care of a little scratch on your arm?"

I didn't even have the energy to get angry at him. "I'll take care of it. Where can I find a needle and some 5.0 nylon?"

"Frank."

"I'll find it myself." I started to walk away.

"*Frank.*"

"What?"

"I was kidding." His brow furrowed. "You OK?"

"Long day."

"Long day? It's eight-fifteen."

"A.M. or P.M.?"

He winked. "Follow me." He brought me into one of the curtained cubicles, sat me down and grabbed a surgical tray. "Let's get a look." He covered the table between us with green draping and laid my wrist across it. "I think I can save the hand," he joked. He doused my skin with Betadine, then alcohol.

I winced.

"It burns," he smiled.

"Thanks for the warning."

He repositioned my arm. "You want a little lidocaine before I start?"

"No."

"Ah, an ascetic."

I had to chuckle. "I don't want a little. I want a lot of it. Unless I'm mistaken, you trained in family practice, not surgery."

He laughed with real pleasure, and I realized again why his patients adored him. Still in his thirties, he exuded the warmth of an old country doctor. He filled a syringe and deftly injected the margins of the wound. The skin tented up, then flattened as the anesthetic was absorbed. By the time he placed the first stitch, all I felt was a little tugging.

"So what happened?" he asked. "Some pretty thing tie you up too tight?"

"I wouldn't say *pretty*."

He took another bite with the needle. "Naming names?"

"Sure. General William Westmoreland."

"I didn't know you swung both ways. And you landed a military man. Good for you."

"Actually, he's a paranoid schizophrenic. I was evaluating him down at the jail, and we got into a little tug of war over sharp objects."

"All in a day's work, I guess. *Your* work, anyhow." He tied the second knot. "He's not the one who killed Sarah Johnston . . ."

"Word's out, huh?"

"Front page of the *Item* last night. I didn't know her, but I think I met her once or twice in the cafeteria. Thank God they caught that bastard." He sprayed some saline over my wrist to wash the blood away. "I hear half the nurses on the psych unit called in sick. We're short down here, too. I can't imagine what this place would be like if the guy was still out there."

"Let's hope things settle down."

"He's real crazy, huh? The paper said he cut her up."

I didn't want to get into it. "We only talked a few minutes."

"Oh." He looked up at me, then back down. He put in another stitch, tied it and cut it loose. His brow furrowed. "This being a work-related injury, I guess I don't need to ask the standard questions."

I watched the needle pierce my skin again. "Standard questions?"

"You know. There's a whole protocol that goes along with wrist lacerations. I'm even supposed to get a psychiatric consultation. But since you *are* a psychiatrist—and a friend—I figure you'd tell me if I should be worried about you."

"Worried? You're not thinking I'm *suicidal?*"

"It's routine to ask."

"Nels, I didn't try to off myself. I'm too narcissistic to even think about it. I'm more likely to try cloning myself."

He smiled and cut the nylon thread over his last knot. He had put in five stitches. "I just wanted to be sure, with Kathy and everything." He dropped the needle on a plastic tray and peeled off his gloves. "Not that you two haven't had your ups and downs before."

"I didn't know the rumor mill here was so goddamn efficient."

"Trevor's as discreet as a bonfire."

"Trevor? He's old news."

He folded the surgical drapes in on themselves, threw them in a laundry bin and walked over to the sink to wash up. "Eh, fuck him."

"Nels . . ."

He turned around and looked at me. "Why don't we grab coffee or something?"

"Save the bedside manner for grieving relatives. Just tell me."

"Tell you." He exhaled audibly, then leaned back against the sink. "OK. I was covering Buck Berenson's shift last night. I get a kid with a bad facial laceration—ran through a glass door. So I call Trevor in for the plastics. I don't happen to like him. I think he's nuts. But he's a gifted surgeon, no denying that. If I got hurt, he's the one I'd want working on me. Anyhow, he gets here maybe eight, nine o'clock and starts rushing me. . . . You sure you don't want to get a quick coffee?"

"Thank you. No."

"No problem." He looked at the floor. "I call Trevor, and he comes in and starts saying how he wants to get through the job on the kid fast, because . . ."

"Spit it out."

"Because he's got Kathy back at the house waiting for him." He looked at me like he'd just told me I had cancer.

I let my breath out all at once. "I should have seen that coming."

"I feel like an asshole," he said, shaking his head. "It wasn't my place to say anything."

"I'd rather hear it sooner than later."

"You want to talk?"

"There's nothing to say. Kathy was close with Sarah Johnston. Where she takes comfort is her own business." I rolled down my sleeve and stood to go.

"You sure there's nothing I can do?"

"There is one thing."

"Shoot."

"Let me know if anything odd walks through the door. Scratch marks. Bite wounds. Signs of a struggle."

"That's not a reassuring request from someone working on Lynn's latest murder. They do have the right guy, don't they?"

"I think we'll know soon enough."

◆　　◆　　◆

I went into the men's room and locked the door. I let the cold water run, then doused my face again and again. I needed to stay awake and to stay in control, but my mind kept flipping through images of Trevor and Kathy together. Even taking the sudden loss of Sarah into account, I couldn't make sense of her shacking up again over my cocaine. What kind of insulation from the randomness of the universe could she hope for spending the night with a playboy? Unless randomness—the unpredictable life and death of relationships—was exactly the thing she was replaying. But that seemed like a reach. Maybe Nels was wrong; maybe Trevor was exaggerating a phone call from Kathy into a rendezvous with her. I wasn't in any condition to see her, but I needed to hear the story firsthand. I opened my packet, spread a pinch over my gums and snorted a line off my key. Then I shot up to the fourth floor and over to the Ob-Gyn Department.

Kathy's office was one of six in a row behind a semicircular reception desk. The secretary, Kris Jerold, a young gay activist with a bleach-blond crew cut, motioned for me to wait until she was off the phone. "She isn't here yet," she said, hanging up. She fingered the three gold hoops through her ear. "She called earlier to let me know she'd be in at nine o'clock."

"I'll wait in her office."

She nodded tentatively.

My fuse was short. "Is there a problem with me waiting in there?" I asked.

"Not that I can think of."

"Well, is there one that you *can't* think of?"

"I love psychiatrists," she smiled, then paused. "There's no problem at all with you being in the office. I was just going to ask how Dr. Singleton is doing after losing her friend."

"I'm trying to get a feel for that myself. How does she seem to you?"

"I haven't seen much of her. She left early yesterday. Now she's missed half of her morning clinic." She shook her head. "They were almost like sisters . . ."

"Yes." I thought again of the fire that took Kathy's sister. "I think that's right."

"I'll hold her calls when she comes in."

"Thank you."

I walked into Kathy's office and collapsed into her desk chair. I could smell her perfume. I smiled at a photograph of me she kept inside a sterling, beaded-edge frame I had given her for Christmas. I was looking smug outside a Lynn hole-in-the-wall called the Irish Mist, straddling the black Harley Fat Boy I'd bought just a few weeks after we'd met. I chuckled, remembering that I'd paid for the bike with money set aside to get back into analysis. "You ought to figure out where you intend to go before you get all excited about how to get there," my psychiatrist, Ted Pearson, had offered when I canceled the appointments we had scheduled.

"I think I'll be alright," I told him.

"Then you're even worse off than I suspected," he said. "Call me when you need me."

There had been at least a few times during the last year when I'd been tempted to seek out Pearson and admit how lost I felt, but he'd gone on to run the state's Impaired Physicians' Program, dedicated to identifying and treating alcoholism, drug abuse and mental illness in doctors, and I wasn't about to throw my hat anywhere near that ring.

The standard hospital-issue furnishings in Kathy's office were institutional modular units, but she had overcome them. Her frilly Laura Ashley love seat filled the space in front of her desk. Porcelain-faced dolls sat in a row atop a few yards of ivory lace on the credenza. Instead of the usual collection of degrees and awards, original oils of children at play hung on the walls. A piece of antique stained glass blocked the view of the tenement houses out her window and cast orange and yellow and red light across the gray carpet.

I noticed one of Kathy's blond hairs coiled on the edge of the blotter, picked it up and pulled it straight between my fingers. The muscles in my neck and shoulders relaxed. I tilted the chair back and closed my eyes. If a single hair of hers moved me, I wondered, why not take the final step to marry her? What was I afraid of?

I fell asleep for several minutes, then woke to Kathy's hand gently massaging my shoulder. Her scent enveloped me. I kept my eyes closed and didn't move.If she was part of a lingering dream, I didn't want to scare her off.

"Frank," she whispered.

I took a deep breath but said nothing.

Sharply: "Frank. You fell asleep." She raked her knuckles across my collarbone.

"Ahh! Shit!" I cursed, wriggling away. I looked up and saw her standing over me, looking half-amused, half-annoyed. She was wearing blue scrubs that made her eyes seem even brighter. Her hair was damp.

"What are you doing here?" she asked.

"Jesus Christ." I rubbed my shoulder.

"What are you *doing* here?"

"I was looking for you. Alright?"

"What for?"

"I missed you last night."

"Really." She sat down on the love seat. "Why?"

I took a deep breath and straightened up in the chair. "Oh, I don't know, Kathy. You sleep with someone hundreds of nights in a row, you kind of get used to it."

She shrugged. "Does that put me above or below cocaine on your list of habits?" She noticed my wrist. "What happened to you?"

I looked at the bandage. Blood had seeped through. "Nothing. I was interviewing the man who . . . It happened at the jail."

"The man who killed Sarah," she said flatly. "You can say it. I won't fall apart. I hope they electrocute him. I'd throw the switch myself."

"Falling apart is allowed," I said. "So is rage."

"You would know. Let me look at your wrist."

"It's all set. Nels stitched me up."

Her expression turned to worry. "Last night?"

I smiled. "Actually, Nels usually has the morning shift. I just finished up with him. But you're right. He was on last night, covering for Buck Berenson. I think he felt badly interrupting you."

"Me?"

"You and Trevor."

She stood up. "You know what? I don't appreciate being interrogated—or set up—especially by someone as trustworthy as you."

"Did you fuck him?"

"Did I . . . ?" Her eyes filled up. "I can't believe you'd ask me that."

"Did you?"

She looked like a little misunderstood girl. "No."

"The two of you just visited? I'm supposed to believe that?"

"Believe what you want."

"You didn't come home."

"I don't have a home."

"Where did you sleep?"

"Your mother's." She wiped away a tear. "She showed me the scratches you made on her dining room table."

"You two are getting closer and closer."

"Maybe you'd like to know if I fucked her."

I stood up and walked over to her. I grabbed her scrub shirt, pulled her toward me and started to kiss her neck.

"Let go of me!" she demanded.

I held her tight, pulled the drawstring of her scrub pants loose and slipped my hand down between her legs. She tried to push me away at first, but stopped struggling as I kept touching her. Fighting me had always excited her. I felt her getting wet. I slipped a finger inside her, then two. She pressed herself against me. Her breathing quickened, and her pelvis rocked slightly toward and away from me. But just as she began to tighten around my fingers, her whole body froze. She dug her nails into my arm. "Don't," she said.

I pushed to keep my fingers inside her.

She took a step back and yanked my hand out of her pants.

She looked confused and needy and angry and very, very beautiful. I brushed the hair back from her face.

"I want to, Frank. You know I do. But I won't until you get help. I'm not going to be with someone who could be gone tomorrow."

"Any of us could be gone tomorrow."

"See how it feels, then." She tucked her top into her pants and took a few steps toward the door. "I have patients waiting in the clinic. Call me when you're off that shit. If you start to care a little more about yourself, maybe I'll start to care again, too."

"Where will you be?"

"Somewhere a little safer," she said.

•   •   •

I left the hospital and started toward Boston, hoping the V.A. Medical Center on Huntington Avenue might have more information on Westmoreland. Halfway there, my eyes fixed on the two-story, pink neon greyhound outside the Wonderland Dog Track.

I knew stopping would be the wrong thing to do. A lucky bet would be another drug—and I didn't have time to waste getting high. But insight doesn't necessarily produce self-control. Sometimes you just see your destructiveness more clearly. I pulled off Route 1A, lined my car up next to a thousand others and bought my two-buck program on the way to the betting windows.

I didn't really know whether Kathy had slept with Trevor. I didn't know whether she'd come back to me. I didn't know if Emma Hancock would report me to the Board. I didn't even know for sure whether I was officially off Westmoreland's case. I had no idea where I would find the $4,815 mortgage payment Eastern Bank wanted for September. What I knew was that Pompano Beached, whose name I liked immediately, was running in the fourth race of the afternoon, paying twenty-five to one, to win.

Manny, the clerk at the window, beamed when he saw me. "Help ya, Doc?" he urged. He was a little, round-shouldered, obese man with gold crowns that shimmered when he spoke.

"I need all kinds of help." I winked.

"You and me both," he nodded. "Missed you Saturday. Trifecta came in. Twenty-dollar bet paid out twenty-three grand."

"Don't tell me: A little old lady from Revere who lives in a triple-decker and bet her address."

"Nope. Guy was flashin' a gold-and-diamonds Rolex. Nobody wins when they need to."

"Don't say that, Manny. *I* need to."

"Then get back in your car."

"Give me fifty bucks on Pompano Beached to win."

"Hmm. Pompano?" He ran his fingers over his bald head like he still had hair. "Fifty?"

"Bad idea?"

"There are no bad ideas," he chuckled. "Not at *Wonder*land." He looked past me, right and left. "I might have a better one."

I slid a five-dollar bill under the window. It was Manny's standard fee. He moved his hand to a panel of buttons but didn't press any. "If I had fifty to spend," he said, tapping his diamond pinky ring on the countertop, "I'd lay it on Belle Dango." His eyes lit up. "I watched that bitch on a couple practice laps this morning. I never seen hound like that. Every muscle carved like stone, Doc. Fucking poetry in motion." He shook his head. "Pompano's built OK, but she's too pretty in the face. Dog that pretty don't need to run, and she knows it."

"Ain't that the truth. What are the odds on Belle?"

"Four to one."

I wasn't about to turn down a tip from a gold-toothed gnome like Manny, but I didn't want to kick myself for getting off a winner, either. "Twenty-five on Belle to win, twenty-five on Pompano to place."

"I'd go thirty-five, fifteen," he nodded.

"Done."

He slid the five-dollar bill back to me. "I'm in for ten percent."

"Deal."

Manny keyed in the bet just before the race began. I heard the starting pistol fire and walked to the wall of television monitors adjacent to the betting windows. The bunny flew down the track. Pompano had faded well back by the first turn. Belle Dango was stuck in the middle of the pack. "Boxed in," I muttered.

"She's setting the pace from the center," Manny said with confidence. "Cagey little bitch. I love that. Fuckin' beautiful." I glanced at him and saw that he was talking to himself, not to me. "Wait . . . wait . . . wait . . . wait . . . now! Go!"

Belle's spotted torso began flying past the other greyhounds. I felt my heart begin to race. My palms were moist. She moved just behind the leader, started to fade a bit, then advanced. The two dogs looked like one. They turned the last corner into the home-stretch.

Out of the corner of my eye I saw Manny looking at the program, not the monitors. "Homestretch," I called to him.

"No way to beat Belle in the stretch. Come get your money."

I stayed put. Belle opened a lead and kept it. Pompano Beached finished next to last. I could hear my pulse in my ears. I waited out the few people who were placing bets with Manny, then walked back to his window. "My God, what a dog. I thought she'd panic there in the pack. It didn't look like she had anywhere to go."

"You and me, we'd run scared in that much traffic," Manny said, shaking his head. "A dog like Belle sees the whole race before it starts. I know it's hard to believe, but she meant to be where she was every step of the way." He counted out seven twenties and slid them under the window. "I'd marry that dog."

I pushed one back toward him. "Here's your engagement gift."

"Too much."

"You earned it. What's next?"

"What's next is you should walk away," he joked. "Buy yourself a nice sweatshirt or something in the gift shop."

"Next dog."

"I like Maiden Voyage."

I slid my six twenties along with four more from my wallet under the window. "To win."

"You sure?"

"I guess not."

"Bet her to place. She gets in trouble near the finish line. Fear of success."

"I'm glad I'm not chasing bunnies. I think I got that fear worse than she does."

"*Everybody's* chasin' bunnies, Doc. Two hundred to place?"

"What are the odds?"

"Eleven to one."

"Two hundred."

I took my spot in front of the monitors. Maiden Voyage led from the beginning, then, twenty yards from the finish, gave up two lengths to Silly Puppy.

Manny and I had won and lost over the years, but this time he was definitely on a roll. I was up around twelve hundred. I didn't even think about stopping. "Hit me again," I said when I got to the window.

"You got it bad." Manny winked.

"I need—"

He covered his ears. "Don't say that."

"You're right. I'm sorry."

"Maybe you should go home."

"One more. Then we're done."

"Stay Safe."

"Jesus Christ, Manny. Just one more."

"That's it. *Stay Safe*, to show. Nine to one."

I looked down at my program. "Sounds like a brand of tampon."

"Ya, well, that's about right. She's been on the rag. Twice a favorite, never won. I say she's due."

"Why not bet her to win?"

He rolled his eyes. "There you go having ideas of your own. You really should call me for what to wear every morning."

"Alright. A thousand to show."

"A grand?"

"You really think she's due?"

He nodded.

"OK, then."

Laying that much cash on one dog pushed Westmoreland and Kathy and Hancock way, way back in my mind. I had outdistanced all of them. I took deep breaths of the musty Wonderland air. When the starting gun fired, I felt, of all things, confident.

Stay Safe took a long lead and never lost it. My skin turned to gooseflesh. I experienced my luck as something more than random, something *meant* for me. I felt Belle Dango and Maiden Voyage and Stay Safe and all the other dogs who had run and would run that day and Manny and me were somehow connected. It was just one of the many times I have found God in peculiar places.

I collected three thousand dollars and handed three hundreds back to Manny. "We'd be up nine grand if we'd bet her to win," I said.

"Ya. Unless she hadn't."

"One more?" I asked him.

"Go home."

"That a dog?"

"No. It's advice. We've been here before. Remember?"

That sobered me up. Manny and I had held three grand a dozen times and never kept more than a quarter of it. And I really did need the money. I slipped another two hundreds under the window. "Tip for a tip," I said. "Thanks."

"You don't have to do that."

"I know. That's why I'm doing it. See you, Manny."

Five

I got back on Route 1A and took it toward the Tobin Bridge into Boston. My mood was a little lighter. Sending the bank two thousand would probably keep them quiet a few weeks, and I'd still have cash to prevent myself from crashing off coke before I was ready to. Maybe I could even throw a little something at Hancock to lose whatever video she'd shot near the Emerson. I figured anybody who talked about church as much as she did was using it a little like cocaine anyhow. At a stoplight I took out my package and did a little blast.

It took me half an hour to reach the V.A. Medical Center. The Medical Information and Benefits Office hadn't changed its location since I'd been a resident, and Cliff Pidrowski, a recovering alcoholic who'd lost his legs in Vietnam, was still running the place. He recognized me immediately. "Oh, Jesus," he laughed, "hide the money." He wheeled himself out from behind his desk.

"I didn't cost you guys much," I chuckled, shaking his hand. I was glad to see he hadn't cut his hair, which hung in a braid down his back.

"Didn't you? Shit. Every skid row vet in the state must have had the word on you. Show up in the emergency room with a little depression or posttraumatic stress and watch the spin doctor make your benefits flow. *Spin*; they still call you that?"

"You were the only one who called me that." I took a seat. "And

I was just convincing you to give away what you wanted to give away in the first place."

"Oh, I did? I must have buried that real deep in my subconscious. I seem to remember sweating bullets to get it through your head once in a great while that being on the streets isn't always service-connected. You can be plenty fucked up before you fight a war."

"Then you shouldn't have to fight it. Uncle Sam's got to take his victims as they come."

He covered his ears. "I'm having déjà vu. Tell me you're not here on a job interview."

"You think the government has its head *completely* up its ass? I'm still chasing forensic cases on the North Shore."

"You always liked the real sickos," he chuckled. "I got to admit, though, you could settle them right down. They must have sensed they were with someone as dangerous as them."

"I'm harmless."

He rolled his eyes. "Not to shortcut the journey down memory lane, but if you're already gainfully employed, what are you here for?"

"A favor . . . if you're willing."

"Sure. Anything that doesn't cost Uncle Sam a monthly check."

"I need a service record."

"That's confidential information."

"That's why it's a favor."

He wheeled himself over to a computer station. "Anybody asks, I never helped you with a thing," he said.

"I won't have to convince anyone who knows you."

"Still a wise ass. What's the name?"

"First name's George. Second name starts with '*La*.' "

He entered *L* and *a*. "That narrows it down to a group about the size of Rhode Island. And cross-referencing with '*George*' . . . I'm down to several hundred. What war?"

"Vietnam."

"That's progress. Got a diagnosis?"

"Schizophrenia."

"Eye color?"

"Blue."

"Height?"

"About six feet."

"I got a blue-eyed, six-one schizophrenic by the name of George LaFountaine. Born, April 5, 1949. Drafted, Army, April 16, 1969. Court-martialed, November 28, 1970. Charges dismissed. Medically discharged, December 1, 1970. Diagnosis: Schizophrenia."

"Court-martialed? Anything in there say what happened to him, what he was charged with?"

"That wouldn't be on the computer." He swiveled toward me. "But he was treated upstairs on 13B after discharge. And about a dozen times since then. The records should be in storage."

"How would I get those?"

"With a release of information from the patient."

"No chance."

"Then you're shit out of luck. Medical records isn't my department. They're touchy about details. Like the Fourth Amendment."

"I've already examined the guy, Cliff. He'd want me to see his chart, but he's locked up. I can't get to him right now."

"Sorry."

I sighed. "I didn't want to use it up, but I guess I'm gonna have to call in my debt."

"Debt?"

"Helena?"

"You can call me Charisse, if you want to. It won't get you anywhere."

"Not Helena. Helga. That social work intern. Bright red lipstick. Tight skirts. I let you borrow my call room with her. You said you owed me one — a big one."

"That was ages ago. Like ten years."

"Lucky for you I'm not charging interest."

"She wasn't even that good."

"She was good enough to tie up my room for three fucking hours in the middle of the night." I smiled.

"I think I'm getting it where the sun don't shine," he said, shaking his head. "You really, absolutely need this . . ."

I nodded.

He picked up the phone and dialed. "Rusty, Cliff. I hope you can help me. I need to pull whatever records you've got on George LaFountaine, capital *L-a*, capital *F-o*. First admission to 13B, December 3, 1970. Social Security number 010-16-3024. I'm gonna send down a shrink—Doctor Clevenger. . . . No. . . . No release. . . . He's doing a study on benefit payments for psychiatric disabilities. I forgot to get him clearance." He winked at me. "Thanks, Rusty. I owe you one." He hung up.

"I appreciate it."

"Forget it. Rusty should have it for you in about ten minutes. Basement level."

"It was good seeing you."

He nodded. "You, too, Spin. Try to be careful out there, will ya?"

"You bet."

· · ·

I found Rusty, who turned out to be a thin, jittery woman about fifty, eating a brown bag lunch deep in the three thousand square feet of wall-to-wall records that comprised Patient Information Retrieval. She was sitting Indian-style on the floor, leaning against one of the floor-to-ceiling files. "You can't take it with you," she said, struggling to hand an eight-inch thick folder up to me. She turned away, bit off the top of a carrot stick and swallowed it without chewing.

"*Can't take it with you,*" I kidded. "That's catchy. You should write it down."

"Sure, everything's a joke—until something gets lost. Then somebody comes down looking for that something, and, suddenly, it's not funny anymore." She looked very serious. "It's the end of the world."

"Yeah. Well, sorry." I sat down against the file opposite her.

She kept staring at me.

"Am I OK here?" I asked.

"If you don't watch me eat."

You can figure out a lot about people's minds by the way they feel about putting things in their mouths. I had to remind myself that I didn't have the time to get into it with her. "No problem," I said. I flipped open the chart. There was a black-and-white photograph of George LaFountaine glued to the inside cover. He was handsome, even with a crew cut. His smile was full and confident. I focused on his eyes, looking for Westmoreland in him. They gave away nothing. I fanned the pages of the chart and stopped at a color photograph, marked 1985. I shook my head in disbelief.

LaFountaine had become Westmoreland. His cheeks had hollowed, and his smile had contorted into a fierce showing of teeth. His hair had grown into a tangle of snakes. Terror had taken over his eyes. I felt like a burglar walking through another man's home. Or was I digging up a grave? Westmoreland had wanted to bury LaFountaine, and I had unearthed him. The moral thing to do may have been to put the chart back on the shelf, to leave undisturbed in that tomb of records what Westmoreland had intended to. Wasn't I justifying his paranoia by violating his confidentiality?

Perhaps it was my own morbid curiosity that convinced me in that moment that there was a *reason* I had his chart in my hands— that it was not by chance he had let slip enough of his name to unlock the door to his past.

I went back to the beginning of the chart and read the cover sheet. It listed Westmoreland's date of discharge from the service and his date of admission to the hospital. His family address was recorded as 12 Warren Avenue in Charlestown, a tough, blue-collar neighborhood on the north edge of Boston. Next of kin was his father, John LaFountaine. I turned the page to the first of two handwritten sheets labeled "Initial Psychiatric History":

> George LaFountaine is a 22-year-old white man medically discharged from the Army due to the onset, following military action, of

paranoia and auditory hallucinations. These psychotic symptoms were believed to be responsible for Mr. LaFountaine's recent bizarre behavior, which resulted in a court-martial. All charges have been dismissed, and the patient is remanded for psychiatric assessment and definitive treatment.

On November 21, Mr. LaFountaine, who previously had been decorated for bravery, participated as a member of an elite group raiding the Son Tay prison camp near Hanoi, an operation for which he had trained extensively. The camp was believed to house U.S. POWs but was found abandoned. The patient spent several hours searching vacant buildings, some of which were booby-trapped. A close friend, searching with the patient, was killed by explosives.

I looked up and tried to imagine the muddled surges of hope, fear, hate and sheer panic that must have swept over LaFountaine as he burst into each empty room in that abandoned camp. I pictured him holding his dying friend, blown up on a mission to free no one, by an enemy nowhere to be found.

"Don't," Rusty scolded.

"What?"

"You were looking at me eating. I asked you not to."

"I wasn't. I was just thinking."

"Right. About what a pig I am." She gathered her Baggies of vegetables and got to her feet. Standing, she looked even bonier. "I'm not going to play your game."

I couldn't leave it alone. Pain has always been irresistible to me. "The truth is, Rusty, that you were never fed enough, not that you swallow too much."

She took a step toward me. "Who the hell do you think you are coming at me with that slick analysis crap? You wanted a record. I got you one. I don't remember askin' to lay on any goddamn couch."

I nodded. I could tell I was already deeper into some crevice of Rusty's unconscious than I wanted to be. "You're right. I'll just finish my reading." I made a point of hanging my head over the chart so that I couldn't be accused of looking at her.

"And to say I wasn't fed enough. Another goddamn shrink who thinks he knows everything."

I stole a glance at her feet. They weren't moving. She wanted the couch. Deep down, everybody wants to tell the truth.

"You probably grew up with a silver spoon in your mouth, Doc," she prodded. "My father worked three jobs to put food on the table."

I closed my eyes, hoping she'd let me off the hook.

"Dad cooked for us, too. I ate plenty well. Better than well." No footsteps. "So what's your point? Or don't you have one?"

I looked up reluctantly. "Did your mother work?" I surrendered.

She seemed startled. "Huh?"

"Your mother. Did she have a job?"

"She wasn't around. But . . ."

"Why not? Where was she?"

"Why would I tell you?"

"I don't know. You certainly don't have to." *You need to*.

"What the hell. You want to know so bad, she got sick—mentally sick—right after I was born. Killed herself in this very hospital." She put her hands on her hips. "Happy?"

My shoulders sloped under the burden of her revelation. I sighed. "Pretty big job," I said quietly, "filling the space she left behind. Especially as the only child."

"How did you . . ."

"Just a guess. But I can see how it would make things that much harder for you."

She shrugged.

The rest of what I had to say forced its way out, like a child being born. "He couldn't give you enough by himself. Your father, I mean. No man could—no matter how good he was. And you couldn't let him know that. That's what I was getting at when I said you weren't *fed* enough. I meant emotionally. A mother's love." I looked straight into her eyes. "I'm sorry you ended up feeling guilty about your needs."

"I feel guilty all the time. About everything. Even . . ."

"Of course you do. That's why you think everyone's watching you eat. You're not allowed to have an appetite, let alone a big one."

She tightened her grip on her vegetables. "I don't know about all this," she said. She walked to the end of the corridor and around the corner.

I stared after her a few seconds, warmed by the very part of her—the neediness, the capacity to be loved and filled—that she feared letting anyone know. I took a deep breath and started to read more about LaFountaine:

> According to scant records sent with the patient, his symptoms were present by November 23 when he sought out a senior officer and reported that assassins were stalking him for "crimes of cowardice against mankind." He was sedated and observed in the camp infirmary, for an apparent acute stress reaction. His symptoms subsided, and he was allowed to resume his routine.
>
> On November 25, however, Mr. LaFountaine, using a scalpel he had apparently smuggled from the infirmary, took hostage a nurse who had cared for him there, insisting she was involved in the plot to capture and execute him. After holding her in a storage shed for four hours, he released her. He had cut deep horizontal gashes at the corners of her eyes, presumably to investigate his suspicion that she was equipped with robotic surveillance devices.

I read the last sentence three times. My stomach churned. He had done it before. It was all there: the woman, the knife, the search beneath and behind. I let my head fall back. Could I have missed the drama Westmoreland was playing out? Did he need to know whether his lover, his Madonna, was a robot under her soft parts? Was he repentant now because he had found only flesh and blood? Even with the Amytal on board, maybe he couldn't tell me what he had done because he feared I was part of the plot to kill him. I didn't want to read any more, but I needed to:

> Mr. LaFountaine was apprehended and contained. A court-martial was held November 28 at which charges against him were dropped,

as it was determined he was suffering a psychotic disorder. The patient was medically discharged, processed and transported to this facility. Mental-status examination on admission revealed a well-kempt, muscular white male whose speech was rapid, sometimes to the point of incoherence. His affect was labile. Mood was reported by the patient as "horrifying." He was quite paranoid, continuing to believe others were pursuing him in order to exact revenge for his "crimes of cowardice." He denied auditory, visual, olfactory or tactile hallucinations (although his report may not be reliable). He is oriented to person and to date, but mistakes this hospital for an "experimental lab" where his brain will be "analyzed for radio transmitters"—the theme of robotics and mechanization again being prominent.

This is the patient's first known psychiatric admission. He denies previous psychiatric symptoms.

Developmental history is significant for severe beatings by both parents during childhood. It is not known whether the patient sustained head trauma or loss of consciousness.

I closed my eyes. Every violent person I have ever treated was victimized as a child. I took out my package of coke, snorted what was left and started to pace with the chart.

There are no known serious adult medical illnesses. There is no known alcohol or illicit drug abuse.

Mr. LaFountaine will be treated with antipsychotic medication, most likely haloperidol. The goal of treatment must be to eliminate his paranoid delusions and any other psychotic symptoms and, hence, his potential for violence. Given the patient's recent assaultiveness, we anticipate an extended stay.

Bruce Rightwinder, M.D.
Attending Psychiatrist, 13B

LaFountaine's first admission lasted five months. Haloperidol didn't stop his paranoia. Thorazine didn't work, either. Dr.

Rightwinder started to wonder whether his patient's symptoms might be due to an underlying psychotic depression. He had lost a friend, after all. When a six-week trial of the antidepressant imipramine failed, Rightwinder prescribed twelve sessions of electroconvulsive therapy.

The patient improved steadily. He became more trusting. He stopped talking about robots and transmitters. But there was a significant side effect from the shock treatments. "The patient has no memory of the events preceding his hospitalization," Rightwinder wrote. "He cannot recall participating in the Son Tay raid. He denies anyone close to him having died. While obviously worrisome, we believe this memory loss to be a temporary phenomenon."

It sounded to me like they had temporarily nuked LaFountaine's trauma into the deepest recesses of his cortex. But psychological conflict always works its way back to the surface. He was admitted with paranoid delusions ten more times over the next decade. On each occasion he was given more antipsychotic medication and more electroconvulsive therapy, and his condition gradually stabilized. Noting the relapses, another staff psychiatrist decided Mr. LaFountaine should return to the hospital every two months for *maintenance* shock treatments. But the patient stopped showing up during November 1985:

> Mr. LaFountaine failed to present for his maintenance electroconvulsive therapy. Given his history of violence, and recurrences of intense paranoia over the past several years, a Section 12 commitment has been filed with the court. Boston and V.A. police have been notified to locate the patient and bring him to the emergency room. They have been provided with his address in Charlestown and with a description.

The police apparently hadn't found him—until now. I closed the chart and walked around the corner to find Rusty. She was working on some filing two aisles away. I held the chart out to her.

She didn't take it from me. "You look awful," she said. "Are you alright?"

"Tired. That's all."

"I'm not sure I got everything you told me, but when I thought about it, it kind of made sense."

I was finding it hard to focus on what she was saying.

"Where do you practice? You have a card?" She waited a few seconds. "Did you hear me?"

I could have told her *my* truth—that the most I could pull off reliably was a ten-minute analysis on the fly, not much more than you'd buy off a decent psychic in a coffee house. I could have told her that she needed someone braver and more honest than I to take her all the way back to whatever fires of hell burned the child in her. I could have told her that I'd probably disappoint, leave her lost and alone somewhere in her past, unable to finish the journey into her pain and back out again. "I don't see patients anymore" was what I managed.

Injured people know one another. Her tone of voice dropped to a croon of empathy. "Don't see patients? But why?"

"Long story." I forced a smile. "You've got your own to think about." I laid the chart on an empty shelf and walked away.

Six

The sky had gone gray behind a driving rain. I wanted to fly home, to clear my head, but could only lurch from traffic jam to traffic jam. I cursed my wipers, worn nearly to the metal, and leaned to peer through the windshield. Everything looked hopelessly distorted. I rolled down the passenger window to edge my way right, onto Longwood Avenue.

Longwood runs past four Harvard teaching hospitals that have grown around and over one another. I had to lower the window again to squeeze past two construction cranes jutting into the road in front of the Dana-Farber Cancer Institute. The place had swollen three times the size it was when I worked there as an assistant to Dr. Hyman Weitzman during the summer of my sophomore year at the University of Massachusetts. I was majoring in neuroscience, and Weitzman, an oncologist, had teamed up with neurosurgeons to investigate whether placing radioactive disks directly into glioblastoma brain tumors could slow their growth.

Even back then I had felt like an outsider. The other students working on the project were fascinated by the haphazard shapes of the malignant cells under the electron microscope, the technique of implanting the disks in the brain, the changes in patients' reflexes and vision as the cancer invaded, then retreated. None of that excited me. I stayed late at the institute to ask patients how it *felt* to harbor a deadly intruder, what they fantasized had caused their illnesses, what they believed would heal them.

At the end of the summer Weitzman, a bespectacled, obsessive man who had survived Auschwitz, called me into his office. He handed me a letter of recommendation highlighting my statistical analysis of our data. "You did a complete and thorough job," he told me. "I appreciate your efforts." He gazed out the window of his Spartan office. "May I share a concern with you?"

I adored Weitzman in the way I adored every older man who showed me any hint of the kindness I had missed from my father. I worried he knew I had been playing grab-ass every lunch hour with his research assistant Lisa in her studio apartment down the street. "A concern?" I asked.

"More a piece . . ."

I cringed.

". . . of advice."

"Of course."

He leaned toward me. "I have worked as a researcher many years, Frank. I have known great investigators. Mountcastle, Snyder, DePaulo, Coyle. These men love biochemistry and anatomy and physiology. Structure and function. Cause and effect." His voice rose and fell like German music. "They are perpetually fascinated by the body. They see the whole universe in a single cell." He held his hands in the air like a conductor. "Such a man feels his pulse in the contraction of a single muscle fibre of another man's heart."

I was drawn in by his passion. "Yes!" I said.

He shook his head and leaned back in his chair. "You are not one of these men."

"No?"

"I have been watching you, listening to you. You are interested in philosophy—the meaning of things. Big questions. You are concerned with the soul."

I felt as if I was being disowned. "Well, it isn't that I don't—"

He held up a hand to stop me. "A suggestion."

I waited in silence.

"Have you thought of studying at a seminary, of becoming a minister?"

"A minister?"

"A spiritual guide. A moral leader in the community. Such individuals are sorely needed at this time."

"I've never thought of it," I said.

"Are you a religious man?"

I considered telling him about my contempt for organized religion — organized anything — but I knew he was a devout Jew. "I think I believe in God," I said.

"You think . . ." He nodded and sighed. "I see."

Longwood ended in a traffic signal near the on-ramp to Storrow Drive. The car in front of me didn't budge when the light turned green. I waited a few seconds, then hit the horn. The car finally started to move, but at a crawl. I stepped on the gas and swerved around it.

Weitzman's advice had seemed bizarre to me, but some of it must have hit home because I went back to U. Mass. that fall as a double major in neuroscience and philosophy. And after four years studying, prodding and dissecting every organ in the body at Tufts Medical School, I picked a specialty concerned with healing the spirit. At least that's what it used to be about before insurance and pharmaceutical companies cut the heart out of it.

Now, with Westmoreland looking more and more like a killer, I wondered whether my choice had been such a good one. Maybe I would have done better to devote myself to the kidneys or the retina, where pathology can be measured in milliliters of urine output or degrees of visual acuity. Because something kept going horribly wrong with me and psychiatry. Emma Hancock liked to dredge up Prescott, but his wasn't the first case I'd botched.

During 1988, while I was in private practice, I had begun treating an adolescent named Billy Fisk. Billy had been abandoned by his biological parents at the age of four and raised by one set of foster parents after another. By age twelve he was drinking steadily; by age fourteen he had stolen his first car. Six grand larceny arrests later he was sent to me for therapy. He had just turned sixteen and was serving time in a Department of Youth Services detention facility.

"You've got to stop stealing," I told him during our first meeting.

He was already as tall as I was and even broader in the shoulders. A scar from a street fight ran from the corner of his mouth across his left cheek. "Cause you say so?" he sneered.

"You think I'm an asshole?" I sneered back. "Why would you give two shits what I say?"

He shrugged but looked me in the eyes for the first time.

"You should stop stealing because you're lousy at it. You get caught every time."

"Not every time," he smirked.

"OK, *pretty* lousy at it."

"How would you know? You never stoled nothin'."

"I haven't?"

He rolled his eyes. "You're a doctor."

"Let's see. . . . . A bike. A crate of oranges. More street signs than I could find places to hide. A stereo. A forklift, once, when I was about your age."

"You grabbed a forklift?"

"I didn't want it. I mean: What the hell was I going to do with a forklift, right? But I wanted *something*. I just couldn't figure out what it was."

He nodded. "It's like being hungry, but it don't go away when you eat."

"It only gets worse."

Having presented my bona fides as a thief, I went on meeting twice a week with Billy for a little less than a year—about a hundred hours tossing a football around my office, talking about loneliness and fear and rage, splitting enormous cheese steaks at Sunrise Subs down the street. Then his sentence was up. He was scheduled to join another foster family—the Worths—out in the western part of the state.

"Too bad I can't live with you," he said, chuckling.

I had thought about that possibility, but not seriously. It would have raised concerns at the Department of Youth Services about my "clinical boundaries." More important, it would have meant giving up the independence I loved. "You're going to do fine," I told him.

Within two months Billy was drinking heavily again. His "family" was talking about getting rid of him. He called and asked me to visit, but I told him I didn't want to interfere with him and the Worths working things out. "You hang in there, and I'll give you a call in another few days," I said.

He was sobbing.

"OK?"

"OK," he managed.

The next day Anne Sacon, a Department of Youth Services case manager, called me at the office. "Dr. Clevenger," she said, "I have bad news about Billy."

I figured he'd stolen another car and been locked up. Part of me welcomed the chance to work with him again. "Where's Billy the Kid now? Maximum Security?" I asked.

She exhaled audibly. "Billy's dead. He killed himself."

"Killed himself?"

"Mr. Worth found him in the garage. He used a rope and one of the beams."

"When?"

"Early morning."

"What happened? Did he leave a note?"

"It was eerie," she said. "It said, 'Hang in there.'"

I was trembling.

"Are you there?"

"OK," I said.

"Since you two already terminated, we'll finish all the paperwork, including the incident report."

What a strange word for saying goodbye to Billy, I thought— *terminate*. "Is there anyone else to contact?"

"He didn't really have anyone else."

After we hung up, I thought how Billy had never really had me, either. I'd been available, for a fee, two hours a week. When push had came to shove, and he'd needed a real father, I hadn't been able to do any better for him than my own father had for me. Not even when he'd reached the end of his rope. I hadn't even heard the final desperation that must have been in his voice the day he called.

I worried more and more that I was a dabbler in life stories, rather than a student of them, that I would skim over another critical page. Three months after Billy died, I terminated with the rest of my patients and closed up my psychotherapy practice.

A couple of BMWs were traveling side by side down the two eastbound lanes of Storrow Drive, like a moving roadblock. I tailgated in the passing lane, but got nowhere. I leaned over for a clearer view, veered all the way into the breakdown lane and whipped in front of them.

I had hoped forensic work would be more about facts than feelings, more about the evidence than about me. It wasn't turning out that way. Something inside me kept blinding me to the destructiveness in people—in Prescott, and now in Westmoreland.

I sped through a yellow light at Bell Circle in Revere and tried to cut across two lanes to make the entrance to Route 1A. When I turned the wheel, the car kept going straight. "Christ," I muttered. "Not now." I steered into the skid and pumped the brakes. Just as I felt rubber grabbing the road, an old, red Mustang tried to slip past me. I flipped into low gear and pumped faster. I managed to miss the driver's side door but smashed into his rear quarter panel.

I got the Rover back in control and kept driving around the rotary. Part of me wanted to race toward Boston. My insurance had been canceled for nonpayment, and I had six delinquent parking tickets in the glove compartment. If the police got involved, they'd boot my car and confiscate my license. I checked my rearview mirror and saw the Mustang pulling into the Dunkin' Donuts parking lot off the rotary. I shook my head. The last thing I needed was a hit-and-run on my record. I finished the lap, swung into the lot and parked between two other cars.

The driver of the Mustang, a short, stocky kid about twenty, was pacing in front of the dent, holding his head in his hands. I walked over and looked at the car. The rear quarter panel and taillight were crushed, a hubcap was mangled and the bumper was dented and hanging loose.

He glared at me. He was pulling nervously at his Grateful Dead T-shirt. "You stupid sack of shit!" he spewed.

The best way to exhaust someone's rage is to run ahead of it. "What an asshole I am!" I sputtered. "What was I thinking?"

He glanced back at me. "Damn," he said, almost calmly. He paced a little, then started in, again. "How goddamn fast—"

"I'm such a shithead, I can't believe it." I looked around to make sure no cops were driving by. "What is this, a '67?"

"Sixty-four and a half."

Just my luck, crashing into a classic. "Perfect condition."

"Until now, you mother—"

"I can't fucking believe what I did."

"I drove to Vermont to get that hubcap," he said, his voice cracking. He shook his head. He was winding down. "Let's exchange everything and get this over with."

I didn't want to exchange anything. "Why don't I take care of it so we don't have to get insurance companies involved?"

"Take care of it?"

"The repair." I took the wad of hundreds from Wonderland out of my pocket. "How much do you think is fair?"

He looked at the money. "I'm not sure about this. I think we should do it the regular way."

"The regular way? With a '64½?" I walked around the back of his car to check his license plate. "You don't even have this registered as a classic. The insurance company will never ante up for original parts."

He looked sick to his stomach. "The taillight alone goes four, five hundred, if you can find it."

"You'll find it. Let's say fifteen hundred, total."

"Like I told you, the light's five by itself. I got no idea about the bumper, let alone the panel. There could be axle damage."

I thought about bringing up the fact that his license plate also carried a code for people who are supposed to be wearing glasses when they drive—which he wasn't—but I couldn't afford to piss him off. "So what's fair?"

"I don't know. Twenty-five, at least."

"Twenty-five?" Out of the corner of my eye I saw a police cruiser entering the rotary. You can't stay ten minutes at a Dunkin' Donuts without a cop turning up. "Done," I said. I started counting.

The kid took my cash, and I dragged myself back to the Rover. The right front corner was flattened, and the fog light was ripped off. It would probably cost a grand to fix—money I didn't have. I pulled myself inside, picked up the phone and dialed Stonehill Hospital. The operator put me on hold while she paged Kathy.

"Dr. Singleton," she answered.

As soon as I heard her voice, I knew I wouldn't be getting the comfort I longed for, but I stayed on the line. I wasn't willing yet to admit how alone in the world I really was. "Kathy, Frank," I managed.

No response.

My throat tightened. "I, uh . . ." I took a deep breath.

"What's wrong? Where are you?"

"Dunkin' Donuts."

"What's wrong, no honey-dipped?"

I forced myself to chuckle. "I had an accident with the car. That's all. I stopped here."

"Are you hurt?"

"No." I took a deep breath.

"You're shaken up?"

"I'm fine," I lied.

"Frank. I've got three minutes before my next OR case. Why, exactly, did you page me?"

"I've been telling Emma Hancock she's got the wrong man, and now it looks like the guy might have done it."

"Well, he's still locked up, right? It's not like you let him go."

"He's locked up."

"I hope they—"

"I know. I know you do. The trouble is the evidence still doesn't make sense to me. And even if Westmoreland's guilty, that doesn't mean he's rational enough to confess. He's out in the stratosphere. If they'd let me give him one of the new antipsychotics, like Clozaril, he might have more to say."

"You'd go out of your way to give Sarah's murderer a hand?"

"He was abused half his life."

"Abused how?"

"Beaten."

"Spare me. Another killer as victim."

"I haven't met any killer yet who wasn't."

"Even Marcus Prescott?"

My stomach fell. "Why are you—"

"Even him?"

I closed my eyes. "Yes. Even Prescott."

"You know what? If you want to go on painting yourself as some sort of messiah to psychopaths, that's your business. But don't screw up Sarah's case over it. *She's* the victim." She paused. "The truth is, Westmoreland is just another of your addictions."

"Huh?"

"I don't think it much matters to you. Coke, booze, girls, the occasional mind-fuck with a patient. Me, when everything else runs out."

"You're not an addiction. Neither is Westmoreland."

"Oh, thank you. I'm in good company. Listen to me: You need to get yourself to a detox."

"I have to see this through."

"You're too polluted to be of any use to anyone—the police included."

"I don't know. The facts don't add up. I can't say it's the coke."

"Then you'll have to learn the hard way. Hitting bottom. Just don't expect me to pick up the pieces. I'm sick of playing second fiddle to your crazies."

"You really think I should go to another detox? Now?"

"I've said what I think."

"I can stop on my own."

She laughed. " 'The drug's not the problem. I can stop on my own.' You sound like a junkie."

I did sound like a junkie. I let all my breath out. "I'll think about admitting myself to McLean."

"Don't think too long." She hung up.

I sat there a few minutes, planning my next move. I didn't think I'd be able to sit in therapy groups at McLean and pay attention while bankers started to foreclose on my house and repossess my car. I drove over to my mother's apartment building. I had to press the intercom button on the directory five times before she answered.

"Hello?" she sang. Her voice sounded tinny and distant.

"It's Frank." I stood there with my hand on the door, waiting for the lock to click open.

"Oh."

"The door isn't clicking open."

"Are you here for money again?"

I didn't have the energy to lie. And I didn't have the courage to tell her I needed much more than money from her. Things she'd never been able to give. "The three hundred you gave me doesn't really make a dent. I've got my mortgage and—"

"Kathy told me to expect another demand for cash."

"Let me in."

"No."

I let out all my breath and leaned on the wall to get my mouth closer to the speaker. "You can send checks directly to the finance companies, if you want. I'm in trouble. I could lose everything."

"You always take the easy way out of trouble, Frank. That's the problem."

Funny. I didn't remember taking the easy way out of any beatings from my father while she was locked in her bedroom.

"Kathy says I have to stop being one of your . . . I forget what she called it. Disablers?"

I smiled in spite of myself. "*Enablers*, not disablers. And the only thing you'd be enabling me to do is keep a roof over my head and wheels under my ass."

"Well, I'm sorry. I have to be firm."

"You won't help me."

"Not with money."

"Not even, say, a thousand?"

"No."

"Five hundred?"

"Not a dime."

I leaned to get my mouth even closer to the speaker. But what I had to say was vulgar and venomous and, though I hated the woman at that moment, I couldn't bring myself to say it. I walked out of the lobby.

•   •   •

I didn't get home until dusk had draped the house in shadows. The phone was ringing. I let my machine answer.

"Hellooo. You there? Pick up!"

I grabbed the cordless from the end table in the living room and collapsed onto the couch. "Paulson."

"Screening your calls. What are you, paranoid?"

"Absolutely."

"I guess not paranoid enough . . ."

I reached for a Marlboro from a tiger's-eye box on the coffee table. "Meaning?"

"Malloy tells me they shook you off the case. Actually, he said, 'That cocksucker shrink got canned.' "

I lit up. "*Cocksucker* and *canned* in one sentence, huh? It's looking more and more like his rage stems from repressed homosexuality."

"I'd like to go searching for that with a scalpel."

"His baton might be more effective."

"I'll try anything once." He paused. "You really off the case?"

"Sounds that way. Hancock and I went at each other badly this morning."

"Maybe she'll cool off."

"It doesn't matter much now. She only gave me thirty-six hours to work with Westmoreland. Even if she stuck to the deal, I'd be almost out of time."

"I hear Fitzgerald found Westmoreland competent to confess — and to stand trial."

"Naturally. He's bought and paid for." I looked out the window at the ocean. There was just enough sunlight left to make out the spray of waves as they crashed against the seawall. "I'm not sure I was seeing the case clearly myself."

"It's not my call, but maybe you got too close, too fast." He paused. "Did you really slice your wrist to get Westmoreland to stop biting himself?"

I took a drag off my cigarette and blew the smoke out in a thin stream. "Malloy told you that, too?"

"So it's true. Unbelievable."

"I knew Westmoreland wouldn't let me do much damage." I shook my head, thinking about what he'd done to the nurse he'd taken hostage. "At least I didn't think he would. After today I'm not sure about anything."

"Sounds like one for the record books."

"I'll tell you about it when my mind's a little clearer."

"You're not alone in the fog. It's getting more and more confusing down here at the lab."

"How so?"

"Remember I told you Sarah had fibrotic changes at the margins of her wounds?"

"Sure."

"I figured she had fibrocystic disease."

"Or scleroderma."

"No. Not scleroderma. I specifically ruled out scleroderma as unlikely."

"Whatever. What do you think now?"

"It's not *whatever*, Frank. I never seriously entertained sclero-derma. I told you her esophagus was too pink and moist for scleroderma. Scleroderma leaves the tissue like rawhide. I don't want . . ."

I pictured him at home in a starched white button-down, squir-reled away in his spotless study, surrounded by the hundreds of pathology books and journals he kept precisely aligned on the floor-to-ceiling shelves. "I wasn't accusing you of misdiagnosing the corpse," I reassured him. "I was just hoping you'd get to the point."

"Patience, Doctor. You do remember our discussion. We were at the microscope."

"I remember. I remember."

"Then you'll remember I never formally put forward sclero-derma as a diagnosis."

"Fine," I strained.

"I never broke my wrist on that swing."

I felt like hurling the phone through the window. "You're ab-solutely right. You didn't."

"I stated that I didn't know the specific etiology of the fibrosis. And believe me, I've suffered over that."

"I can only imagine."

"Exactly. You can only imagine. Because—and I mean no offense—yours is a soft science. A set of theories. When all the an-swers must be in flesh and blood, when nothing counts that cannot be seen, a man can be brought to his knees by the whiplash of a loose end."

"Beautifully put. Especially for a hard scientist. I take it you have a plan to stay on your feet."

"Of course I do. I sent slides from the wound margins to Ed Mc-Carthy at Johns Hopkins. Ed's the best pathologist I know."

"And what does he think caused it?"

"He couldn't say for sure."

"Paulson, I've had a bad day," I pleaded. "What did this Ed guy find?"

"This *Ed guy*? That's a little like calling DiMaggio that *Joe guy*."

He chuckled. "Anyhow, he couldn't say *for sure*, but he had a pretty strong idea."

"I promise not to hold him to it."

"Fair enough. He thinks the tissue was exposed to a toxin."

"A toxin? Like what?"

"We don't know. Ed cleared the way for me to send a sample to the FBI crime lab in Quantico, Virginia. They've seen everything."

"I'd like to hear what they come up with." I looked at a photograph of Kathy on the coffee table. She was perched on the rocks outside my house in a little white sundress, holding her knees and pouting. The ultimate nymphet. "I might be hard to reach for about a week, though."

"Is that right? Good for you. It's about time."

"About time for what?"

"To stop polluting yourself. You've got the same twitching in your eyelids that you had before the last detox."

"It's that obvious? Have I seemed out of it?"

"If you'd been out of it, I would have locked you up myself until you were off that poison. On your worst day you're sharper than any psychiatrist I've met. I just miss your best days."

"When were they?"

"Soon, I hope."

I smiled. "Thanks."

"Get better, my friend."

I clicked the phone off. I knew Kathy and Paulson were right. I was like a ship taking on water, fast. I searched my wallet and pulled out the napkin Rachel had given me. I dialed her beeper. If I was going to a detox, I was going after one last big night. The phone rang a minute later.

"Rachel?"

"Who's this?"

"Frank."

"Very funny."

"I didn't mean it to be." I took a drag off the cigarette and blew the smoke out through my nose. "I'm the psychiatrist who offended you at the Lynx Club last night."

"I'm sorry," she laughed. "You never told me your name."

"I got yours off a napkin."

"It's been worse places. I had to pay Max twenty bucks to get that napkin to you."

"I tipped him ten."

"He ended up making out alright, for a complete pain in the ass."

"He was just doing a job."

"That's very understanding of you."

I had started to pace like a schoolboy. "I called to see if we could have dinner tonight."

"You and Max, or you and me?"

"I don't know. I didn't get a chance to see him dance."

"The truth is, he's your only choice tonight. I'm working."

"Oh."

"But if you visit me at the club, we could have a drink after closing."

I wouldn't have turned down an invitation like that when Kathy was sleeping at home, let alone with her unaccounted for all night. Maybe that was a weakness in me worth pondering, but I wasn't about to ponder it just then. I told Rachel I'd stop in at the Lynx Club around ten.

I had time to kill. I walked into the study, turned on the antique standing lamp and dropped into a worn leather wing chair. The cigarette had relaxed me a bit. I grabbed another from a crystal cup on the side table and lighted it. I imagined the empty rooms of the house stacked like a maze around me. It was a much larger place than two people could make use of, let alone one. Four thousand seven hundred and thirty square feet. In that way, my mother's question about what I needed it for was on the mark, even if she had played a part in creating the need. I couldn't deny that the house was partly my reaction against an inner fear of being insubstantial.

Kathy had not wanted to see that fear in me—or I had kept it from her—which explained why my coke habit brought out only her anger and no compassion.

I glanced at the bookcase against the far wall. It was an English piece with griffins carved at each corner. The top shelf was filled with Kathy's collection of Trixie Belden books. She had told me more than once that the stories, about a teenage heroine who solves mysteries, were her favorites when she was a girl. She was petrified of the dark, and they relaxed her enough that she could fall asleep. I had never taken the time to read one.

I got up, walked to the bookcase and reached for one of the volumes. It was number three of thirty-nine, *The Gatehouse Mystery*. I sat back down in the wing chair and opened the cover. The title page was marked with the word *Mouse*, written in pencil. Crude whiskers emerged from the *M*, and a tail curled off the *e*. Had that been Kathy's nickname? I wondered. She was anything but a mouse now. I flipped to the first chapter and started to read:

> *"Oh, Moms," Trixie wailed, twisting one of her short blond curls around the pencil she had stuck behind her ear. "Do I have to write Brian and Mart? They'll be home Saturday, and then I can tell them everything."*
>
> *Mrs. Belden looked up from the sweater she was knitting for Bobby, Trixie's young brother. "That's the point," she said with a smile. "Your older brothers have been at camp all summer, and you've never sent them anything but a few scribbled postcards."*
>
> *"There just wasn't time," Trixie said, staring down at the sheet of paper on which she had hastily scrawled, "Crabapple Farm, Sleepy-side-on-the-Hudson, New York, Tuesday evening, August 22nd."*

I liked thinking of Kathy young enough to lose herself in Trixie. I looked back at the long line of canary yellow volumes on the shelf, put my feet up and kept reading.

Seven

My last big night had to include coke. I wasn't about to risk another buy in front of the Emerson, or a delivery to the house, so I headed over to Pug's, a watering hole on the Lynn line. Willie Hightower, one of my connections, worked there on and off. He spent the rest of his time drumming for a heavy metal band called Four Point Restraints, a name I had come up with. Luckily, he was in.

I didn't have to tell Willie what I wanted, which felt a little like getting breakfast automatically at a neighborhood restaurant. I just threw my box of Marlboros on the bar. "How's the music?"

"Hard and fast," he said. He cleared his throat and flipped his long, dyed black hair out of his face. He looked around as he poured me a Miller. "Malloy was in earlier. He was asking if you bought here." He put the drink down in front of me and picked up the Marlboro box.

I nodded. My heart had started to race.

"Of course, I didn't say jack. Never worry about that. But I thought you should know." The Marlboro box disappeared behind the bar.

"Thanks."

"It's not like I haven't been paying the fat shit three-fifty a month for the past year and a half to stay the fuck away." He cleared his throat again. It was a nervous habit. "I think you're alright. He was probably just putting me on notice to be discreet, because you do work for the city. With Hancock running for mayor, they don't want to be embarrassed." He lighted a cigarette and put the Marlboro box back on the bar.

"Hancock? For mayor?"

"You know, tough on crime. All that crap. It's like she thinks she's *Isis* or something." He turned around and grabbed a *Lynn Evening Item.* "See for yourself."

"*Hancock Seeks Mayor's Post*" was the lead story. I read the first few lines:

> Emma Hancock, a veteran of the Lynn Police Department and the state's first female police captain, has announced she will seek the position of Mayor, currently held by the Honorable William McGinnis. Hancock, who has complained that her department is being strangled by City Hall budget cuts, promised a major crackdown on drugs and violence if elected.

No wonder she needed to wrap up Sarah's case. "She'll have power and religion. The age-old cocktail." I tossed the paper back on the bar. "We know what she's running *for.* The question is what she's running *from.*"

"That's your deal. I just pour drinks."

I smiled. "Did you contribute to the campaign?"

"Of course. That's the other reason Malloy stopped by. He's got to fill Emma's campaign purse."

I drank half my beer and stood up. "On my tab."

"Like Bogart said, 'Your cash is good at the bar.'"

"I figured." I pushed five twenties toward him. "Spend it wisely. I'm heading for detox tomorrow."

"Always glad to lose a customer. You know that. Good luck."

•   •   •

The Lynx Club parking lot was nearly full by the time I got there. I took my package out of the Marlboro box, sprinkled a thick line onto the blade of my hunting knife and inhaled it. Within thirty seconds a delicious numbness had spread through my nasal passages and down my throat. I closed my eyes and swallowed. I felt nothing. "Emma Hancock for Mayor" meant nothing. All my worries receded from consciousness. I sucked up another fat line and went inside.

The rhythm of "Hit Me with Your Best Shot" surged through me. Pulses of red and blue light flooded my eyes. I drank in the ripe curves of two blondes dancing naked on round platforms at either side of the runway, gripping chains anchored in the ceiling. As the music peaked, they pulled themselves up off the platforms, legs spread, and spun around in midair like jewelry box figurines. I took a seat under the one wearing a pink patent-leather dog collar and inhaled deeply of the musty Lynx Club air. I gazed up between her legs and felt the last of my anxiety leave me. Few things in life steady me; my primal connection to that soft flesh is one of them.

I ordered a Black Label straight up, lit a Marlboro, then reached into my pocket and tossed a dollar bill on the platform. The dancer, who looked about twenty years old, dropped off the chain and crouched like a crab in front of me. She was pretty, but a bit severe, with high cheekbones and a prominent chin. I looked her in the eyes because I feared staring at her crotch right away would be impolite. She met my eyes for a second, blushed, then looked down between her legs. I followed her lead. She was mostly shaved, just a little dirty blonde triangle left, and when she used two fingers of one hand to spread her lips, I saw she had pierced herself with a gold wire ring. I guessed it was a symbol of submission to a lucky truck driver somewhere. She picked up my dollar bill and rubbed herself with it, then slipped it in her garter. She struggled to her feet, turned around and bent over. I looked her in the eyes again, feeling especially foolish since hers were upside down. She winked, struggled up on her spike heels and pranced to the other side of the stage.

My scotch had arrived. I took a sip, then downed half the glass. I looked around the room for Rachel but didn't spot her. Perverts' Row along the runway and the long tables to either side of it were full of the usual potpourri of businessmen, construction workers and bikers.

I turned around and checked out the bar that spans the wall opposite the runway. My eyes passed over, then returned to, a man sitting on the stool nearest the door. His back was to me. "Couldn't be him," I muttered. I studied him to find something inconsistent with the man I knew. And yet, I could not deny that the wavy salt-and-pepper hair and tailored blue-black suit could only belong to Trevor Lucas. My jaw tightened and my heart began to race. He threw his head back to finish a drink, and, sure enough, his gold Cartier wristwatch and bangle bracelet came into view. He turned and faced the runway.

I quickly did the same and pretended to be watching the dancers. But I wasn't watching anything. My eyes were closed. Rage was boiling up from some primitive place inside me. I gulped the rest of my scotch and put the glass down quickly to avoid whipping it at the bastard's smug face. I couldn't afford to lose control and get myself in a jam, especially in a strip joint. I took a deep breath, opened my eyes and tried to concentrate on the dog-collar girl, who was smoothing oil onto her immense breasts and tugging at her nipples. They glistened as the colored lights fell on them. Then, just as I tossed another dollar on the pedestal, I felt a hand on my shoulder. I looked over at it—black hair down the fingers, buffed nails, a gold signet ring. There was no turning back. I stood up. My fists were clenched.

"Frank Clevenger. I thought that was you," Lucas smiled, holding out his hand. His voice was melodic—an announcer's voice. Even in dim light his teeth gleamed. "Good to know I'm not the only perverted doctor north of Boston."

I stood there, glaring into his piercing eyes. Why hadn't he left when he'd spotted me?

He leaned past me and picked up my empty. He smelled the glass, then held it in the air. "Peggy," he shouted to the portly woman tending bar, "another Black for my psychiatrist, and another double bourbon Manhattan for me." He sat down in the chair next to mine and looked up at me. "You don't mind if I sit here, do you? I know some guys like to be alone in a crowd."

"I didn't think you were the type to worry about another man's space," I said, taking my seat.

He threw a ten down on the pedestal and nodded at the dancer. "Nice tits!" he yelled.

I cringed.

She chuckled and licked her lips. Then she crouched down and picked up the ten by squeezing her breasts against one another. "Thanks," she grinned. She sat on the pedestal, spread her legs and held her ankles while she rocked back and forth. The ring through her lips jutted out and receded rhythmically.

The waitress put our drinks down in front of us. Trevor handed her a twenty and waved off the change. He glanced at me, then went back to watching the girl. The song had changed to "Ride Like the Wind," and she was pretending to straddle a motorcycle. "Terrible about Sarah Johnston," he said. "Damn good nurse."

"Yes."

"Damn good-looking nurse, too."

I took a sip of my scotch but said nothing.

"Wrong-place, wrong-time kind of thing, huh? Just bad luck."

"Looks that way."

"I hear you got up close and personal with the nut who defiled her."

Had Nels Clarke been talking to him? Had Kathy? "No one's convicted yet," I said, still staring straight ahead.

"The papers don't seem ambivalent." He gulped his drink. "You have a shadow of a doubt?"

I was tired of being civil. "Not about you." I looked him in the eyes.

He pursed his lips, shook his head. "Why come down on me, Frank? Nobody's forcing Kathy to play both sides."

"I don't doubt the whole thing's a game to you."

"Cat and mouse," he grinned.

Mouse. If he meant to irk me by mentioning Kathy's nickname,

I wasn't going to give him the satisfaction. I turned away and tossed a dollar bill onto the runway.

He took another gulp of his Manhattan. "I've never thought of her as more than a good fuck, but I think she fell pretty hard."

My fingers went white as my fist tightened around my scotch. I glanced back at his face, dark from a day's growth of beard, and pictured shards of glass splaying open his Grecian nose and cleft chin.

"It wouldn't solve anything," he said, looking down at my glass.

"Huh?"

He leaned a bit closer. His face seemed to undulate under the red and blue lights. "You could do it. You're bigger and stronger than I am, and I've heard you're capable of almost anything when you're angry. But I'm not your problem. Kathy is."

I was infuriated with him but captivated by him. "You don't take any responsibility for what you did? What does that make you, some sort of mindless, sexually transmitted virus?"

He laughed. "On the contrary. I take full responsibility. That's why I'm sitting here with you. I could have disappeared."

Out of the corner of my eye, I noticed Rachel leave the dressing room and start toward the bar. My eyes tracked her. She was wearing sweat pants and a white tank top that hugged her pert breasts.

"Flat," Trevor said.

"Excuse me."

"The girl you're ogling. She's flat."

I looked at him. "Maybe she'd excite you more if you knew she was shacking up with someone else."

"Probably. Are you doing her?"

I picked up my glass and grimaced. Trevor threw up a hand to shield his face. I tilted my head back and drank half my scotch. "You are one sorry fuck. You mistake rivalry for passion because no one ever really gave a shit about you."

He smiled. "Interesting theory. But then how would you explain it if Kathy actually loves me and just screws you? Not that you could blame her, Frank. I get closer to her than you'd ever dare. I get closer than she gets to herself."

I reached into my pocket. "You need to leave now," I dead-panned.

He nodded to himself. "Last night we really had fun. She was phenomenal. But tell me something. You seem to dabble in this analytic stuff: Why does she scream 'Daddy!' when I put it in her ass?"

I used my thumb to open my silver knife and kept it hidden under the counter.

"It's kind of like 'Dadeeeeh!' "

With a flick of my wrist I slashed the bulge in his trousers with just enough force to lay open the cloth. I knocked my drink over with my other hand.

He jumped up and nearly fell backward. "Jesus Christ! Are you crazy?"

"It's razor sharp," I told him. I smiled to reassure the other cus-tomers and patted the spill with my napkin. "If you're planning to sleep anywhere other than the operating table tonight, you'd want to get going."

He took two steps back. "Maybe you're right. I wouldn't want to miss Kathy. She gets so angry when I'm late." He turned and headed for the door.

I could have gone after him, but I didn't. Somewhere under-neath all the scotch and cocaine and nicotine, in a part of my brain where the chemical messengers still flowed according to plan, I knew what he had said was true. He was irrelevant. My problem was with Kathy.

Had she lied to me? Was she really screwing him again? It cer-tainly sounded that way. The image of her on her stomach, ass up in the air, looking back at him through her blond hair nauseated me. But even my reserves of narcissism ran shy of letting me judge her from where I sat: Perverts' Row, waiting around to send it home to a naked dancer with freckles who called herself Tiffany.

I drained the quarter inch of scotch left in my glass and headed for the men's room. My vision was slightly blurred. Too much booze, not enough coke, I thought to myself. I had to concentrate to walk normally, reminding myself to swing my arms and put heel to the ground before toe. I walked through the door, past a couple guys standing like soldiers at the urinals, staring straight ahead. It's alright to blow a kiss at a dancer's genitals at the Lynx Club, but glance at another customer's and you could get to know the cement floor real well. I locked myself in a stall and took a leak. Then I got out my package, shoved a pinch in each nostril and inhaled. The dizziness was gone in a minute. I walked out.

A new girl with shiny black curls had started to dance to that Bonnie Raitt tune about *chargin' by the hour*. She was dressed like a cowboy, with holsters and guns, but she had nothing on under her chaps.

Rachel was sitting with an old man at the bar. She had her hand on his knee. I took a seat diagonally across from them and ordered a cup of coffee. Peggy, the barmaid, a slow-to-move woman who looked about fifty years old and about fifty pounds overweight, set it down on a cocktail napkin for me.

"Five dollars, honey," she said. She had a warm voice.

"Five bucks for coffee?"

"You want a little Kahlúa or Baileys in it? Same price."

"I better not." I paid her six.

She pulled down on the collar of her polyester crew neck to show me her cleavage. "Enjoy the show," she chuckled.

I took a sip and looked over at Rachel. Her eyes met mine, and she smiled, but her attention never really drifted from what the man was saying. I noticed a bottle of champagne on the bar. She leaned over, ran her hand all the way up his thigh and whispered something in his ear.

The girl on stage had dropped her chaps and was on her knees, her eyes closed, the barrel of a revolver in her mouth. She slid it all the way in, pulled it out, licked the length of it, then slid it in again. I imagined the panic that would erupt if the gun were loaded, and she turned it on the crowd. Would that not be a poetic mass murder, a stunning expression of rage? Step up to every man with a dollar in front of him and fire into his lap, then turn around, bend over and fire into his face. "I just killed the tippers," she could testify. "Mercy killing. I thought that's what the dollars were for." I wondered if I could get her off on an insanity plea.

I felt a pair of hands fall lightly over my eyes. They were delicate and soft, and, even with the sudden darkness, I felt comforted by them.

"I'll be hurt if you watch the other girls," Rachel said. She let go and took the stool next to mine.

Her hair was pulled back in a ponytail. Her strong forehead and the amber color of her eyes impressed me even more than they had before. "I was starting to feel lonely," I said.

"Trevor gone?" She glanced back to where he and I had been sitting. "I figured it was doctors' night out."

Was I having a nightmare? "How the hell do you know Trevor?"

"We all do. He's a regular. Candy, the girl with the ring, knows him from . . . well, professionally."

So Trevor had been buying it, too. I wondered what Kathy would think of having traces of Candy—and probably half of Revere—inside her. "How well do *you* know him?" I asked.

"Just to say hello." She smiled. "You certainly didn't think *I* saw him professionally."

I thought about it for a second. "No," I said. "I didn't." I took another sip. It was very bad coffee. "Who's the old guy?"

"Joe Smith."

"Ah. Very creative."

"It doesn't matter if he's lying. I think it's easier for him to talk without telling me his real name."

"What's he talking about?"

"I shouldn't say."

"I won't tell a soul."

"On your oath?" She squinted at me. "Do you guys still take an oath?"

"Absolutely." I held up a hand. "I swear on the oath of Hippocrates. 'Whatsoever I shall see or hear in the course of my profession I will never divulge, holding such things to be holy secrets.' "

"You memorized it?"

" 'I will abstain from all intentional wrongdoing and harm, especially from abusing the bodies of man or woman.' "

"We can talk about that part later. For now, maybe you can help me out with Joe."

"Sure."

"OK. He had a skin cancer removed from his inner thigh, near his groin, three months ago. There's a bad scar, he says, and I guess part of it hasn't healed up." She squinted at me. "Can it take that long?"

"At his age, especially if there was any infection."

"OK," she shrugged. "Anyhow, he says it's still partly open. So he won't let his wife see him naked, let alone touch him. He thinks he looks like a freak down there."

"That's what he's talking about? To you? Here?"

"It's probably cheaper than talking to you. And you won't stroke his leg."

"I wouldn't have guessed that was allowed."

"It isn't. But it makes him feel better, and he's buying champagne—unlike some customers I know—so Peggy told the manager to fuck off."

I glanced over at him. "People will get what they need."

"Really? I'm not sure. I think some people hurt so much they can't take what they need, even when someone wants to give it to them."

You figure you're talking to a stripper and you end up talking to a healer. God headlines at the Lynx Club.

"So what should I tell him?" she asked.

"He's thinking of himself as a victim, something less than what he was. For all we know, that's why he's not healing up in the first place. You need to help him see himself as a survivor. He's beaten cancer, stared death in the face. The wound is his badge of courage. Ask him why he thinks he lived when so many other people die from malignancies. Ask him how he stood all the pain."

"That will help him?"

I shrugged. "Maybe. The truth is, anything you say will help him as long as you keep touching his leg."

"Good," she smiled. "That's kind of what I thought." She stood up. "I dance next. I should finish getting ready."

"I'll wait here."

"Why not sit up front?"

I couldn't argue with that. I took a seat back at Perverts' Row, next to two young guys in pinstriped shirts and club ties who were talking about selling Porsche and Mercedes automobiles.

"The problem with Porsche buyers," the one nearer to me was saying, "is that they're wannabes. They're a bitch to get financed because they can barely afford the cars. It's an ego thing with them." He took five one-dollar bills from his pocket and laid them on the counter. "Whereas the Mercedes buyer is within his means. He doesn't *need* an image boost. He needs quality transportation."

"What about Range Rovers?" I piped up.

"Snobs with bad credit," he said, turning to me.

"Big repossession car," his friend added.

"Oh," I said.

"You drive a Rover?" the first one asked.

"Yup."

"Sorry," he chuckled.

"Don't worry about it."

"It's true, though. If you want a truck, get a truck. A Ram or a Suburban. I mean, why pretend you're in the middle of a jungle?"

"I'll have to think about that."

He handed me his card: JERRY STEIN, MANAGER, MEL'S AUTOWORLD. "We take in a lot of preowned trucks. We can find you a real one."

"Great." Diagnosed fake by a car dealer.

Rachel's music, "Purple Rain," by Prince or whatever the fuck his name is, had started. She came out wearing white lace panties and a black leather jacket, with silver zippers and a chrome buckle. I didn't know whether etiquette would dictate my laying down a five or abstaining. I put down the five.

She swayed her way over and stood in front of me, biting her lower lip. Her auburn hair fell over her eyes. She sat down with her legs spread, the panties not quite covering her, and ran a finger over the lace. Then she turned over and pulled the panties down to her thighs, letting me look at her from behind. I wanted to touch her. To taste her. Maybe she remembered my request from the night before, because she reached behind herself with one hand and slapped herself. Then she stood up, without taking my money, and let her panties slide down to the floor. She stepped out of them, left them there and danced to the other side of the stage.

The car guys were staring at the five. "You know her or something?" Stein asked.

I felt strong. Chosen. Because *I knew the stripper*. They could only imagine what that might mean. I winked at them.

When the waitress came closer, I asked her to bring me another Black Label, straight up.

She brought it right over. I reached for my wallet. "Tiffany told us your drinks are on the house tonight," she yelled over the music.

My relationship was fractured. I had no money in the bank. My car was a mess, not to mention a fake. Westmoreland's case had gone sour on me. I might never see any more work out of the Lynn Police Department, which had been most of my work for the past year. I needed a detox. Badly. Yet for that moment, on Perverts' Row, with a little cocaine left in my pocket, a free scotch in front of me and lace panties within reach, I could still fool myself into thinking I was OK. More than OK. I was on top of the world.

Eight

Rachel had danced last at the Lynx Club, and the Rover smelled like sex by the time I drove her from Revere to Chelsea, two square miles of urban blight just north of Boston. I watched from behind as she climbed the stairs to her apartment, the fifth floor of a five-story industrial building on the waterfront. She was wearing no panties, and her jeans were worn through where her legs met her ass. With each step she took, I could see creamy flesh pressing against the last denim threads.

Intellectually, I know a woman's rear end is nothing more than gluteus maximus—a strap of muscle anchored in pelvis and femur—but I have never achieved any scientific distance from it. Much of my adult life has been spent in pursuit of that bowing flesh.

My brain was mostly adrenaline and testosterone by the time Rachel slid open the iron door to her apartment and stepped inside. I grabbed her and pushed her against the wall. We kissed, tonguing and biting each other's mouths and lips. I tried to unbutton her jeans, but she batted my hand away and unzipped my fly.

"You need to come," she whispered. She licked her palm and slipped her hand inside my boxers.

The wetness against my skin made me sigh. My tongue found her ear.

"Relax," she said, tilting her head away. She started to move her hand faster.

I rested my head on her shoulder and closed my eyes. Then, without warning, she spun us around so I was pressed against the wall. When I reached down to feel her ass, she grabbed my wrist and pinned it at my side. I could easily have overpowered her, but I didn't want to. Did that mean, I wondered, that she had overpowered me?

"What's this?" she asked, looking down at my bandaged wrist.

"A long story."

"We don't have time for a long story," she said. "Don't move. I want to watch your face." She licked her palm again and reached back inside my pants. "Tell me when you're about to come."

It usually takes me a while on coke, but her hand was doing pretty much what I would do to myself, only I wasn't doing it, couldn't anticipate the exact pressure and pace, and that excited me to the point of exploding after just half a minute. I hesitated to tell her I was about to lose control, maybe because she had asked me to, maybe because I feared she would slow down and tease me, keep me hanging, a puppet to my own pleasure. But I did tell her. "I'm going . . . to come," I strained.

She was on her knees with her lips around me when the spasms started. My back arched against the wall, and the muscles in my legs contracted all at once. I looked down, saw her staring into my eyes and pulled out of her mouth.

She kept looking at me as my sperm splattered her lips, chin and cheek. She waited a few seconds, slowly wiped her face with the back of her hand and stood up. She leaned into me, touching her forehead to mine. "Did you like coming on me?" she cooed.

The lilt in her voice was familiar. I had a memory of being ten, dressed in cutoffs and a T-shirt, sitting on a love seat with my mother as she stumbled through the facts of life. I'd been found fondling the breast buds of Kim Daney, a nine-year-old blond-haired girl with green eyes who lived two houses down. "When a little boy likes a little girl, sometimes his little penis gets hard," my mother had said in that same singsong. She glanced down at my crotch. "That hasn't happened to you with Kimmy, has it?"

I didn't know how much trouble I might be in. "No," I said.

"*No?*"

"Yes," I admitted.

"Don't be embarrassed, Frankie." Her tone became severe. "And don't lie to me." She paused. "Did you like that? Your thing being hard?"

"No . . . yes," I shrugged. I tried to hide behind my bangs.

"When people are older—older than you—the man puts his hard penis into the woman, into . . . a slit between her legs. He pushes it in and out, and, for some reason, that gives him a good feeling." She watched for my reaction. "You haven't done that to little Kimmy, put your hard thing between her legs, have you, Frankie?"

I hadn't done anything remotely like that. It sounded interesting, but I had one practical concern. "What if you need to pee when it's in there?" I asked.

"If you need to *pee?*" She started to laugh.

I tried to rescue myself. "No. I didn't mean . . ."

It was too late. She was already shaking my father out of his drunken sleep on the La-Z-Boy to tell him what I'd said.

I had started to cry.

My father shook his head as he listened, glanced over at me, then backhanded my mother so hard she collapsed to the floor. "You don't make fun of my kid like that," he muttered. He looked at me, nodded—one man to another—then fell back into his stupor.

Rachel pinched my gut playfully, and my parents disappeared. I was back with her. "I asked you if you liked coming on me?" she cooed.

Her forehead against mine suddenly felt oppressive. I took hold of her shoulders and pushed her off me.

She stood there in my grip. "Well, did you?"

I thought of telling her not to flatter herself, that I had ejaculated on better-looking faces, which happened to be true. But in my heart I didn't feel she meant me any harm. "Yes," I said, "I liked it."

"And you liked watching me spank myself at the club."

I stayed silent.

"Didn't you?" she insisted.

"Yes."

"You'd like to spank me yourself. Across your lap."

I shrugged.

Her voice dropped. "Not just my ass. Between my legs, too. You'd like to slap me there."

My gusts of breath betrayed me.

"You should say what you want, Frank. There aren't any rules."

"Tell me what *you* want," I managed.

"But it doesn't matter to you what I want."

"Yes, it does."

She smiled and pressed forward to kiss my cheek. "Liar." She twisted back, out of my hands, and started toward the galley kitchen.

I felt exposed and alone. I fumbled to tuck myself back in my pants.

"Scotch alright?" she asked.

My boxers were damp and uncomfortable. I cleared my throat. "Scotch," I rumbled, "will always be alright." I sounded like a caricature of John Wayne. I shut the front door with such force that it bounced back along its track.

"Tricky door," she called out.

I closed it more gently.

"Feel free to take a look around."

"Thanks." I was glad for the chance to get my legs—and my brain—working again.

Rachel's apartment was a loft with exposed posts and beams and lots of brick. A mahogany sleigh bed covered with a velvet patchwork quilt sat atop a three-foot-high platform that was centered against the wall opposite the door. The other walls were covered with oversized black-and-white photographs of people down on their luck. Men with despair in their faces huddled outside a soup kitchen called A Day's Bread. A black boy not more than eight slouched against a wall of graffiti. An old woman in a wheelchair grimaced in pain. I turned toward the kitchen. "The photographs are your work?" I asked.

"I shot all of them here in Chelsea," she said. "Did you want ice?"

"Straight up." I looked back at the old woman. A clear plastic tube delivered oxygen to each of her nostrils from a tank strapped to the chair. "No one would accuse you of being a romantic."

"No? I think their will to live is beautiful. Just like my customer and his cancer. 'Staring death in the face,' as you put it." She started over with our drinks.

My eyes drifted to a piece of taxidermy that served as the base for a glass coffee table in the middle of the room. It was a coyote with a raccoon trapped in its jaws. The coon's eyes were wide with terror, but it had managed to sink its claws deep into the coyote's muzzle.

"You do believe what you told me about the scar, don't you?" she asked. "About him being a survivor?"

That was a good question. When I had been in private practice, I sometimes felt like a salesman peddling reasons to stay on this dismal planet. Again and again, I had patients sign "contracts for safety," assuring me in writing that they would not do themselves in. But would I have lived their lives? Would I have lived Billy's? *Hang in there.* Why? "It doesn't matter if I believe he's a survivor," I said, taking my scotch from her. "He's the one who has to believe it."

I walked with her to a set of French doors at the end of the room that opened onto a deck overlooking the Tobin Bridge as it crossed into Boston. The massive arch of steel was faulted with ruining Chelsea by extinguishing the neighborhoods where its concrete feet touched down. I had never spent any time looking at it before and was struck by its grandeur. I sat down on an old church pew Rachel had positioned in front of the doors. "What was this building used for?" I asked.

"A sweatshop," she said, sitting down with me. "They made uniforms for the military during Vietnam. They closed it after the place caught fire." She pointed up at a few feet of charring along one of the beams. "This floor wasn't badly damaged. The other floors were gutted."

I knew from listening to relatives of mine who had followed the path of upward mobility *out* of Chelsea, to North Shore towns like Nahant and Swampscott and Marblehead, that most of Chelsea had burned down twice, first in 1908, then again in 1973. "You know what they say: What Chelsea really needs . . ."

". . . is another fire. I've heard all the jokes." She sipped her scotch. "They say that to be cruel, but they're right, in a way. Nothing ever gets better gradually. You have to die to be reborn."

"Not exactly a vote of confidence in my profession."

"Sorry, but let's face it: Most of you guys can't see the potential in a nervous breakdown. A real collapse. There's more chance of finding yourself in a major depression than there is in a bottle of Prozac." She leaned toward me. "Or a gram of cocaine."

"Cocaine?"

"*Cocaine?*" she mocked. "You really are a terrible liar. I tasted it when my tongue was in your mouth."

"I have more if . . ."

"No thanks. I don't do drugs. But go ahead, if you want to."

I didn't need much encouragement. I'd been thinking about a trip to the bathroom for a little blast since starting up the stairs. I took out my package.

"I tried it for a while—that, marijuana, Valium, Percocet, heroin, Prozac, Zoloft." She paused. "Oh, yes. Ritalin. A lot of Ritalin."

I wasn't sure I wanted to delve into Rachel's psychiatric history. If I ended up feeling sorry for her, I might not be able to screw her the way I wanted to. But I have never been satisfied on the surface of anything. "You were depressed."

"Very good, doctor." She turned over her arm. Four vertical scars ran from her wrist several inches up her forearm. How had I missed them? "I tried overdosing on Prozac, too. Nobody told me you have to take a jug of the stuff to do the trick. It doesn't cure you and it won't kill you. What the fuck good is it?"

"What saved you?"

"A healing professional, like yourself," she smirked. "Is that the right answer?"

"Not in my experience."

"Mine, either. The truth is, stripping saved me. I started feeling better the day I started dancing."

"A more powerful anesthetic?"

"I think of it as a safety valve."

"How so?"

"In shrink lingo, it allows me to direct my anger outward, rather than inward."

"I thought *we* were the ones abusing *you*."

"Hardly. I know what the customers are going through when I bend over in front of them. I know most of them have overweight, aging wives at home who wouldn't put dick in their mouths if their lives depended on it. I know I get them stiff, and they imagine what it would be like to put their cocks in me. They can get close, but never close enough. I see the pain in their eyes."

"So you're a sadist."

"Onstage. Absolutely. And that's enough for me. I don't have to kill anybody."

"You're still young." I took another pinch, spread it over my gums and put the package away.

"My question is, where's your anger?"

"Huh?"

"Your anger," she smiled. "It was dripping down my face a few minutes ago. Where else does it show up?"

I licked the crystal of my watch to get the last of the powder. "I specialize in evaluating murderers, to figure out if they're crazy. I listen to them describe how they strangled, cut and bludgeoned their victims. I go to morgues and visit corpses."

"You enjoy it?"

"It's a job. A strange job, but a job."

"C'mon."

"C'mon, what?"

"You could be a professor if all you wanted was a job. You don't have to go to morgues."

I smiled at her determination to get at the truth—that anyone who makes a life of trying to understand killers is connected to them at some basic level. "I guess I like it, then."

"But it's not enough."

"It's plenty."

"I don't think so, or you wouldn't need the tootie." She took a long drink of her scotch.

"If you're going to be my analyst, you should start charging me," I said. "Especially since you seem to be so good at it."

She put her drink down on the pew, stood up, unbuttoned her jeans and let them drop to the floor. She came over and stood between my legs. "So pay up."

I ran my hands down her graceful arms, over her hips and squeezed her ass, burying my fingers between her cheeks. Her body was younger than Kathy's, firmer, further from death.

She backed up a few steps and let me look at her, motionless in the moonlight, wearing nothing but her white, ribbed tank top. I could see the folds of skin beneath the sparse triangle of red hair where her legs met.

She turned and walked toward the bed. I started after her. She climbed the three stairs up the platform, picked up a coiled black leather belt from the nightstand and laid it on the patchwork comforter. Then she knelt over the mattress.

My heart was racing as I took the stairs behind her. I picked up the belt with a trembling hand. But after the first thwack of leather against her bottom, watching a band of creamy skin start to redden, I lost all fear. I lashed out again, then again, enjoying Rachel's groans, her quivering as she waited for the next blow. "Say 'Please,' " I told her.

She looked back at me. "Please," she whimpered.

I hit her again.

She arched her back, bringing her bottom up off the mattress. "Do what you want."

I leaned over her and used the belt to bind her wrists. Then I knelt down behind her. I had never sodomized a woman before. I wet myself with saliva and pushed my way inside her, slowly, reveling in her resistance.

She screamed.

I pushed deeper.

•   •   •

I left Rachel at five in the morning. The Rover was covered with dew. I pulled myself inside, rolled down the windows and breathed deeply of the morning air. Four hours sleep in two days had left me light-headed. My legs felt weighty. I still had about a quarter gram in my pocket, but I didn't reach for it. I wanted to linger on empty, really let myself touch bottom.

I looked up at the Tobin Bridge. The first commuters were making their way toward Boston, probably unaware that beneath them, in Chelsea Harbor, the day was already going full throttle. I could see three tugboats bullying a tanker toward a fueling station onshore. Only a faint drone from their engines reached me, but the force they generated was obvious from the cottony wake they churned. I once shared a bottle of scotch at the Surf Lounge with a tugboat captain out of Salem Harbor who had laughed at me when I used the word *romantic* to describe his work. The tug's charm, he had explained, is an illusion: Onboard, the mismatch between the vessel's size and its power means constant danger.

I started the car and turned down Broadway, toward Route 16 east. I needed to pick up some clothes in Marblehead before heading over to McLean. During my residency I had joked with the staff on the detox unit at Tufts about the way the place filled up around the third week of each month, when the addicts had blown through their welfare checks and couldn't afford to get high. As soon as the next month's checks were issued, the place cleared out again. Now it didn't seem so funny: I was the one who had waited to admit myself until my pockets were almost empty.

I wondered whether I would find Kathy at home. If she had waited up for me all night, I could count on a scene. Once her anger was kindled, my trying to reason with her only fed the flames. Usually, she'd end up belting the wall or kicking a couple of antiques to pieces. Even fracturing her fingers hadn't stopped her the last time, when she'd borrowed my copy of *The Pugilist at Rest* and found a Polaroid of Isabela Cadronale, a twenty-two-year-old Brazilian journalist we'd met together on the beach at St. Croix, wearing nothing but a bow tie. My bow tie. Kathy had kept flailing away with her swollen fist, as if she felt no pain. I ended up having to hold her down a good ten, fifteen minutes until her jealousy burned itself out. Then the silent tears started, as they always did, a prelude to our best sex.

Why didn't I feel guilty about my indiscretions? I mean, not even a little guilty. Not even with the salt of Kathy's tears on my tongue. And why had she always come back for more? Were we laced together by love or by the promise that I would hurt her, again and again?

I hadn't agreed with Ted Pearson, my psychiatrist, when he'd suggested that my drinking, drugging and philandering were all fueled by a deep-seated ambivalence about intimacy, but why else would I keep Rachel close to me, but in pain, for hours? Why else would I caress her naked body, yet penetrate only her ass? Why delight in the fact that we moved in a perfectly coordinated rhythm, but only because she dared not move at all without my hands guiding her hips, lest I tear her with an ill-timed thrust?

There was little traffic, and the road was dry, but I drove slowly around Bell Circle in Revere. I didn't have the money to repair anybody else's car. As I passed the Wonderland Dog Track, I lighted a Marlboro. It frightens me to admit it, but I would have stopped in at Manny's window if the place had been open—to bet one dog, maybe two. How could I explain that? Why couldn't I feel alive unless I was living at the edge of ruin?

I had reached the Lynnway when I heard a siren. I looked in my rearview mirror and saw a police cruiser about a hundred yards behind me. I checked my speedometer, saw that I was under the speed limit and pulled right to get out of the way. The siren stopped, but the cruiser followed me into my lane and started to close the distance between us. I could feel my pulse quicken with the irony of being nabbed the day I planned to detox. With the videotape Emma Hancock had of me buying in front of the Emerson, I worried she could claim her men had reasonable cause to search me. And if they found the cocaine, I could be looking at a couple months in the Essex County jail. Maybe more. What a meaty *Evening Item* headline my sorry life would make: "Doctor Heal Thyself: Local Psychiatrist Arrested for Cocaine Possession." I accelerated back up to the speed limit and took the package out of my pocket. The siren started to sound behind me again. I checked the rearview mirror to make sure I wasn't likely to be seen, unfolded the package and snorted what was left. Then I popped the paper in my mouth, chewed it up and swallowed it. I veered into the breakdown lane and slowed to a stop. The cruiser parked behind me.

The way my luck had been going, I should have guessed that Kevin Malloy would get out of the passenger side. He hooked his thumbs over his belt and started toward my window. An older cop I didn't recognize stayed behind the wheel.

I left the car running and turned on the CD player. Big Mama Thornton was singing the blues. I upped the volume.

Malloy plopped his hairless arm on my door. He was holding a pair of cuffs. "You know, we've been behind you with the siren since the fucking dog track."

I smiled, trying to imagine the clumsy race a *fucking dog* would run.

"Something wrong with you? What's so funny?"

I sobered myself. "Big Mama Thornton." I nodded at the stereo. "That's her, singing 'Little Red Rooster.' One of the greats, Mama was. And one funny lady. I do lose myself in her." I couldn't resist needling him. "Sorry I didn't hear your siren sooner. It's really neat, and the blue lights are very cool, too."

He was looking around the interior of the car. "Glad you like 'em," he said evenly.

"Stop to chat?" I asked.

"Afraid not."

My anxiety level was climbing. "Let's see: You thought I was the Good Humor man and you wanted a Nutty Buddy."

He squinted and pointed at me like he was about to say something. Then, without a word, he reached through the window and lightly touched my chest.

I looked down. My denim shirt was speckled with tiny white rocks of cocaine. When I looked back at him, he was licking one off his fingertip.

"Looks like we've got a problem," he said, clicking the cuffs like castanets.

My stomach sank. I thought about mentioning the $350-a-month payoff he'd been taking from Willie Hightower at Pug's, but I figured it was better to wait for his next move.

"I bet when we vacuum this shitbox for tootie we'll understand why you plow into other people's cars."

"Plow into other people's cars?"

"Spare me. The kid with the 'stang filed a hit-and-run at the Revere police station late last night. Says you smashed into him, then took off. The on-duty officer over there let us know, seeing as you work with us—or used to."

"I paid the sonofabitch in cash."

"Oh, good. Then we're all set. Got a receipt?"

"Sure." I couldn't hold back. "Like the ones you give Willie Hightower every month."

Malloy's upper lip thinned, exposing those yellow teeth of his. "You'll have to follow me back to the station."

A crazy thought came into my head. If I was going to take a fall, why not really dive deep? My hunting knife was right under my seat. I stared at his belly, then focused several inches higher on the point where the aorta emerges into the abdomen, no longer shielded by the sternum.

"You want to follow me like a big boy, or you want to ride with us in the cruiser?"

I looked him in the eyes and saw my father. *You want to walk up to your room and take your punishment like a man, or you want I should carry you up like a little baby?*

Malloy clicked the cuffs together again.

I could smell the booze on my old man's hot breath. Didn't he have the knife coming to him? Would justice not be served? *Where's your anger?* I heard his voice again.

"*OK, I guess we'll do this the hard way.*"

Or was it Malloy I had heard? I shook my head. Too much damn cocaine, I told myself. I wasn't thinking right. I needed that detox. I needed sleep. I rubbed my eyes, and Malloy was back. I took a deep breath. "Lead the way," I told him.

Nine

The door to Emma Hancock's office was open when I got to the station. She glanced up at me as Malloy and the older cop, who had introduced himself simply as Grillo, hustled me into the same cell where Westmoreland had been held. I stood at the door as they locked me in. "Where's your other guest?" I asked.

He didn't answer.

"What am I charged with?"

"That's a tough one. So many choices. Cocaine possession. Driving to endanger. Resisting arrest."

"*Resisting arrest?* I followed you here."

"Details," Grillo said. He slapped Malloy on the back.

"Do I get a phone call?"

Malloy chuckled. "I thought *I* was the one going to bad movies." He turned, and the two of them started for the door.

I sat down on the cot and looked around the cell. My eyes lingered on a spray of dried blood along the wall where Westmoreland had stood as he bit his tongue. A few red smudges were also left on the floor where I'd taken him down after he had attacked me.

I turned and checked out the other cells: All empty. With Sam Fitzgerald's stamp of approval Hancock had probably transferred her prize prisoner to the Massachusetts Correctional Institution at Concord, to await trial for murder.

My head had started to throb. I worried my pressure might be rocketing from the coke and decided to lie down. The odor of decay wafted off the cot and blanketed me. I stared at the bunk overhead, then raised myself on my elbows to read a word scrawled in blood on the flip side of the mattress. It said GEORGE. "George LaFountaine," I said out loud. I collapsed back on the mattress and closed my eyes.

I woke just a few minutes later to the jangling of keys as Emma Hancock stepped inside the cell. I rubbed the sleep from my eyes and sat up.

She leaned against the wall. "I warned you," she said.

"I underestimated you, Emma. I thought you were worried about me screwing up the commissioner thing for you. It didn't cross my mind you were gunning for the corner office. I would have been more careful dealing with the future *Mayor* Hancock."

"I could do a lot for this city. But it's a long road from here to there."

"You take curves pretty well." I pointed up at the dried blood on the wall. "You moved the general along. That's one less roadblock. Fitz is a lousy psychiatrist, but he knows where his bread is buttered."

Hancock pressed her lips together and shook her head. She looked drained. "I didn't move him."

I nodded automatically, then realized I didn't understand. "What do you mean, *you didn't move him?*" I glanced around the cell block again. Empty.

She looked down for a few moments, then over at me again. "He's dead, Frank. He killed himself."

"Killed himself."

"He shoved a sock down his throat. Tobias Lucey found him late last night."

I got to my feet and spoke through my teeth. "I told you to watch him."

She shrugged. "Nobody wanted this to happen."

"Nobody?" I could feel the blood rushing to my head. "How about you?"

"I don't wish death on anyone."

"No? Not deep down, where those nuns at Sacred Heart couldn't reach? Think about it: Isn't it easier to have Westmoreland out of the way than to risk some smart-ass public defender taking him on as a cause?" I took a step toward her. "Who's gonna squawk over what happens to a bum?"

She straightened up. "I didn't kill him."

"Not in a way you could be punished for. Not in this life. But it does seem to tie any loose end that could snag your campaign. Nurse murdered. Killer caught. Killer dead. End of story. Right, Mayor Hancock?" I took another step toward her.

"No, you're wrong."

"*Wrong?* Oh. I want to hear it, Emma. Tell me how sorry you are, how you wanted Westmoreland to get the justice he deserved."

"We've got another body."

"Another . . ." I felt like I had been kicked in the gut. I stared at her a few seconds, then staggered backward and sat on the cot. "Same MO?"

"Not exactly. But close."

"Who was she?"

"*She?*"

"The victim, Emma."

"Why do you say *she?*"

"Oh, little things. Like the fact that the killer likes cutting tits off."

"She was nineteen years old," Hancock said in a monotone. "Single. Lived on Park Street. Her roommate found her in their apartment a few hours ago."

"Nurse?"

"Dancer."

I looked up at her.

"She works over at the Lynx Club." She studied me for my reaction.

"My God. I was just there."

"I know that. That's one reason I had Malloy bring you in. The owner keeps a list of the plates of everyone who parks in his lot. Just in case there's any trouble." She crossed her arms. "You're on the list."

"And . . ."

"And you were pretty steamed about not getting your way with Westmoreland."

"So?"

"So I don't know how steamed you get, Frank, especially on coke. I'm not sure I know you at all anymore."

I squinted at her. "You think I did the dancer? What, to prove a point?"

She shrugged.

I got up and walked within arm's length of her. "The guilt is eating at you, Emma," I said quietly. "You're responsible for her death and you know it. You let her murderer walk the streets without even having to look over his shoulder. Because your life is so pitifully empty of everything else that you'll do anything to be mayor." I leaned closer to her. "Mayor of Lynn. A goddamn job. What a pathetic motive. You make me . . ."

She turned away. She seemed to be fighting back tears.

I just stood there.

She took a deep breath, then looked back at me. "Her name was Monique Peletier," she said. "She was my niece."

◆   ◆   ◆

Training in psychiatry is supposed to make you comfortable sitting silently in the presence of another person's pain, but I longed for the shelter of words.

Hancock rubbed the heels of her hands into her eyes, crossed her arms again and gazed out the bars of the cell. She looked even more confused than sad, as if she couldn't believe her instincts had failed her so miserably. I knew the feeling. "My brother passed away a few years ago. I looked in on her now and then, hoping to get her interested in the church. She was a beautiful person, just lost."

"Were you close with her?"

"I think you know I don't let myself get very close to anyone."

I stayed silent, hoping she might tell me more about herself.

She stood there looking at me for several seconds, then stiffened. "I can't say for sure that the same man killed both of them. The *North Shore Weekly* came out with a piece yesterday that described what happened to Sarah Johnston in detail. This could be a copycat."

I nodded. I suspected she was reaching for any explanation that would help absolve her of guilt, but I didn't know enough about the case to argue the point. That suited me.

She clicked her nails so hard I thought they might break. "Whoever did this to Monique, I'll find him," she vowed. "As God is my witness." She looked back at me. "Whether we're dealing with a serial killer or not, the psychological profile will be crucial. That's where I'll need your help."

I shook my head. "You were on target the first time, Emma. I'm not up to it. If I were you, I'd avoid Fitz, but Chuck Sloan would probably take the case."

"I don't want Sloan. He's a plodder."

"Andrew Rothstein at New England Medical Center is a reliable man."

She squinted at me. "I'm not looking for a *reliable man*, Frank. Not anymore. No ordinary shrink is going to be able to think like this monster."

"I wouldn't be any good to you. My head isn't clear."

"I hear you. Two-fifty an hour. Ten hours up front."

"It's not about money."

"Thirty-five hundred up front, and I send somebody to straighten out the kid with the hit-and-run. They tell me he's hot for the Police Academy."

I rolled my eyes. "Great. Another sterling character with a license to carry."

"What else do you want? Name it."

I looked over at Westmoreland's dried blood on the wall. I gritted my teeth. I felt like telling her that I wanted her to feel the terror that consumes a paranoid man when he's caged like an animal. I wanted her to experience the psychological suffocation that makes shoving a sock down your throat seem like a reasonable escape. I wanted her to admit that she didn't have the capacity to grieve for her niece nearly so deeply as Westmoreland had for his friend. But she was already suffering in her own way. "I don't want anything from you, Emma," I said.

She pursed her lips. "You're looking at possession of cocaine."

"I'll do my sixty days. I've got it coming to me," I shrugged.

"Could be longer. The court could make an example of you."

"Maybe."

"Then there's the Board of Medicine."

I stared at her.

"You're sure about this." Her eyes bore down on me. "I won't ask you again."

I nodded, but tentatively. I didn't know what else she had up her sleeve.

"I understand," she said. "You're going your own way." She started for the door but turned back. "I'll fix the drug charge against you and the hit-and-run and see to it you get paid for the work you put in on the case. Nobody's squealing to any Board. This whole thing—Westmoreland and Monique—was my fault. You were right from the beginning." She took a deep breath and let it out. "For whatever it's worth, I don't care what they say about you, not about Prescott or the coke or anything else. You're the best there is at what you do. Whether you think so or not." Then she walked out.

•   •   •

So much for McLean. I was following another cruiser, this one carrying Emma Hancock and her driver, headed for the morgue. It was just after 8 A.M., and garbage trucks were fanned out on both sides of Union Street. The stench seeped through the Rover's window seals. I fantasized about peeling off for Route 1 north, driving straight to the clear air of Vermont, but Hancock's mea culpa had gotten to me. I would help her catch the psychopath who had butchered her niece.

There was another reason I wasn't running away. A selfish one. I needed to find the killer, too. With Prescott and Billy and, now, Westmoreland, I was wondering more than ever whether I could follow a trail of rage and destruction all the way to the end. Days before Westmoreland's death I had read in his Stonehill Hospital medical record about his history of suicidal thinking. Yet I hadn't asked him whether he planned to do himself in. Not even after he had nearly spit out his tongue. What if that question alone would have reassured him that someone understood his desperation?

And why hadn't I gone back to see Westmoreland after reading the Boston V.A. medical record about the horrors he had witnessed in the Son Tay raid? Did I lack the courage to help him face his friend's random death, to see that George LaFountaine had died needlessly in that prison camp, too?

The cruiser pulled up to the curb. I parked behind it. I walked to the door of the morgue with Hancock. "You sure you want to look at this?" I asked her.

She opened the door and walked in.

I followed her to the autopsy suite.

Paulson Levitsky was standing to one side of another gray body, holding a clipboard. He looked up when we were halfway to the dissecting table. "The second one always brings out the brass," he deadpanned. "Nothing like a serial killer to get people working on the same team."

Hancock stopped and grabbed my arm with her meaty hand. "He doesn't need to know it's family," she whispered.

"It'll come out eventually."

"I'll settle for eventually."

"Fair enough."

We walked to the table.

"This one's worse than Ms. Johnston," Levitsky said, tightening the Windsor knot in his tie. He took the stainless steel pointer from his pocket and flicked it open. "There has been trauma to Ms. Peletier's genital area."

I glanced down at the hacked flesh between Monique's legs.

"Lord God," Hancock muttered.

"Note that the clitoris has been excised," Levitsky pointed out, "in addition to the breasts. Again, the offending instrument appears to be a razor-sharp blade not greater than five centimeters." He gently raised the head of the corpse, exposing a blue-purple depression behind the right ear. "Cause of death, however, is trauma to the head with a blunt object. Something like a tire iron. Mutilation occurred thereafter." He eased the head back down. "We don't have the missing body parts."

I looked at the girl's mangled chest, then at her face. I shook my head. "I saw her dancing at the Lynx Club hours ago," I said.

"Where?" Levitsky asked.

I turned to him. "*The Lynx Club*. The strip joint in Revere. I had a couple drinks there last night. She's one of the dancers. Her stage name was Candy."

He raised his eyebrows, but said nothing.

I glanced at Hancock, then turned back to Levitsky. "She wasn't completely shaved then, Paulson. She had a triangle of hair right above her labia." I pointed.

Hancock grimaced. "How do you remember something like that?"

I had to go on. "Another thing. Her clitoris was pierced. She wore a ring through it."

"A ring?" Hancock said.

"It takes all kinds," Levitsky said. "In some cultures piercing the clitoris is commonplace. In ours I believe it's a ritual among sado-masochists. She did have calluses and minor abrasions around her wrists. Handcuffs could explain them."

I noticed Hancock's hand drift to her own set of cuffs. "Was she raped?" I asked.

"Semen was recovered from the vaginal vault. I can't know if it belongs to the assailant or a lover."

"You'll analyze it for a match with the sample from Sarah?" I asked.

Levitsky winked at me. "You think I should take the time? Or better to let it go? You know, the police department hasn't wanted me to get bogged down in details."

"You take all the time you need," Hancock said evenly.

"I guess we're not in a rush to close the case now that Jack the Ripper has struck again." Levitsky looked knowingly at me. "Patience bestows its gifts a little late for Mr. Westmoreland, I fear."

Hancock had it coming to her, but not with her niece laid out on a stainless steel table. "Let's move on, Paulson," I said.

"OK. Onward. But first, what else do you know about her that I should know?"

"About her appearance?" I stalled.

"You've been at the table before, Frankster. I need to know anything that might help me interpret what I find."

I instinctively turned my back to Hancock. "I think she was a pro," I said softly.

"A what?" Paulson said. "Speak up for the microphone."

"A pro," I said, feeling defeated. "A prostitute. A friend of hers told me she was for sale." I felt Hancock's hand grip my shoulder.

"Don't hold back on anything that could help us nail this guy," she said. Her voice had the distant quality of someone lost in thought.

Levitsky squinted at the two of us.

"That's all," I said.

"OK. At least we know the reason if I come up with different blood types for the sperm inside her." He was still on Hancock's case. "I hope my analysis of the semen in this young lady won't embarrass any of your contributors. This being campaign season."

Hancock's forehead was red. She took a deep breath. "Let your work take you where it leads, Doctor."

"Thank you." Levitsky bowed slightly. "That's a great gift to me." He pulled the cuff of each sleeve briskly to get the wrinkles out.

"You have anything that can help me with the psychological profile?" I asked him.

"Just that the sculptor has more than a passing interest in his craft. I prepared slides from the tissue margins where the breasts were removed. The same scarring is present as in the first body. He's doing something to the wounds. Maybe sprinkling something on them. I'm still not sure."

"Nothing back from the FBI lab?" I asked.

"FBI?" Hancock asked pointedly.

"Paulson has a pathologist friend at Hopkins who forwarded tissue samples from Sarah's wounds to their lab in Quantico," I said.

"This damn thing will be on *Inside Edition* before long," she said.

I was taken aback. Was she still hoping for damage control before the election?

"I'm thinking of the girl's mother," she explained. "She's having a hard time."

The door to the autopsy suite swung open, and Malloy bounded in. He swaggered up to the table, planted himself between Hancock and me, and looked the corpse over. "Wow," he grinned. "Talk about razor burn." He sensed his humor was lost on us. "I've heard of close shaves, but . . ." He looked from face to face, then shrugged.

Hancock was staring at him.

"When do we open her up, Doc?"

"Not surprisingly, you're just in time," Levitsky said. "Officer Malloy stayed with me until every one of Ms. Johnston's organs had been dissected. He has an insatiable interest in physical evidence."

"Absolutely fucking right," Malloy said. "And we're gonna need every clue we can get. I just interviewed the fag this whore lived with."

Hancock closed her eyes.

"An unemployed pastry chef. A *true flake*. And when you're dealing with white trash like her, you can't expect—"

I drove an elbow into Malloy's mouth. He hit the ground with a thud and started writhing on the floor.

Hancock grabbed my arm and glared at me, one hand on her gun, then slowly let go. Her whole body seemed to deflate. She turned back to the table, reached out and rested her hand on Monique's ankle. "This girl is my niece, Dr. Levitsky," she said. "Please give us all the help you can."

"Shit! My teeth!" Malloy screamed.

Hancock stood there, staring at her fingers lightly stroking Monique's skin, then turned around and walked over to him. She grabbed him under the arm and pulled him to his feet. "I need everybody I've got on the job. So don't try taking sick time," she said. "Go visit your dentist, get yourself fixed up and get back to the station." She let him sink back to the floor. She looked at me. "Remember. Anything you need."

◆　　◆　　◆

I left the morgue around nine. I was past fatigue, into a kind of foggy second wind. I got in the car, turned it over and popped an old Ray Charles album into the CD player.

I wanted to visit Monique's apartment to get a sense of any other signature the killer might have left at the crime scene, but I felt the need to stop by the hospital to see Kathy first. I couldn't say why. Maybe she'd been right; maybe she was another of my addictions. I put the car in gear and started onto Union Street, then stopped short when I noticed a small manila envelope—the kind I stored my stamp collection in as a kid—taped to the underside of the glove compartment. I grabbed it and ripped it open. A ziplock bag of what looked like cocaine was inside, along with a small card. I took out the card first. One side was a schedule of church services at Sacred Heart. On the other, Hancock had written, "Whatever you need." Talk about picking your drug of choice. I tossed the card on the floor mat, fished out the plastic bag and rolled it between my fingertips. It felt soft and inviting. A pillow to rest my head. I swallowed and imagined not being able to feel my throat.

I pulled apart the plastic seal, took a pinch and spread it along my upper gums. They went numb immediately. *Numb.* Even as I basked in the absence of sensation, that word started to bother me. I thought again of Rachel's comment that I wouldn't need the coke if I was in touch with my rage. I knew this was fact, knew it with dead solid conviction, yet I took a second pinch to dull my lower gums, then a third for my nose. *Dull*. Another word to dwell on.

The fog cleared, but I worried my clarity was another illusion of distance, like the romantic vision I had of the tankers in Chelsea harbor.

I hit the gas, flew down Union and weaved through traffic on Boston Street to get to Stonehill Hospital. I took one of the spaces out front reserved for doctors. At the end of the row, Trevor Lucas' red Ferrari Mondial was parked, nose out. I shook my head at his vanity plate: CMENOW. It had taken me a while to decipher it the first time I'd tried. I thought he was being lewd. Now I read it automatically as "See Me Now," the cry of a certifiable egomaniac. I hurried up the steps, past the lobby and toward the elevator.

Kris Jerold, the receptionist, told me Kathy was still at rounds. "They're over in less than an hour," she said, fingering the three hoops through her ear. "I'll tell her you stopped by."

"You've changed your hair."

"It's salmon-colored now," she said.

"I think that's what caught my eye. It's very different."

"Thanks."

"How has she been?"

"Dr. Singleton?"

"Well, yes. Are we worried about someone else?"

"She's fine."

"Fine?"

She bit her lip. "Well, not exactly *fine*. She's . . . See, I'm buried right now. I can't really talk."

Just then the door to Kathy's office opened, and Trevor Lucas walked out. He took a few steps, spotted me and stopped.

I looked at Kris. "Not fine at all." I stepped to the corner of the reception desk.

"The slasher," Lucas said. "Do you know that was a Brioni suit? Four thousand dollars."

The one he had on looked at least that expensive. I glanced at the gold, monogrammed buckle of his belt, then at his alligator loafers. "I'm sure you've nipped and tucked your way into quite a wardrobe."

"People are addicted to different things."

Kris shuffled some papers, excused herself and walked off down the hall.

I noticed deep, raw scratches that started under Lucas' right ear and ended at his tab collar. They were the only part of him that didn't look perfect. "Something attack you?" I asked. I squinted to get a better look.

He touched the broken skin. "One thing our little girl does not lack is passion. I don't believe you've ever really tapped into it. But you and I were over that ground last night."

"All I remember is you running away."

"I'm here now."

I was about to start toward him when Kathy appeared in her doorway. She looked as angry as I had ever seen her.

Lucas noticed me staring over his shoulder. He glanced back at Kathy, then moved off to the side so that the three of us were standing there like the points of a triangle. "Why don't you tell Frank why you clawed me," he grinned.

"Go fuck yourself," Kathy seethed. "I didn't touch you."

"I made you jealous, didn't I?"

"Jealous of what? You're insane."

"No lying, Mouse."

Kathy looked at me. Sadness took over her eyes. "Please make him leave," she said.

Part of me wanted to see her pushed further, but a tear had started down her cheek. "Why don't you just take off?" I told Lucas halfheartedly.

"*Tell him.* Tell him how angry I made you. He hardly knows you."

Tears streamed down her face.

Lucas shook his head. "Amazing, isn't it. The way she changes moods on a dime." He looked back at me. "What do you make of it? One minute a scorned woman, the next a helpless child."

Kathy turned away. The side of her face was red and puffy.

My jaw tightened. "Did he hit you?" I asked.

"It doesn't matter," she sobbed.

I stared at Lucas. "Get out of here."

"You want to let her slide that easy, partner? A little damsel-in-distress routine, and she's off the hook. Don't you even want her to explain what I'm doing here? What *we* were doing in *there?*" He nodded toward her office.

I did and I didn't.

"You're calling the shots," he said after several seconds. "Shall I stay or go?"

"I told you to leave. I meant it."

He looked over at Kathy. "She'll tell you everything in due time." He headed for the elevator.

I walked up to Kathy and lightly touched her face. Even after finding her with Lucas, I wanted to be close to her. But I didn't know exactly how. "Are you through with him?" I asked.

"I'll never see him again. Ever."

"I've heard that before."

She pulled her face away from my hand. "Leave me alone, then, if that's what you want."

"That's not what I want."

She softened, took my hand in hers.

"I want to try to understand what's been going on. With you. With us."

"I thought we agreed the first step was you focusing on your own problem. You know I don't want anyone else, but it's like you're not even here when you're on that shit."

I nodded. "I was all set to go to McLean."

"And . . ."

"It turns out I was right; Hancock had the wrong man. There's been another murder."

"What? What do you mean?"

"Another woman was hacked up last night."

"Tell me she wasn't from the hospital."

"She wasn't. She was a dancer at the Lynx Club."

"A *stripper?*"

"Yes. A stripper."

"Well, Sarah never did anything sick like that. What's the connection?"

I tried to be gentle. "The wounds were a lot like Sarah's."

She closed her eyes.

"Hancock wants me on the case."

She let go of my hand. "That doesn't change the fact that you need to detox."

"I will. When this is over."

"It'll never be *over*. You'll always have a reason to stay high, Frank. I don't think you're doing this for Sarah or me or Emma Hancock or anybody. We're just the excuses you use to justify your habit."

"I can't walk away from this."

She rolled her eyes. "Then, please, stay away from me. OK?" She stepped back into the office and started to close the door.

I stuck my foot in the way.

Her face went blank. No sadness. No anger. "I'm not going to stand by and watch you destroy yourself. If you don't leave, I'll call security."

"You'll what?"

Her breathing quickened. "Get out, before I lose control."

I could tell she meant it. "Fine." I moved my foot. "But remember—"

She slammed the door.

Ten

I heard Lucas rev the Ferrari as I started down the steps outside the hospital. It lurched out of its space, then stopped short in front of me. "I could have told you: She's in no mood for company," he shouted.

I was in no mood to be fucked with. I walked over to him.

"My God, what a barracuda," he smiled, pulling on a pair of black leather driving gloves. "She'll chew both of us up, given the chance."

I rested my arm on his roof and grabbed his side mirror with my other hand. "She tells me you hit her."

He winced. "Could you move your hand? I just had the car detailed."

I left my hand where it was and looked over the hood. "Shines like new. Not that I would expect anything less from a cosmetic surgeon." I stuck my head inside. The champagne leather upholstery was in showroom condition. Matching burgundy and beige oriental carpets covered the spaces where floor mats would sit. The gearshift knob had been replaced by a high-gloss ebony ball, inlaid with a pearl yin-yang symbol. "Obsessively maintained," I said, straightening up.

"And I'd like to keep it that way. So move your hand."

"I will. Don't worry. Just admit it. *You smacked her.*"

He squinted up at me. "Do I look like Santa Claus?"

"Huh?"

"Don't let the color fool you; this is no sleigh. I have no reindeer. You do not get a wish list. I do not slide down your chimney to spread cheer and goodwill. I do not wear black boots and—"

"Enough, already. What the hell are you talking about?" I pushed on the side mirror. The metal creaked.

"Jesus, let go!"

"Tell me you hit her. What's so hard about that?"

He shook his head. "Look, I hear what you're asking. And I agree. She desperately needs to have the shit knocked out of her. I mean, a severe thrashing. But that's not my job. It's yours. And you can't even stand to see her shed a tear. Go ahead and wreck the car if you want; I'm still not going to do your dirty work."

I stared at him.

"I'll tell you my bottom line: I'll drive her until you get up the courage to look under the hood and fix her yourself. I'll keep her oiled up nice. But I can't take responsibility for a major overhaul. After all, you're the one with the analytic training."

I focused on the point where his nose met his upper lip. A quick blow there can snap the nasal bone and splinter the maxilla almost beyond repair. But part of me was fascinated by Lucas' character, in the way Paulson Levitsky would be fascinated by a voracious bacterium. He was a living, breathing specimen of psychopathy.

"Hey, speaking of head cases of the female persuasion," he said, "you'll appreciate this." He pointed toward the windshield.

I meant to only glance where he was pointing, but my eyes stayed glued on a gold wire ring hanging off the rearview mirror from a few inches of blue nylon suture. How had I missed it? My pulse quickened. "What's that?" I asked.

"You'd never believe it."

"Try me."

"Let go, first."

I moved my hand to the doorframe.

"You don't recognize it?"

"No," I lied.

"Do you want to spin or buy a vowel?"

"Neither. This isn't a game."

"*Everything's* a game, Frank. Here's a hint: It belongs to one of the dancers we saw last night. Candy—the girl with the perfect tits. I threw her a ten-spot."

"The one that was pierced."

"Bingo."

"It's the ring she was wearing."

"The *ring she was wearing*. Don't be afraid of words. It's her *pussy ring*. Can you say that?"

"How did you get your hands on it?"

"Say it. *Pussy ring*."

"OK. How did you get her pussy ring?"

"It's a long story. You probably have places to go."

"I've got time."

"I knew you'd be interested. We're a lot alike." He flicked the ring gently with his gloved fingertip. It swung back and forth from the suture. "I drove by her apartment late last night. She likes getting off in the car." He gunned the engine and looked at my hand. "Feel it? She says it's like straddling a jet."

"Incredible. You had her naked? Right there?"

"Right here, my friend." He patted the seat. "And I grab her pretty much whenever I want. That's our deal."

"What deal is that?"

"It's a secret."

I didn't want to press too hard too fast. "Don't keep me hanging. Was she any good?"

"Good? She was *phenomenal*. No gag reflex whatsoever." He shook his head. "Do you know how few women can actually deep-throat? I don't mean take half of it. I mean swallow it whole." He moved his hands up and down over his lap as if he were guiding her head. "I had her going like a piston."

"Fantastic," I nodded. "But why do you have the ring?"

"You'll think I'm crazy."

"Hey, it's like you said: You're not the only perverted doctor north of Boston."

He reached up to the mirror, snapped the suture free and

dropped the ring into the palm of his hand. Then he closed his eyes and sniffed it. "You can still smell her." He held the ring out toward my face.

I felt like strangling him, but I leaned over and sniffed it. I couldn't smell a thing, maybe because of the coke. I kept my eyes closed as I straightened up. "Imagine if you could bottle that and sell it," I sighed.

"How about Eau de Candy scratch-n'-sniff trading cards? You'd have kids turning over Mo Vaughn and Jose Canseco like the Red Sox were a farm team."

I laughed. "How'd you get it from her?"

"You want all the details?"

"Every single one."

"You really are as sick as I am." He looked around as if someone might be listening. "Picture her sitting there wearing a tight little lime green skirt that's hiked up around her waist. No panties. That's the rule: She has to be naked from the waist down when she sits in the car."

"OK."

"She's leaning over, blowing me." He used his left hand to simulate the motion of her head bobbing up and down. "I'm reaching around back, between her legs, and I've got two fingers going like a sonofabitch—in and out, in and out, in and out." He used his fingers to show me the frantic movement. "She's gasping for air, cause she's got me down her throat and she's gonna come, especially when I'm tugging on that ring, right? Cause she likes the pain."

"Right." I was getting excited myself, which disturbed me.

"But I've got my hand on top of her head to keep her on me. And I'm pumping away like a jackhammer." He moved his hips like he was riding a horse. "See?"

"I'm with you."

"I take a handful of her hair—nice, blond, soft hair—and I use that like a handle, you know? Like her head's a goddamn maraca. And she likes that, too."

"Nice."

"Then I blow my wad, and she swallows it, doesn't spill a drop, which is another rule, but I must have lost it there for a minute, because I pulled hard on the ring. I mean *hard*. And it rips right through her. She screams like I stuck a knife in her snatch . . ."

"Is that when she clawed your neck?"

He rolled his eyes. "Did you leave your ears at the office? I told you the Kathy monster did that."

"The Kathy monster?"

"That's what I call her when she's mad."

"Oh."

"May I continue?"

"I'm listening."

"Good. Because we were at the most exciting part of the story. You'll appreciate this as a shrink."

Whatever excitement I might have felt was lost in the image of Monique's bloodied flesh. "Go on," I managed.

"Well, right after I rip the ring out, she just comes and comes and comes. She's shaking and moaning like a cow in heat. And then, talk about crazy, what do you think she tells me?"

I couldn't hide my disgust any longer. "I have no idea," I scowled.

"Don't get down on yourself. How could you know? She leans over and whispers in my ear that she . . ." He started to laugh.

"She . . ."

"She tells me that . . ." He was laughing hysterically and could barely get the words out. "She tells me . . . she loves me."

I felt sick to my stomach. "So you killed her," I said.

"Perfect. You're beautiful." He laughed, but then turned serious. "I don't know which of us is sicker."

"Why did you cut her up?" I asked.

"Cut her up, like how? What do you mean?"

"Her breasts and genital area were mangled. I just came from the morgue. Why did you do that?"

"From the morgue . . ." He looked at me blankly. "I don't know. Why would I do that?" Without warning, he hit the gas.

I barely managed to dive clear of his back tire as it swerved in my direction. I smashed into the ground. My side felt like it had caved in. I struggled to my feet and looked down the parking lot. The Ferrari was stopped at the exit. It lingered there a few seconds, then started racing back toward me. I stumbled toward the stairs.

Lucas skidded to a stop where we had been talking. He got out of the car and came toward me.

I figured the best way to defend myself would be a head butt to his abdomen. I crouched down on one knee, ready to spring.

He stopped about five feet away, just out of striking distance. "I'm sorry, Frank," he said, "but I've had enough of you demeaning my character. I happen to be the most honest man you'll ever meet. If I killed somebody, it would be for a good reason, and I'd be the first one to take credit for it." He turned around, got back into his car and drove away.

* * *

I brushed myself off and dragged myself into the Rover. I locked the doors, then tapped my fingers along my side to find any point tenderness over the bones. I had learned the exam long before medical school. When I was thirteen, my father had landed a punch that fractured two of my ribs. I couldn't remember any longer what had gotten him angry, and he probably didn't even know himself at the time, but I did remember having lied to Henry Harris, our family doctor, that I'd injured myself diving for second base during a pickup game down at the park. Harris had been a boxer in the Marines, and every one of his movements still seemed exquisitely choreographed. I had watched him as his fingers danced up and down my torso, his eyes searching my face for the slightest twinge of pain, homing in on the breaks, all the while talk-ing me through the proper way to slide, feet first, keeping the bag in sight at all times. After he'd fitted me for an elastic rib binder, he'd picked me off my feet effortlessly, set me down on that crinkly, white paper that covers every examination table in the world and given me another piece of advice. "You go home now and rest. I'm going to talk to your father a few minutes about the risks of sports injuries. If you get hurt again, you come right down here and let me know."

When my father had come home, his lip was split, and one eye was swollen shut. Later that day, my ear to the bathroom door, I heard him cry for the first time and realized—also for the first time—that I loved him, would always love him, in spite of everything. And that made the beatings even harder to take.

I couldn't find any fractures. My breathing was steady, so I wasn't worried about a punctured lung. But I was badly shaken. Almost on instinct I reached into the glove compartment for the pillow of white powder. For comfort.

Comfort. Was that what I really needed? How far was comfort from numbness? Could I uncover the secrets of a murderer, laced as they always are with great suffering, when my own goal was to escape suffering?

I could almost hear Ted Pearson telling me again that the roots of any evil deed can be traced to the perpetrator's refusal to experience pain. "That makes facing your demons a moral duty," he'd told me. "It's the only way you'll ever be any different than your father."

Pearson's warning hadn't kept me from blowing off my psychotherapy sessions, but now I could see that he had been right. How many people would I have to hurt before I allowed myself to hurt?

I held the pillow between my fingertips. The powder shifted seductively. I pulled apart the seal, plunged a wet fingertip inside and enjoyed the coke's sour taste one last time. Then, absent any great drama, I poured about three grams of the stuff out my window.

I sat there a minute, convincing myself not to open the door to see whether any of the powder could be retrieved off the parking lot pavement. It wasn't until I pictured myself on my knees licking the ground that I banished the idea from my mind.

I needed to tell Hancock that Lucas had Monique's ring, but I wanted to be certain of what I told her beyond that. My jealousy and anger could easily make me paint Lucas as the killer when all I really knew was that he had something in his possession that belonged to the second victim. It was true he had seen her just prior to her death, but so had I. And I was troubled by the question he had put to me. *Why would he do it?* If he harbored rage toward women, he had found the perfect profession to deal with it: He sliced women every day and got paid handsomely for his handiwork. Maybe that wasn't enough for him anymore, maybe the fact that his patients wanted to be cut up took all the excitement out of it. In the OR, after all, his rage was channeled according to *their* whims. Maybe he was sick and tired of being a blade for hire. Making precise cuts on a woman's face or breasts or buttocks might not satisfy a man who is, at heart, a butcher. Yet why would he show me the ring? Did he want me to stop him? That seemed like a cliché.

Lucas' motivation still didn't make sense to me. Maybe there would be a clue at Monique's apartment.

I started the Rover and backed out. I had the impulse again to search for the coke on the ground. After all, I needed to think. But for the first time since I could remember, I was even more convinced that I needed to feel.

•   •   •

Union Street turns into Joyce Street, which heads into the Highlands, the part of Lynn that houses its most dispossessed citizens. It is a neighborhood of broken glass—little pieces glittering in the streets, jagged sheets tilting out of window frames, half-crushed bottles lining the curbs. I took a left onto Monroe Avenue and pulled up in front of No. 115, a puke green triple-decker with a rusted pickup in the driveway. Two cruisers were parked on the dirt where a front lawn belonged.

Of the three doorbells at the entryway, the only label was for the third-floor apartment. A piece of yellowed paper carried the names Marzipan and Peletier.

I let myself into the foyer. The smell reminded me of the stale air in the triple-decker where I'd grown up, but there was something sweeter mixed in. I recognized it as the odor of melting cocaine. The door to the apartment right of the staircase was missing, and I could see mattresses lined up on the orange shag carpeting. Balls of aluminum foil were strewn everywhere. I knew why. The place was a crack den. For ten bucks, you got a rock, a piece of foil to make a pipe and a place to sit while you smoked. The amount of trash in the room testified to a thriving business. Malloy would probably let it reopen—for a monthly fee—after the crime scene closed down. Not that it mattered much what he did; crack cocaine is inevitable in a dying city.

I started up the stairs. The wood creaked under my boots.

The door to the second-floor apartment was closed, but I could hear a man and a woman shouting at one other in Spanish.

I hurried up the steps. A length of yellow tape stenciled with the words POLICE BARRIER—DO NOT CROSS was stretched across the doorway to Monique's apartment. Angel Zangota, the officer who had first escorted me to Westmoreland's cell, was inside speaking to a lanky man with a shaved head. He spotted me and started over.

I ripped the tape away from the door. "Don't give me any crap about this place being off-limits," I said. "I'm working directly with Hancock. You have questions, call her."

"Kevin Malloy—"

"Fuck Malloy."

He held up a hand. "Malloy called with your clearance a few minutes ago. I guess he had some sort of medical emergency. Otherwise he'd be here himself."

"His teeth are bothering him."

"That's right. He was at Dr. Plotka's office. How did you know?"

"Never mind. What did he say?"

"He needs two molars bonded."

I shook my head. "I mean about me."

"He told me to make sure you had access to whatever you wanted—including the first floor."

"What does the first floor have to do with anything?"

"The contraband we confiscated is in the cruiser." He winked. "Back seat, passenger side. Matches are in the glove compartment."

Two-fifty an hour and all the cocaine I could snort or smoke. What would I have done for a deal like that two days before? "Thanks, anyhow," I told him.

"You sure?"

"Maybe later."

"It'll be gone later. It's good stuff."

I looked into his eyes and realized he was wired himself. "Obviously." I walked past him and offered my hand to the man with the shaved head. "Frank Clevenger," I said. "I'm a psychiatrist helping out with the investigation."

He took my hand in both of his. His willowy fingers ended in long red nails. "I apologize for the place being such a mess," he lisped. "They wouldn't let me touch a thing."

I took my hand back and glanced around. The coffee table was overturned. A lamp lay in pieces on the ground. My eyes settled on the couch; the middle seat cushion was soaked with blood. The walls were splattered in places, too.

Zangota joined us. "Dr. Clevenger, this is Mercury Marzipan."

"*Mercury Marzipan?*"

"We can't all be cookie-cutter, *Frank*," Marzipan said.

"Thank God for that. Did you change it from something?"

"My parents were Roman caterers," he smirked.

I smiled back.

"I changed it when I left the CIA."

"You worked for the Central Intelligence Agency?" Zangota asked.

Marzipan turned to him. "I was a double agent," he mocked, "until the Wall came down." He looked back at me. "CIA, as in Culinary Institute of America. My thesis was a five-foot marzipan statue of Mercury, wings, cap and all."

"Hence, Mercury Marzipan."

"The name was a better fit with the position I had accepted."

"What position was that?"

"Associate pastry chef at the Ritz." He became solemn. "You see, I was born Elliot Stankowitz."

"I understand," I said.

"Mr. Marzipan lived with Monique Peletier for two years," Zangota broke in.

"Wrong, Zorro," Marzipan said.

"Zangota," I corrected him.

"Well, maybe now he knows how it feels. I'm Ms. Marzipan. At least that's the way it's supposed to turn out. You might understand, being a shrink. I'm undergoing reassignment. I was already a wreck over it, and then this . . ." He looked around the room.

For the first time I noticed that Marzipan had breast buds showing through his yellow linen shirt.

"I've been reassigned plenty myself," Zangota nodded. "Salem, Saugus, now Lynn. I know how you feel. It's a big adjustment."

"He means sexual reassignment, Angel," I said. "Mercury is becoming a woman."

"Congratulaciónes," Zangota said flatly.

"Zorro won't let me put on my hair," Mercury said, pointing to the mantel. A brown, flowing wig sat atop a ceramic head. The white face was speckled with blood.

"They need it for evidence," I said.

"I need it, too. I feel naked."

"Why did you say you're *supposed* to become Ms. Marzipan? Are you reconsidering?"

"Not for a nanosecond. And seeing a fine male specimen such as yourself only confirms what I know about myself." He gave me the once-over. "You really could model. You know that, don't you?"

"Thank you. But if you aren't reconsidering, why the doubt about becoming a Ms.?"

"Circumstances beyond my control," he said, shaking his head.

"Such as?"

"Such as Monique being dead."

"Why does that change anything?"

"She was part of the deal."

"What deal?" Zangota asked.

"I'm not saying another word, unless I can put on my hair. I'm the one standing here exposed for your pleasure."

"You're right. Put it on," I said.

Marzipan headed over to the mantel.

"He'll contaminate the—" Zangota started.

"Look, this isn't the O.J. case. He's worn the thing a hundred times. Let's not get jammed up over nothing."

"OK. But I didn't see him do it."

"No problem. I'll tell Court TV you were too coked up to know what the hell was going on."

I could see Marzipan fixing himself up in the bathroom mirror. I walked over and stood just outside the open door. He was putting on mascara. "So what deal was Monique part of?"

He leaned close to the mirror to check his lashes.

I waited.

"It won't go in the newspaper or anything, will it? My parents would absolutely drop dead."

I figured he was doing a bit of wishful thinking. "There are leaks in every investigation. I can't promise anything."

"It would embarrass my whole family. They're very conservative people. Dad's the commandant of the Essex Yacht Club in Marblehead." He reached for the blush. "When I was arrested for possession last year, he had a mild heart attack."

"If what you're about to tell me is as sensitive as you say, I'm sure it could devastate them," I said. "Him especially."

I noticed a hint of a grin on Marzipan's face as he twisted open a pink lipstick. He covered his lips, then rubbed them together to even out the color. He turned to me.

With his hair and makeup in place he looked every bit a woman. Pretty, even. "You make a very convincing Ms.," I said.

"That's kind of you to say." His voice was softer. He seemed calmer. He sat down on the edge of the bathtub and crossed his legs. They were shaved. "It was surgery for sex. My doctor could have me or Monique whenever he wanted, in exchange for his work. But now, with Monique gone, I don't know if he'll honor the deal. I think he liked her better."

"Why do you say that?"

"No reason," he frowned.

"C'mon now, Mercury. You're talking to a shrink."

He shrugged. "He only had sex with me in the apartment, with the bedroom door locked, like he was ashamed of me or something. But he had Monique here, there and everywhere. Even in his car."

I stood there in silence for several seconds. "What kind of car?" I asked finally.

"His substitute cock, if you ask me. The man's built like a sparrow."

"What kind of car?"

"Talk about showy. A red Ferrari."

I tried to keep my breathing even. "Why would Monique sell herself so you could become a woman?"

"Surely you jest. That little bitch wouldn't sell a French kiss if my life depended on it. No disrespect for the dead intended." He reached over and knocked on the wood trim around the door. "The deal was for both of our surgeries."

"Both? What surgery did she want?"

"She *got* hers. She had itty-bitty titties before the implants." He looked down at his chest. "I was hoping mine would come out half as nice. You couldn't see her scars at all."

"This doctor—was his name Trevor Lucas?"

"He's not a friend of yours, is he?"

"No."

"But you know him."

"More and more."

"Could you put in a good word for me? So I don't get left hanging?"

I wasn't going to let that word sneak by me again. "You're not feeling desperate enough to do yourself in, are you, Mercury? You could tell me if you were."

"I seem that bad off to you?"

"No. But whenever someone mentions hanging. . . ."

"It was a joke." He grabbed his crotch. "Don't you get it?"

"Yeah. I get it." I shook my head. "Here's my advice: Stay away from Dr. Lucas. It's a lot less bloody to change your mind than your sex."

"Easy for you to say, big shot. You're not trapped in the wrong body." He got up, walked back over to the mirror.

I watched him spreading more blush onto his cheeks. I felt like burrowing into his psyche to find out who had cleaved him from his manhood. I even came up with an opening line: *Your dick was cut off a long time ago.* That might get him mad enough to trot out a few of his demons. But then what? What was he supposed to do ten minutes later, when he was edging toward the truth, and I was finished with him? I sighed. "You're right," I said. "It would take me a long time to really understand what it feels like to be in your predicament."

He stopped putting on makeup and watched me in the mirror.

"So if you ever want to talk about it—you know, get deep into it—I'm listed in Marblehead and, uh. . ." I stopped myself. "I could probably find somebody, a therapist, for you to talk to. Somebody who's good. Top-notch."

"Thanks," he said, tentatively.

"Not at all." I touched his arm on my way out. "Good luck, Mercury."

•   •   •

I stood with Zangota on the landing as he replaced the barrier tape I had torn away. My mind was racing. Lucas had been with Monique the night of her murder. He had operated on her breasts, and I had a feeling he was also the one who had pierced her. Maybe she had held back on the sex she owed him, and he had decided to collect the body parts he had worked on. But that was still a theory in search of proof. "No trace of the murder weapon?" I asked.

"We've combed every inch of the place, including the yard." He nodded toward the apartment. "What did he—or she, or whatever—tell you in the bathroom?"

I wasn't ready to swing the formal investigation toward Lucas. I was afraid there would be no turning Hancock back, regardless of the evidence. And wasted time could mean more bodies. "He didn't tell me anything that made sense," I said.

Zangota squinted at me. "He took a long time to say nothing."

"Oh. OK, then. He confessed. He murdered Monique and Sarah. And JFK. And John Lennon."

"He was supposed to tell you about a *deal*."

"That was some silly thing about Mercury's landlord cutting him slack on back rent. He liked having a pretty girl like Monique around. With her gone, Mercury has to pay up, which puts his surgery—"

There was suddenly a great deal of shouting in Spanish coming from the second-floor apartment. "What the hell are they arguing about?" I asked Zangota.

"She's saying, '*Leave him alone. Leave him alone.*'"

The woman screamed.

I started down the stairs. Zangota followed. "What's the man saying?" I called back to him.

"He's gonna '*teach the little bastard a lesson.*'"

Halfway to the second floor I heard a slap. I picked up my pace. When I got to the door, a child cried out. My movements were automatic, directed by something deep inside me over which I had no control. I reared back and aimed my foot at the center of the door. It splintered free of its hinges with a single kick. I took in the scene as snapshots. A man about thirty was standing toward the far corner of the room. He turned to me, but I didn't look at his face, only his arms and chest. They were dark and muscular. The next snapshot was of a woman sitting cross-legged on a couch nearer to me, covering her face with her hands. My eyes flicked back to where the man was standing. A boy seven or eight years old was cowering on the floor in front of him. Blood trickled out of his nose. I instinctively began walking toward the two of them. My mind was clear of thought. The man stepped into my path. I kept walking. He flailed at me, but I grabbed his wrist, pulled his arm straight and drove the heel of my hand into his elbow. The joint popped. He backed up, cradling his unhinged appendage, then leaned over and charged me, like a bull. I waited until he was inches away, stepped aside and slammed my knee into his chest. He lurched forward onto the floor, gasping for air.

Out of the corner of my eye, I saw the woman rushing toward me. I grabbed her, spun her around and threw her back onto the couch. Then I started after the man on the floor.

Zangota stepped between us. "Enough," he said. "I'll take care of him."

I tried to shove past him, but he stayed right in front of me.

"I said *I'll take care of him*," he sputtered. "Help the kid, why don't you?"

"Who?"

"The kid. He's a mess."

I turned around. The boy was standing up, shaking. There was terror in his eyes. I walked over, kneeled in front of him and wiped the blood off his lips. Then I took one of his shoulders in each of my hands. He leaned toward me and started to cry. I held him. I thought I felt his tears running down my cheek, but realized that couldn't be. His head was on my shoulder.

The tears I felt were my own.

Eleven

I waited in the back seat of Zangota's cruiser ten minutes or so before a Lynn Police Department van rolled into the driveway. Zangota came out a few seconds later with his prisoner. The man's dislocated arm was hanging limp at his side. His other hand was cuffed to his belt. Zangota shoved him into the back of the van, slammed the doors, then walked over to my window.

He pointed at the metal box next to me. "The best you'll ever have," he said. "And you look like you could use it. I know I could."

"What do you figure will happen to the kid?" I asked.

"We both know what's gonna happen. The Department of Social Services will investigate and make a recommendation."

"The mother's no use."

He shrugged. "So they'll yank him out of there."

"And put him in a foster home where some other lowlife can get at him."

"There are good foster homes."

"Yeah, right. Go live in one, then tell me."

"I did live in one."

"You were a foster kid?"

"My parents were a mess," Zangota chuckled. "Up and left one day, out of nowhere. Good people took me in."

"Where are your biological parents?"

"I don't know."

"Ever considered looking for them?"

"Sure. But I never have."

"Too much anger?"

"Listen," he grinned, "there's not enough room for me to lie down back there. Let's light up and lighten up."

I stared at the box. I could picture the little white rocks inside. I could smell the sweet smoke they give off. I was exhausted and full of anxiety—the worst combination. And I wanted relief. I reached over, opened the box and looked inside. There was as much cocaine as I had ever seen in one place, enough to erase the little boy from my memory a thousand times. But which little boy—the kid in the house, or me? I closed my eyes and thought about that.

"Hellooo . . . You still with me?" Zangota asked.

I nodded. "He doesn't need it," I said.

"Who doesn't need what? What are you talking about?"

I looked up at him. "Our murderer. He doesn't need coke or booze or anything else. He's got a drug: the kill. He avoids feeling pain by inflicting it. He turns his suffering inside out so he can feel powerful, instead of weak. It puts him back on top of the world."

"*His* suffering?"

"You don't leave victims lying around unless, deep down, you feel like one yourself."

"Spoken like a liberal shrink from Massachusetts."

"Thank you."

"If he's been hurt so bad, why wait until now to vent? Why two bodies in three days?"

"I'm not sure. My guess is that he managed to keep himself in control, probably barely in control, until something pushed him over the edge—a chink in his armor. A slight of some sort."

"You think he'll stop?"

"If he can repair the damage to his ego, restore the balance of his psyche, he'll stop. Otherwise he has to keep going. It's the only way he knows to hold back the tide of self-hatred ready to drown him." I closed the box.

"What are you doing? How about my goddamn balance?"

"It's a free country. Sort of. Go ahead if you want."

"You telling me you don't?"

"Of course I want it. I'm just sick and tired of *needing* it."

•   •   •

I picked up Route 1A south, headed for Chelsea. Several hours had passed since I'd learned of Monique's murder. I hadn't spoken to Rachel and didn't know if Monique was simply a coworker of hers at the Lynx Club or her friend. Halfway to her apartment, at the entrance to Route 16, I dialed Paulson Levitsky's lab.

"Levitsky, chief of pathology, City of Lynn," he answered.

"Big fucking deal."

"Where the hell have you been?"

"The hospital. Monique Peletier's apartment. Why?"

"We've got a preliminary report on Sarah from the folks in Quantico. I've been trying to reach you."

I grabbed a Marlboro out of a package on the dashboard. "What did they find? Scleroderma?"

"Not funny. I've clarified that I . . ."

". . . never put forward . . ." I lit up.

"Exactly."

"So what's the finding?"

"I wouldn't call it a *find*ing until it's *fin*al."

"I wouldn't expect you to."

"Even the best labs screw up."

"Understood," I yielded. "What's the *preliminary result?*"

"A toxin, like they thought. But it wasn't anything the killer sprinkled on the wounds. It was already inside Sarah when he cut her up."

I blew a long stream of smoke out the window. "Are you saying she was poisoned?"

"In a way. The tissue samples I sent them were contaminated with silicone."

I veered into the breakdown lane and stopped. My chest was tight with a mixture of anxiety and excitement.

"I should have come up with the idea myself," Levitsky said. "The crap only sparked one of the biggest lawsuits of our time."

"You do mean silicone as in breast implants."

"Well, she wasn't stuffed full of computer chips. Sarah must have undergone augmentation at some point. The implants leaked and caused fibrosis. Our killer didn't slice away all the affected tissue."

"Did he try?"

"I don't think so. This guy isn't shy with a blade. If he'd wanted to go deeper, he would have. My guess is the implants adhered to the surrounding musculature. He had to cut away the underlying tissue to free them up."

I took another drag and blew the smoke out my nose. "Why not rip them out?"

"They'd rupture. There would be silicone gel everywhere."

"Which obviously mattered to him."

"I'd certainly say so. It took real time to get those implants out in one piece—maybe five minutes each. He wanted them."

"Or wanted them back."

"Huh?"

I was less reticent to implicate Lucas. "Maybe he put them in there to begin with."

"What do you mean, *put them in there?*"

"Maybe he's the one who enlarged her breasts."

"You think the murderer is a cosmetic surgeon?"

"Anything's possible."

"You saw the wounds, Frank. There was nothing elegant about them. They were hack jobs. He'd have to intentionally make a mess."

"Unless he was intoxicated by the kill, shaking from it. Think of the power, Paulson: creating, then destroying a woman."

"Maybe . . . except a surgeon's skills become part of him. They crystallize under pressure. They—"

I wasn't in the mood to be lectured. "I get your point."

"You don't think Mike Tyson would beat a man to death with haphazard blows, do you?"

"I don't think Tyson had anything to do with this," I said dryly.

"He'd fire off fierce, crisp combinations."

"How do you know that, Paulson?"

"The laws of stimulus and response. People react predictably, especially when they don't have time to think. They aren't much different than birds pecking for seed."

"Psychopaths don't conform to traditional behavior patterns. That's the problem with them."

"Granted."

"Thank you."

"How does Monique fit into your theory?"

"She had implants, too."

"Her, too?" He was silent a few moments. "If the killer is a doc, that helps me settle on what sort of weapon left so many short, clean lacerations. I was picturing a straight edge. I think I mentioned a razor blade."

"But . . ."

"But now that I think about it, they're even more consistent with a scalpel."

•   •   •

I pulled onto Route 16. My head throbbed along a thick band running ear to ear like headphones. My fingers trembled so much that I dropped my cigarette and had to grind it into the carpet with my heel. I didn't know whether my nervous system was clamoring for cocaine or overwhelmed with what I had learned. At minimum, Lucas was swapping surgery for sex with patients, male and female. He was even more predatory than I had imagined. And if he had been Sarah's surgeon, then he was the common denominator in two murders.

I was beginning to question whether rage was the only force

driving him. Levitsky's comment about the billions in legal settlements over silicone implants hadn't been lost on me. With Dow Corning, the largest manufacturer of silicone implants, filing bankruptcy, every ambulance-chasing lawyer in the world was looking for other deep pockets. Doctors were their next logical targets. And not every cosmetic surgeon carries malpractice insurance. Was Lucas killing off his liabilities? Had Sarah and Monique threatened to sue? The idea seemed outlandish, but I reminded myself of what I had told Levitsky: Psychopaths act in ways that test society's capacity for reason.

I switched lanes, shot past a school bus, then remembered my mishap with the Mustang and slowed down.

Was Kathy blind to Lucas' dark side? I couldn't believe that. Relationships are never chance events. Maybe all my theorizing about how losing her little sister had affected her was bullshit. Maybe she only paid lip service to wanting a stable life. Plenty of people who survive tragedies end up ambivalent about danger—frightened by it, yet strangely drawn to it.

Was that dynamic driving me? I couldn't deny that I had played a part in creating the psychological and sexual ties that bound Lucas, Kathy and me. The actions of any one of us affected the other two. I shuddered as I realized how easily Lucas could strike at me by attacking Kathy. Even worse, I had to wonder whether leaving him on the streets meant I unconsciously wished he would do it. Had I primed Lucas to kill her? Was I really as rageful toward women as he, just less straightforward about it?

I pulled the Rover into the breakdown lane again and waited. When I had the chance, I made a quick U-turn and headed back for the Lynn Police Department.

Hancock wasn't in her office. Mark Meehan, one of the cops at the front desk, told me she was taking target practice.

"Does she usually do that? In the middle of the day?" I asked.

"No," Meehan said. "She usually does it first thing in the morning. Right after church. But she said she could use another session."

I walked through the station to an iron door imprinted with the outline of a human torso and head. I opened it and stepped inside.

Hancock was the only one in the long room, standing at the last of a dozen stations, staring straight ahead. She was wearing safety glasses and earphones. Her arms were outstretched and motionless, her fists curled around her revolver. Her eyes darted my way, then snapped back and focused down the lane again. A paper target was hanging about fifteen yards from her. Without warning, the silence exploded into three echoing blasts that made me shudder and throw my hands over my ears. Three holes appeared dead center of the target's chest. Hancock stood still. Her arms stayed extended, like the first branch off an oak. I walked toward her. Suddenly, she turned in my direction, fixing me in her line of fire. I stopped. Our eyes locked. I smiled, but her expression didn't change. I wasn't certain she even recognized me. I thought about diving for one of the shooting stations, but I knew Hancock could pick me off midair. So I just stood there, alive or dead according to her whim. I felt terror so consuming it bordered, strangely, on complete peacefulness. "Emma," I managed, "it's Frank."

She looked confused.

"Put the gun down," I said softly.

She squinted at me. A smile that seemed forced appeared on her face, then vanished. "My Lord," she said, lowering the gun, "you didn't think I'd fire, did you?"

I swallowed hard. "Your gun was pointed at my head. It kind of threw me."

She took off her earphones and glasses and looked at the gun in her hand. "I was imagining what it would feel like to rid the world of the demon who tortured Monique." She tossed the gun on the countertop in front of her. "I'm sick of ripping holes in pieces of paper. It's driving me crazy."

"And you figured I'd be happy to stand in for the killer?" I walked over to her.

"I'm sorry. I haven't been myself lately." She paused. "You alright?"

"I am now." I shook my head, remembering the combination of panic and peace that had taken hold of me.

"You felt it."

"*It?*"

"The calm at the gates of heaven."

"If you want to call it that."

"Yes. I do. I've been at the wrong end of a gun more times than I care to remember and I've felt it every time." She looked down, lost in thought. "I felt it even as a girl."

"As a kid? You got shot at?"

"No." She looked back at me. "I had Hodgkin's disease when I was ten."

I stayed silent.

"I try not to think about it. But lately I can't stop myself. I wake up thinking about it. Sometimes one, two in the morning."

I kept listening. It finally made sense to me why Hancock was such a loner; children faced with losing everything can grow up unwilling to embrace anything—except their prayers.

"I lost my hair from chemotherapy. There were cankers in my mouth so big I couldn't bear to eat. Most of the time I didn't have an appetite anyhow. But you know the worst part? I couldn't get my hands on the thing that was after me. It was invisible. It wouldn't fight fair."

"So now you catch killers you can lock up." I winced, realizing I'd delivered another punch line to somebody's life story.

"I never thought about it like that." She smiled the shy, wondrous smile with which my psychotherapy patients had always greeted the truth about their lives.

"I hope Monique felt it," I said.

"What?"

"The calm. At the gates."

"I pray she did."

We stood together for several moments. "I wanted to talk with you about the case," I said finally.

"You have something?"

"I've got a bunch of things. I'm not sure they add up."

"Let's hear 'em."

"It's all circumstantial. No hard evidence."

"Let me be the judge of that."

I shared what I knew. I told her about Lucas having been with Monique shortly before she was murdered, about the deal he had cut with Mercury, about the implants, even about the Dow Corning lawsuits. I also let her in on the fact that Lucas was screwing Kathy and that I was frightened for her. Hancock's eyes narrowed. She started clicking her nails. "There are things that don't fit," I cautioned her.

"Like what?"

"Like the fact that Lucas showed me . . ." I looked away.

"Come on. Out with it."

"He showed me the ring Monique wore through her . . . private area. He said he . . ."

"Tell me, damn it."

"He ripped it out of her while they were fooling around in his car."

"He ripped it out of her? Down there?"

I nodded.

Hancock picked up her gun and started to load the chambers she had just emptied.

"Let's think this through, Emma: If Lucas killed her, why would he show me the evidence?"

"Who knows, Frank? Why did the Unabomber contact newspapers? Why do serial killers leave notes?"

"There are other problems."

"Like what?"

"Like I can't quite understand why somebody who gets paid to cut women up every day would risk life imprisonment to do it outside the OR. Even the lawsuit thing doesn't seem quite right. Lucas is so flush with cash he could probably take a couple major hits and still come out smelling like a rose. There's no clear motive."

Hancock clicked the barrel of her gun into place and held it out to me.

"What?"

"Take it. I'm going to teach you something."

"I don't want it."

"Take it. Just for a second."

I took the gun. I had never held one before. It had more heft to it than I would have imagined. My fingers curved around the grip and onto the trigger. I looked at my hand holding the thing.

Just then Hancock grabbed my hand with the gun in it and pulled the barrel against her chest. She pressed her thumb against my finger on the trigger.

I froze. "What the hell . . ."

"You could end it all for me," she said.

I started to sweat.

"Your friend Levitsky wouldn't be able to identify my heart."

"Emma . . ."

My heart was pounding. I imagined what the kick of the gun would feel like against my arm, how Hancock would stumble back, bloodied. It was up to me whether she took another breath.

"I can see it in your face. You're the whole world to me, like I was to you when you walked into this room. Press a little further, and I disappear. I'm nothing. Zero. A half-column obituary in to-morrow's *Item*."

I looked her straight in the eyes. I pressed ever so lightly on the trigger, just to get a little higher. When I did, Hancock jammed her finger against mine and pushed the trigger all the way down. In that split second every nerve cell in my body must have dumped adren-aline into my bloodstream. I felt a high that made cocaine seem like a cup of decaf. I braced for the explosion, but all I heard was a hollow click. I stood there, staring at Hancock's chest.

She took the gun out of my hand, loaded the chamber she had left empty and slipped the gun into her holster. "He wants to feel what you just felt, Frank. Only he wants the payoff, too. The re-lease. The devil playing God. And I'd bet he takes his time at it. He wants to watch his victim start to bleed, feel her flesh give way, guess at which breath will be her last."

"But why? What would drive Lucas to want that?"

"He likes it."

I was still shaken. "You could say that about any killer," I managed. "It doesn't mean Lucas is our man."

"True."

"But you're gonna pick him up anyhow?"

"Well, sure. I don't expect he'll be able to stand up on his own once I'm finished with him."

◆   ◆   ◆

One of the tugs working Chelsea Harbor was forcing a tanker the last fifty yards toward the dock at the end of Rachel's street. The thunder of its engine drowned out the sounds of traffic on the Tobin Bridge and turned a man on the tug's bow into a pantomime act as he cupped his hands around his mouth and screamed silently toward shore.

I was almost on empty by the time I climbed the five flights to Rachel's apartment. I knocked on the door, waited a bit, then pounded.

"Who is it?" she yelled.

"Frank."

She slid the door open and stood there staring at me, a white silk robe tight around the curves of her breasts and hips. She looked worried. She reached out and touched my face.

I was surprised to feel my eyes fill up.

"Are you alright?"

"No," I said. I made an effort to collect myself. "But that's not new." I walked inside and rolled the door closed. When I turned back to her, she had dropped her robe and was standing in pink panties.

"Can I help?" she asked. She came closer and started to unfasten my belt.

I could have urged her to wonder where she had learned to use her body to heal men; my guess was the lesson had come early, probably from an alcoholic father or a depressed uncle. But I needed to be restored myself and I had nowhere else to go.

I took off my belt. She turned around. Part of me wanted to use the last of my energy to yank her panties to her knees and use the leather on her. But another part of me, suddenly the greater part, wanted to give her something other than pain. I stepped around her, so that we were facing one another, and kneeled down. I brushed my lips against her stomach, then held her hips steady as she swayed back. My tongue traced the borders of her panties. She sighed. I helped lower her to the floor. She spread her legs. I kissed her knees and thighs, then moved my mouth along the vertical line of pink cotton caught between her folds of skin. Her breathing quickened. I could smell and taste her excitement. I pulled aside the cloth and moved inside her with my caresses. Her abdomen started to quiver. I moved my tongue faster, biting gently now and then. She groaned, then screamed with pleasure as she arched off the floor. I filled her with my fingers, which made her arch higher and cry out again before collapsing back to the hardwood.

I had nothing left. I laid my head on her stomach and listened as her breathing slowed. Her legs curved around my shoulders, her feet resting on the small of my back. As her fingers moved through my hair, my eyes closed. I forced them open, but only for an instant.

I didn't want to sleep. There was too much I needed to do, and I worried my dreams would leave me anything but rested. But I couldn't fight off my fatigue. I clung more tightly to Rachel and took a last, deep breath.

◆　　　◆　　　◆

I awakened on the platform bed, not remembering how I had gotten there, tangled in sheets so tightly I could barely move. I was naked and soaked with sweat. My legs trembled. I heard the shower running, glanced at the bedside clock and saw that it was six thirty-five in the evening. Chelsea, I reminded myself. With Rachel. I had been passed out a couple hours—time I couldn't afford. I freed my legs, sat up and let reality take me firmly in hand.

My clothes were folded neatly over an armchair. I walked over and pulled on my jeans. Then I grabbed the phone and had the operator connect me to information for Austin, Texas. I got the number for University Hospital.

I dialed. When the attendant answered, I asked her to page Ben Carlson, the cardiac surgeon who had been Sarah Johnston's lover.

"May I ask who's calling?" she asked.

"Frank. Frank Clevenger."

"Will he know you, sir?"

Anyone with an ounce of authority uses it like a sledgehammer. "I'm his analyst," I said.

"Sir?"

"His psychiatrist from Boston, ma'am. He'll want the call."

A minute or so later Carlson picked up. "Prozac is sixty bucks a month. What the fuck do I need you for, Clevenger?"

His tone told me he hadn't heard about Sarah. "Sixty bucks covers twenty milligrams a day," I stalled. "We both know that wouldn't touch your pathology."

"You assume I'm swallowing it. I'm snorting it."

"Doesn't the capsule get stuck?"

He chuckled. "They really are peddling it on the streets out here, you know. It brings five dollars a dose. We're in the wrong business."

"It feels that way sometimes."

"What's it been? Eight, nine months?"

"Around there."

"Still in forensics?"

"Right."

"You're probably better off. HMOs are the only ones making money in patient care. They're reaming everybody." He paused. "You were real good, though."

"Some of the time. When I was bad, I sucked."

"Yes, well. I know. That kid. How long you gonna beat yourself up over it? People get fatal mental illnesses, just like they get fatal cardiac disease. We're not magicians." Several seconds passed in silence. "You probably called for something besides a lecture."

I braced myself to tell him about the murder. "I have bad news, Ben. It's about Sarah."

"She sick?"

"I should have called you sooner, but . . ."

"I've got an emergency bypass on deck, pal. Let's have it."

"She was murdered. They found her in the woods in back of the hospital."

"Murdered? She's dead?"

"She was the first of two victims. Looks like a serial killer."

He cleared his throat. "When did this happen?"

I had to think. "A couple days ago," I said.

"Jesus Christ. Did they catch the guy?"

"No. Not yet. But I'm working on it. That's why I called. I have a question."

"Anything."

"Sarah had breast implants, right?"

"Uh-huh."

The shower stopped. I heard Rachel's footsteps in the bathroom. "Who put them in?"

"Why do you need to know that?"

"Sarah's body was cut up pretty badly. The implants had been removed."

"They were cut out of her?"

"Right."

"Oh, my God." He fell silent again.

"Ben?"

"I don't want to get anyone in trouble needlessly."

"Needlessly? She was killed."

"Well, her surgeon didn't do it."

I didn't respond.

"Look," he said finally, "Sarah had the surgery before she and I met. The guy who did the procedure was dating her at the time."

"Tell me his name."

"I don't see any reason to hang him out to dry in the *Boston Her-*

ald. You know? You screw a patient today, it's a big deal. It's not like it used to be. The Board of Medicine will stick its nose up your ass real fast and—"

"Was it Trevor Lucas?"

"Why would you think Lucas?"

"A wild guess."

"You didn't hear anything from me."

Real moral courage, I thought. "Fair enough."

"He talked her into it, kept telling her she was beautiful, but flat. And Sarah wasn't the most secure girl underneath it all. Anyhow, she regretted her decision. She had problems with the implants."

Rachel stepped out of the bathroom wrapped in a towel, walked to the mirror and started to brush her hair. I wondered whether she had heard about Monique's murder.

"What sort of problems?" I asked.

"Subjective complaints. Fatigue. Joint pains. Migraines, time to time. She thought maybe the damn things were leaking."

"Did she think about suing?"

"Not in a million years. I don't think she ever let Lucas know she was having trouble. She said she felt strange bringing it up, seeing as we all worked at the same hospital. But I didn't buy that for a second."

I watched Rachel drop her towel and wriggle into a flimsy skirt and T-shirt. Even in the midst of talking about a murder, I felt myself getting hard. "How did you figure it?" I asked Carlson.

"My opinion? She was still hot for him. She didn't want to disappoint him."

"Even when you two were together?"

He let out a long sigh. "OK, I might as well tell you: Lucas is one reason I decided to take this position. I was wrecked over Sarah. I thought I loved her." He paused. "Trouble was, she was still screwing him."

My excitement evaporated. I felt light-headed. Did every dark road lead to Lucas? "Why do you say that?"

"Why does it matter?"

"Ben, I'm doing an investigation here. Don't jerk me off. I need to know everything I possibly can about Sarah."

"It's a strange reason."

I sat back down on the bed. "Nothing surprises me."

"She started to shave. Completely."

"Her vagina."

Rachel turned around and faced me.

"I didn't care for it," Carlson said. "I haven't been into little girls since I was a little boy. And when a woman does that, she's doing it because a man asked her to. In this case, another man."

"The good Dr. Lucas."

"I can't even say I hold it against him. I was never one to turn down pussy just because someone else had his name on it. Neither were you, as I recall."

"No argument there."

"Hold on." He covered the mouthpiece. I couldn't make out his muffled words. "Sorry," he said. "I'm due in the OR. Will you keep me up to date?"

"Of course."

"Uh . . . Frank?"

"I'm still here."

"Just for the record, what I said before wasn't true."

"What? Which part?"

"I didn't *think* I loved Sarah. I was absolutely certain of it."

I wanted to reach out to him, but I couldn't come up with anything to say.

"Take care, buddy." He hung up.

I placed the phone back in its cradle.

"Was that about Monique?" Rachel asked.

So she did know. "It was about the first victim, the nurse who was found in the woods, but it looks like the same killer."

"A Lynn cop stopped by. Officer Malloy. He said it was routine. They're interviewing everyone who worked with her."

"I wasn't sure how close you and Monique were."

"Not very. Mostly back room chitchat."

"Did Malloy tell you much?"

"I don't think he spared any details. He told me she was found with her breasts and vagina mutilated. He said her clitoris had been removed." She leaned against the bureau. "He seemed to enjoy talking about it."

"I'm sure he did. Did he frighten you?"

"I've never been shocked by what one person can do to another."

"Why not?"

She shrugged. "I'll tell you some other time—when you've got less on your mind."

I nodded. I was just as happy not to get into it.

"One thing Malloy said did surprise me: He thinks Monique was a prostitute. He wanted to know who her customers were."

"Did you give him any names?"

"I didn't realize she was selling herself. I told him I'd be working at the Lynx Club tonight with five other girls. Maybe one of them would know."

"I thought you said Monique had a *professional* relationship with Trevor Lucas."

"She did. A doctor-patient relationship. She went to him for her surgery. He does all the dancers. Breasts. Butts. Thighs."

"Naturally." At least I could let Hancock know her niece wasn't prostituting—not for cash, anyhow. "I wanted to get here sooner so I could tell you everything myself."

"I wouldn't have put odds on you getting here at all."

I thought about that. "Neither would I," I said.

"But you did." She stared out the window at the Tobin Bridge. "You know, you don't sleep well."

"No. I don't. Did I do anything strange?"

"Not really." She looked back at me. "Grimaced. Twisted. Turned. Screamed."

"I've had nightmares for as long as I can remember."

"What happens in them?"

I was even less anxious to turn Rachel into my therapist than into my patient. "I run as fast as I can," I said, and left it at that.

"But why are you running? What are you afraid of?"

"Nothing."

Her head fell to one side. "I think you need a guardian angel of your own, until you can figure all this out."

I smiled. "I probably could have used one a lot sooner."

Twelve

Rachel left for the Lynx Club, and I started back to Marblehead. My mood was melancholy, and my stomach was in knots. Halfway down the Lynnway, I called Hancock's office from the Rover and learned she was still out, presumably searching for Lucas. I had the impulse to take the downtown exit and stop in front of the Emerson Hotel for a boost. As I thought about it, my tongue flicked back and forth over my gums, and I swallowed again and again, imagining the tissues numb. I started to think that coming clean cold turkey might do me damage. My neurons might be better preserved if I withdrew from the coke slowly, especially given the stress I'd been under. Yet I knew from treating addicts that rationalizations like that one are symptoms of dependency. *Dependency.* That was a good word to describe my relationship with cocaine. I had always searched it out when I needed support, the chemical equivalent of a shoulder to cry on, without ever having to cry to anyone.

I lit a Marlboro, inhaled deeply and accelerated past the downtown exit.

If I found it so hard to share moments of weakness, what had Kathy provided me? Isolation? I shook my head, picturing the games we had played, like competing to stay longer under the cold spray in the shower. More than once we had held lighted matches between our fingertips, betting which of us would blow out the flame first. I was no better at fire than I was at water. Kathy won every time. But why test each other's capacity to deny pain, unless our romantic contract was to help each other ignore it?

I took another drag and blew the smoke against the windshield.

Could I bear life with a woman like Rachel, keeping pain in clear focus? I thought of the photograph of the old woman on oxygen on the wall of Rachel's loft. I remembered the taxidermy scene under her coffee table—a coyote struggling to finish off a raccoon trapped in its jaws. Was my problem with intimacy really a fear of being consumed? Did I think I could cheat death by avoiding life?

"Too many damn questions," I said out loud. I was thinking too much. Obsessing. That can be a defense against feeling, in and of itself. I had tried practicing elements of Zen Buddhism a couple years back, at least the version of it I could pick up by reading books on the subject, but mindlessness and desirelessness had evaded me—except, it seemed, when I was high.

I tossed my cigarette out the window and flew the rest of the way to Marblehead, forked right onto Atlantic Avenue and took another right onto Preston Beach Road. The house was dark, save for a single light in the bedroom. I figured I had left it on by mistake, but as I pulled into the driveway, I saw Kathy's white Volvo. My pulse quickened. Was she there for her things? Or was she coming back to me? My anxiety doubled as I realized she might have been at home the night before—when I had slept out. But why worry over that? She'd been anything but faithful herself.

I parked and went inside. At the entryway I stumbled over something. I clicked on the hallway light and saw Kathy's black leather overnight bag at my feet. I headed upstairs. I had only climbed a few steps when she appeared on the second-floor landing. She was wearing her scrubs. Her hair was wet.

I stopped.

"I figured you'd have packed my stuff and left it for me at the door," she smiled.

My anxiety level dropped, which felt strange, given everything that had happened between us over the past two days. But Kathy's voice had always been a balm. I had no doubt at that instant that I wanted her back.

"I couldn't blame you if—"

"I haven't moved a thing," I said.

"I'm glad."

"Then you're staying?"

She shrugged. "I searched everywhere for your stash. I even snooped in your secret hiding place in the armoire. I couldn't find anything."

"Coke and I have parted ways."

"Good." She nodded, then bit her lower lip. "I heard you had a little rumble with Trevor in the parking lot. Did you try teaching him not to hit girls?"

I thought about what Hancock might be doing to Lucas even as we spoke. "I'd do anything to stop someone from hurting you."

"I'd like to believe that. I don't want to be afraid anymore."

"Trevor's a dangerous man. You were in over your head." I didn't think I should say more until I was certain where she stood with him.

"I know. I didn't see it before, but I do now."

"So you two are . . ."

"It's over. Completely . . ." Her voice broke. She sat down on the landing. "I'm so sorry, Frank. I've been so stupid."

"You'd have to work to catch up to me on that score."

She chuckled and wiped away a tear.

I started toward her.

She stood up and cleared her throat. Her expression switched from sad to bitter. "What about you? Are you done with the stripper?"

I stopped moving, startled by the sudden change in her tone. It warned of a full-scale tantrum. "I didn't really start," I lied. "Did Trevor tell you otherwise?"

"He was trying to hurt me." She smiled again. "He said she was flat as a board anyhow." She smoothed back her hair, then pulled off her scrub top and stood there naked from the waist up. "Not like me." She looked down at herself, then shyly off to the side, like a girl embarrassed over new parts of her body.

I took my time closing the distance between us, watching the night air and the excitement of the moment make her nipples harden. I stopped two steps from her, with my mouth at the level of her chest. I kissed her breasts, squeezing her ass at the same time. A wave of excitement bathed me.

"You don't need a woman built like a little boy," she whispered.

I took her nipple between my teeth, then filled my mouth with as much of her as I could.

She held my head to her. "I want you inside me."

I moved my hand to untie her drawstring, but she took a step back and started for the bedroom. I followed. She turned off the standing lamp near the door. The room went pitch black. I heard her lie down on the bed.

I lay on top of her and kissed her neck, then moved my tongue inside her ear. She sighed. I reached for the lamp on the nightstand and fumbled to turn it on. Before I could, she grabbed my wrist.

"Don't," she breathed.

"I thought you were afraid of the dark," I whispered.

"I like it sometimes. I can't see what's coming."

I didn't like making love in the dark, but I was glad Kathy was telling me what she wanted. That was new for her. Nausea swept over me as I realized the openness was probably something she had learned from Trevor. So what? I told myself. Where was he just then, and where was I? But I was still bothered. I stood up, untied her drawstring and flipped her on her stomach. I pulled down her scrub pants and ran my hands up her legs and over her ass. She was wearing no panties. I forced her legs far apart, aware that my passion was, in large measure, rage. I unbuckled my belt. I wanted to use the leather on her, but I worried she would be shocked. Or perhaps I worried she would not be. Lucas had probably taught her more than I could imagine. I unzipped my pants and let them fall to the floor, along with my underwear. I stood between her legs and leaned to enter her. But a vision of Lucas in the same position, with

Kathy's hair in his fist, stopped me. I stepped beside her, placed my knee on the bed and pulled her over my thigh.

"Hey," she complained. She struggled to get away. "What the—"

I wrapped my arm around the small of her back to hold her steady and used my other hand to spank her. The sound of my palm against her soft flesh made me even more excited than I had been. After three or four smacks she stopped struggling and raised her ass for more. I hit her harder, then very hard. She tried to reach back to catch my hand. Before she could, I turned her over and threw her knees over my shoulders.

"Put it in me . . . now . . ." she gasped.

I rubbed myself against her wetness. Then I stopped and stepped back. Several seconds passed.

"Frank?"

I didn't respond.

"What's wrong?"

Without a word I backpedaled toward the door and turned on the light.

"Frank!" Kathy's eyes flashed with fury. She threw a hand over her crotch, then pulled a sheet over herself.

Too late. I had seen what I had felt moments before.

Her fists were tight around the cotton. "You bastard! What the fuck is your problem? I told you I wanted . . ." She pursed her lips and closed her eyes. She seemed to be trying very hard to stay in control.

I took a deep breath and let it out. "You're shaved" was all I could think to say.

She looked out the window and shook her head. "I wanted to surprise you," she said.

"It worked."

She looked back at me, peeled away the sheet and separated her legs slightly. "I thought you'd like it." She ran a finger over herself.

I did like it. I liked it a lot. But I knew she hadn't done it for me, and I was terrified what it might mean.

"You can see all of me." She spread her legs further apart.

"Kathy . . ."

"Mmm. Hmm?"

"Did Trevor make you shave?"

She pressed her legs together and pouted. "I'm a big girl," she said finally. "No one *makes* me do *anything*."

"Did he *ask* you to do it?"

"Why do you keep bringing him up? I told you: We're through."

"Just answer the question."

"Talk about ruining the moment."

"I need to know."

"Fine. *No.* He didn't order me to do it and he didn't ask me to do it. Satisfied?"

I didn't believe her. I wondered if I could get her to tell me any part of the truth. "Did you let him see you this way?"

She shook her head. "You're so jealous," she said gently.

I thought taking her lead might bring me closer to the facts. "I am jealous," I said. "I was jealous from the moment you went back to him."

"Did you picture us together?"

"It would have been hard not to. He told me all about it."

"What? What did he tell you?"

"He said he put it in your ass, for one thing."

"Were you very angry with him?"

"Very."

"And you felt betrayed."

I wasn't used to Kathy asking about my feelings. I nodded tentatively.

"I know," she said. "It would hurt you even more to think I changed my body for him."

I stayed silent.

She smiled. "Please don't worry." She relaxed her legs and touched her inner thigh. "This is for you, not Trevor. He never saw me this way. I did it when I got here last night."

"Last night?"

"I won't even ask what *you* were doing while I was here all alone. I don't want to think about that slut."

I had the impulse to defend Rachel, but I had the sense to keep quiet. "Why did you think I would want you to shave?" I asked.

"It's a pathetic reason."

I waited.

"I did it because . . . well . . . because Trevor told me your little Miss Striptease was almost all shaved. He said a lot of the girls at the Lynx Club are." She looked down at the bed and plucked at the sheet. "I want to do the things that make you happy. I don't want either of us to have to go to anyone else. Not for anything. Not ever again." She glanced at me. Her eyes had filled up. "We've tortured each other for years. I don't know why. I don't think you can say why. All I know is, I can't take it anymore. I can't stand picturing you with someone else. Kissing her. Touching her."

Maybe Kathy really had shaved for me. Or maybe I just wanted to believe her, wanted to believe that life could throw you savage curves and sliders and fastballs and then lob one right over the goddamn plate so you could knock it out of the park and circle the bases like a hero for once. *Once.* That's all any of us can hope for. But I couldn't take the chance that she was lying and at risk. I walked over to her and ran my fingers through her damp hair. "We should be giving each other everything we can," I said. "We haven't done a very good job so far."

She reached out for my penis, but I took her hand in mine.

"Why can't I touch you?" she whined. "I'm the one who got you hard."

"You can do anything you want to me—in a minute."

She stared at my groin and grinned.

"Kathy, I like thinking you shaved for me." I glanced down at myself. "You can see how much I like it. But I want you to tell me if Trevor—"

"I already—" she interrupted.

I held up a hand. "Tell me, and I'll stay right here. And you should tell me. Because if Trevor asked you to shave, or did it for you, then you're in danger."

"In danger? Of what? Razor burn?"

I smiled, but only for a moment. I didn't see any way around telling her that Lucas was a suspect. I sat down on the bed next to her. "Trevor may be the one who killed Sarah," I said. "Sarah and the other girl, Monique Peletier."

She squinted at me. "You can't be serious."

"He did surgery on both of them. Breast implants. He was also sleeping with them." I paused to let that sink in.

Kathy stared at me blankly.

"Both of the victims were found with their pubic hair completely shaved. Just like you."

"Trevor's not capable of killing anyone."

"I'm not so sure."

She looked away and shook her head. "This is pitiful. You're going after him because he was screwing me." She reached down for her scrub pants. "It's not like he raped me, Frank. It actually took some convincing for me to get him into bed."

I couldn't let my anger get in the way of warning her. "I'm not the one who decided to arrest him," I said calmly. "Emma Hancock made that call."

"*Arrest* him?" she sputtered, pulling on her scrubs.

"And Hancock wouldn't make a move without compelling evidence." Even as I was speaking the words, I realized I didn't believe them.

"If she's so fucking smart, why did she charge that nutcase who thought he was a general?"

I couldn't come up with a decent answer. "She'd be more careful targeting someone else, especially a professional in the community."

"You're forgetting something. I've met Emma Hancock. That bitch would arrest the pope if she thought it would get her a front-page story."

I wasn't pleased Kathy still cared so much what happened to

Lucas, but I tried not to think of that. I walked up to her and took her shoulders in my hands. "Whatever you do, don't go near Trevor 'til this whole thing is cleared up."

She pushed me away. "OK, Daddy," she sneered. "And you stay away from your little cunt at the Lynx Club."

Just then the phone on the nightstand rang. Kathy reached over and picked it up. "Hello?" she demanded. She listened for a moment, then hit the speaker button and laid the receiver back in its cradle.

"Frank? Are you there?" Emma Hancock asked.

Talk about timing. "I'm here with Kathy," I said.

"Well . . . good. We got our man."

"You found him?"

"Not exactly."

"What do you mean?"

"He found me. He swaggered into the station about an hour ago, dressed to the nines, and planted himself in my office. I wasn't back yet, so Officer Zangota told him to get out, who did he think he was, you know? The whole riot act. And our Dr. Jekyll blurts out, 'I'm wanted for murder.' Just like that. Zangota nearly had a coronary getting the cuffs on him."

"Why didn't you call me right away?"

"I wanted to spend some time with him in his cell. Just the doctor, me and a few of my new recruits."

I looked at Kathy's face and saw a mixture of fear and outrage. "For Christ's sake, Emma," I protested, "you can't—"

"Do not denigrate the Lord's name," she interrupted. "This is a time to be thankful."

"I'll be right there."

"No rush. Dr. Lucas is as competent as the day is long. But you're welcome anytime." She hung up.

Kathy started toward the door.

"Where are you going?" I asked.

"None of your business." She stopped and turned back to me. She was near tears again. "You know, I lost a good friend a few days ago." She took a deep breath to steady herself. "The least you could do is tuck your wounded ego up your ass long enough to help find out who really killed her." Then she stormed out of the room and down the hall.

I heard her gathering her things downstairs. I could have gone after her, but she wasn't about to listen to me. I remembered what Ben Carlson had told me about Sarah shacking up with Lucas long after their relationship had supposedly ended. Why should I think I was any better at exorcising Lucas from Kathy's mind? Whatever magic he worked on women was obviously still working on her, too.

The front door slammed shut. I walked to a window in the den and watched Kathy's Volvo lurch down the driveway and disappear into the night. I lowered myself into the wing chair near the window. The leather cushions embraced my naked body. I groped for a Marlboro from the crystal cup on the side table, lit up and watched the tip glow red in the darkness. I inhaled as much smoke as my lungs could hold, then let it flow out my nose and mouth.

Hancock was right; there wasn't any reason for me to rush to the station. No one was likely to suggest Lucas had been psychotic when he killed Sarah and Monique. The police were free to take a confession from him if he offered one. And I had no desire to bear early witness to whatever retribution Hancock and her thugs had exacted while Lucas was locked in his cell.

I imagined him curled up on a bunk, his face swollen and bloodied, his arms and legs contused where Hancock's baton had landed. Every jingle of keys could signal another beating. He was as far from the driver's seat of his Ferrari as he could get. I took another drag and blew the smoke toward the ceiling. Why wasn't I anxious to see that? I wondered. Why not take the opportunity to visit Lucas freshly shelled from his narcissism, at the height of his vulnerability? Hadn't he inflicted that pain and more on his victims? Hadn't he tried to take something I loved from me?

That last question bothered me. I wanted to be certain Kathy had been wrong, that my desire for vengeance hadn't slanted the investigation toward Lucas. I went over the facts of the case in my mind. I had no doubt Lucas was a misogynist capable of violence. I knew for sure he had been sexually involved with both Sarah and Monique. He had performed surgery on each woman's breasts. He was a predator who had grotesquely exploited the doctor-patient relationship. He had been with Monique hours before her death. He had her gold wire ring in his possession.

That was more than Hancock knew. I hadn't told her about my conversation with Ben Carlson in Texas. And what she knew had been enough for her. So why was my stomach in knots? Was I having trouble believing butchery could be the work of a meticulous surgeon? Or hadn't I resolved in my mind why a man licensed and paid to cut women would risk everything for the pleasure of mutilating them?

I sucked in another half inch of tobacco, shook my head and squinted into the darkness. The knots in my stomach were only getting tighter. I stood up, turned on the standing lamp and sat back down. When I reached to put my cigarette out, I noticed a few of Kathy's Trixie Belden books stacked next to the ashtray on the side table. I figured she'd had trouble sleeping the night before and had used the stories to unwind. I picked one up and smiled at the title, *The Mystery of the Phantom Grasshopper*. I opened it and read a few paragraphs.

> Sitting around a roaring fire in the living room, the whole family played guessing games, told jokes and sang songs. Mrs. Belden reeled off a string of tongue twisters that amazed everyone. She challenged the young people to match her skill, and the results had everyone doubled over with laughter . . .
>
> Later, Trixie snuggled in bed and listened to the sounds of the storm outside. Poor old Hoppy, she thought with a shudder. I hope the storm doesn't damage him.

I imagined how reading about Trixie's idyllic life might have comforted Kathy as she grew up in a family scarred by tragedy. I set the book down on my lap. Where had she run off to? She could stay in an on-call room at the hospital easily enough, or she could sit up all night with my mother, cataloging my character flaws. I guessed it was also possible she might head to the Lynn police station to visit with Lucas—a little like a moth drawn to a flame. That image stuck in my mind. I thought again of the fire that had claimed Kathy's little sister. Maybe survivor guilt, the very psychological dynamic that had shattered Westmoreland, was the one driving Kathy. If she believed she should have died in her sister's place, she might unconsciously try putting herself in harm's way, even now.

I realized I couldn't know for sure how Kathy had suffered that night; I hadn't asked her enough about it. I didn't know whether she had jumped from a window or been carried to safety. I didn't know which family members had been at home. I hadn't asked Kathy what she remembered of her sister's funeral, whether she had kept any of her belongings, whether she believed her sister had gone to heaven. It was another black hole in our relationship. How could I have lived so long with another human being, yet kept so much distance from her?

I needed something to stem my anxiety. I walked over to a waist-high art deco wet bar Kathy and I had picked up at an antique show in Vermont. It was made of chestnut, and the top rolled back to reveal an assortment of chrome bottles and a dozen chrome tumblers. I grabbed the bottle that held my 10-year-old Talisker scotch and poured myself a double. The aroma alone was enough to start settling me down. I drank it slowly, but without a breath, enjoying the way it warmed my mouth and throat, then my esophagus and stomach. When the glass was empty, I could almost feel the stuff leaching through my gut into blood vessels that would ferry it everywhere. I let out a deep breath and hung my head, waiting for the wave of calm to carry me off.

I was almost there when I heard a knock at the door. One knock, then nothing. Kathy had the key, so I doubted it was her, unless she had tossed the key out of the car as she sped away. She'd done that more than once before. I realized that I wanted it to be her, but when I looked outside, I saw a pickup, not her Volvo, in the driveway.

I walked to the bedroom, pulled on my pants and started down the stairs. My feet felt lighter with the scotch onboard. When I was a few yards from the door, there was another knock. "Coming," I yelled. I looked through the peep hole, but couldn't see anything. The outside light wasn't on. I flipped the switch, but nothing happened. The bulb must have burned out. "Who is it?" I asked.

No response.

"Who's there?" I yelled.

"Let me in, goddamn it!"

Even through three inches of wood I recognized the precision of Paulson Levitsky's speech, every syllable its own universe. I opened the door.

Levitsky was still in his work clothes—a starched white shirt and club tie. He was clutching a manila envelope to his chest. "We have a problem," he said. He marched past me, headed for the living room. I followed. He sat down on the couch, keeping his back perfectly straight, and took a few sheets of paper out of the envelope.

"Paulson," I said, "we haven't talked. I don't know if you've been in touch with Hancock."

He looked up at me and sniffed the air. "Are you drunk?"

"I had a drink."

He stood up. "Can you think? Or am I wasting my time?" Before I could respond, he held up his hands. "Sorry." He sat back down. "I'm upset."

I took a seat next to him. "I need to fill you in on some things."

"They have the wrong man again," he blurted out.

My heart fell. "What?"

"Dr. Lucas is not guilty."

"Hold on," I said. "Do you know he put breast implants in Sarah and Monique? Silicone implants?"

"Yes. Hancock told me everything."

"She told you what she knew. But I haven't told her that Sarah and Monique *both* had the surgery. And Lucas performed it. He was also sleeping with both of them."

"Reprehensible. The man is a monster." He tightened the Windsor knot in his tie and shook his head. "He is not, however, a murderer—at least, not of these particular victims." He stared at me.

"Why do you say he's not guilty?" I surrendered.

"I *say* he's not guilty because he *is* not guilty. The killer is still killing."

"The killer is . . ."

He held out the sheets in his hand.

I took them from him and glanced at the first page. It was a faxed report from the Revere Police Department. I looked up at Levitsky, hoping for some sort of reassurance.

He offered none. "Go ahead," he deadpanned.

I started to read:

Fifty-one-year-old male homicide victim found in vehicle with ID in wallet. Name: Michael Wembley. Address: 123 Beacon Street, Boston. Vehicle is a black Lexus SC400, plate 887NFT, Massachusetts. Discovered at end of unpaved Foster Road by jogger, Susan Rugeaux (notes of interview filed separately) at approximately 6:35 P.M. Victim is found with eyelids removed (cut off). Victim is naked below the waist (pants at ankles). Genital area is shaved. Penis and testicles are disfigured by multiple deep lacerations.

"Holy God," I said.

"Joshua Belnick, the coroner in Revere, called me immediately and got me the paperwork. Unlike you, he keeps me in the loop when I need to be. He knew we had two bodies with shaved genitals."

"But they were women."

"That's true."

"The breasts were removed."

"What's your point?"

I wasn't sure I had a point. I went back to reading:

Watch recovered from car, propped on dashboard. Rolex. Not running. Stem pulled out. Time: 6:19 P.M. Bagged for evidence.

"What's with the watch?"

"Our murderer apparently wanted to establish time of death. It does seem accurate. According to Belnick, judging from congealing of blood, drying of the eyes, etceteras, 6:19 P.M. is perfectly consistent. Of course, he'll need to do further studies."

"When did Lucas turn himself in?"

"He was booked at six-forty, but he'd been hanging around the station awhile."

"Not enough of a window, then," I said. "He'd have to have flown from Revere to Lynn." I looked back at the sheet of paper. "If the time of death is correct."

"It is, give or take five minutes. Belnick's no hack."

I flipped to the second page. It was a fax of two photographs showing the victim's wounds. The images were coarse, but they showed what they needed to. Without lids, Wembley's eyes seemed to bear witness to an unspeakable horror. Just below that photo, a shot of his genital area looked more like sliced deli meat. "What killed him?" I muttered.

"A blow to the head, like the other two."

"At least he was dead before the rest happened," I said.

"I don't know about that. Pubic hair was found on the driver's seat and floor mat. He shaved in the car."

"Or got shaved."

"Very unlikely. According to Belnick, the direction of the sheared hairs and the abrasions indicate the razor moved from low to high, meaning the hand holding it came directly from above." Levitsky reached down between his legs and used his own hand to show me the upward vertical strokes. "Someone in the passenger seat would have had to reach across and shave downward." He reached toward me to demonstrate.

I blocked his hand. "I get it. How'd this Belnick do so much work so fast?"

"He's a crackerjack. A trained eye. I was one of his instructors during his residency at Boston City."

"Now I understand."

He smiled. "The number of razor nicks—double-edged, by the way, like a Trac II blade—suggests Wembley was either very excited or very frightened at the time."

I looked down at the photographs again and shook my head. "Terrified seems about right."

"I'll leave the psychological postmortem to you. The more urgent matter is convincing Captain Hancock to reopen the investigation."

I nodded. "Why couldn't this be another killer? It's a different MO. Male victim. Revere, not Lynn. Different wounds."

"C'mon, Frank. I don't like being wrong any more than you do, but—"

"It's not about me," I sputtered.

"OK. If you say so."

I settled myself down. "Anyone would say there are differences in the cases."

"The lacerations on the penis were made with a blade identical to those that cut Ms. Johnson and Ms. Peletier. I'd still say a scalpel."

"The very same blade, or the same exact *type* of blade."

"You sound like Hancock. Splitting hairs." He winced. "No pun intended."

"It isn't within the realm of possibility?"

"Anything is within the realm of possibility, Frankster. A second killer is highly improbable. And as you know, I never signed on to the idea that a plastic surgeon would leave such gruesome wounds. I think I mentioned the Mike Tyson thing."

"Yes. You did. You also compared people with birds pecking for seed."

"I stand by the analogy. Human beings have deeply ingrained patterns of behavior."

"But they're not automatons."

He looked out the window. Then, without a word, he turned back toward me and swung an open hand toward my face.

I ducked. "What the hell?"

"Sorry," he said. "I was making a point." He folded his hands on his thigh. "I swing, you dodge. Stimulus, response. Even your irritation with me is a programmed reaction. We're creatures of habit."

I didn't feel like debating the existence of free will. And I wasn't at all sure Levitsky was wrong about the killer still being out there. I stood up. "Let's go find Hancock," I said.

Thirteen

I wanted to drive, but Levitsky refused because he still smelled alcohol on my breath. We took his car, a 1981 Dodge Ram that rode like new. A simulated ivory bust of Einstein was propped on the dash and, to my surprise, an Alpine stereo, graphic equalizer and amplifier were stacked in the open glove compartment. I wondered whether Levitsky harbored a passion for hard rock, but as soon as he flipped the ignition, four speakers began pouring out continuing medical education on the lymphatic drainage system of the lower extremity. "The afferent lymphatic vessels," a man's voice lectured, "run along with the saphenous vein, while vessels from the knee joint run with the genicular arteries."

"Jesus," I muttered.

"Shhh," Levitsky said.

"Most of the efferents follow femoral vessels to deep inguinal nodes," the voice went on. I hit STOP, then EJECT. "Easy listening?"

"It was for me." He nodded toward the glove compartment. "There's a neuroanatomy tape in there, if you like."

I needed a reprieve from thinking about body parts. "Ever listen to music?"

"The flip side of the tape on facial bone structure is Mendelssohn's Violin Concerto."

I found the tape and slipped it into the deck.

Levitsky kept one foot perched on the brake, never topping

twenty miles per hour. Each time the orchestra surged, his thumbs tapped against the steering wheel. I stared at them. "Getting a little carried away there?"

He glanced at me, then at his thumbs. "It's a stirring composition," he said. "Jane Dimitry, the violinist, has perfect pitch. I've charted it with an oscilloscope."

"An *oscilloscope*?"

"It's a device that measures—"

"I know what it is." I shook my head. "See, that's your problem, Paulson. Sound waves don't say a thing about why that violin moves you. Its beauty is immeasurable."

"Its beauty is 40.72 hertz."

"Really? That's it? Then why can't you create the same sounds she does? Just pick up a violin and an oscilloscope and join the orchestra."

"Don't bother me with silly questions."

"You call it silly because you don't have an answer."

He glanced at me again. "The answer is that I don't have Dimitry's eyes or ears or fingers. The cells in my retina and cochlea and the receptors in my dermis were slightly different from birth and haven't been trained by the same stimuli. Her cerebellum, which gives her the sense of balance she feels while seated with a piece of wood pressed to her shoulder and neck, probably works better than mine does. Her neuronal ganglia, linking sensory stimuli and motor output, have lower electrical resistance." He finally took a breath. "Her music is the product of countless smaller ingredients."

"Wrong," I said. "Her music is greater than the sum of its parts. That's the reason people pay good money to hear her play. They want to witness beauty that can't be explained. That's why people flock to exhibits of van Gogh's work. It's the same reason thousands of people would jam a football stadium and wait for a pass from one man to be caught by another man sixty yards away, running full tilt, with several other men trying to get in the way."

"How did we jump from Mendelssohn to van Gogh to football? What motivation are you referring to?"

"The motivation in each of us to prove the existence of a higher power. Nothing about our brains or bodies can explain how that football lands in that receiver's hands at precisely the right place and time. The event is bigger than any of its ingredients. It's a kind of miracle."

Levitsky's thumbs danced on the steering wheel. "I guess that makes Sullivan Stadium a house of worship."

"In a way, yes, it does. That's why we call sports heroes 'idols.' They help us feel God's presence."

"Now I've heard everything."

As we passed the Schooner Pub on the Lynnway, I noticed Emma Hancock's police-issue red Jeep Cherokee out front. "Pull in," I told Levitsky.

"Not a chance," he said. "You drink on your own time."

"Paulson, that's Hancock's cruiser there."

He looked over. "So it is." He made a U-turn at the next break in the median strip, crept back to the pub and took a space at least ten yards from the nearest car. "No sense getting scratched up," he said.

"A dent might set you free."

He turned off the engine. "Don't slam the door," he cautioned.

Hancock was seated at the far end of the bar with Timothy Bennett, a top political strategist who had once run for mayor of Lynn himself. When she noticed us, she motioned him to stay put, signaled the bartender and then walked to a table at the back of the room. A waitress followed her with her open bottle of champagne and extra glasses.

We all sat down.

"Shall we make this the victory party?" she grinned. She filled her glass, then another.

"None for me," Levitsky said.

"I guessed that," Hancock said.

"You have to guess right once," Levitsky said.

Hancock straightened up in her chair. "I know what Dr. Levitsky is here for, Frank. He wants me to release a murderer. What's bothering you?"

"Paulson showed me the documentation from the Revere case."

"And what do you think?"

I grabbed a glass and drank it partway down. "The same type of blade was used."

She nodded. "Same *type*. The *Item* keeps carrying articles that read like a how-to manual. I don't know what happened to journalistic responsibility. The morning edition had a sidebar about the murder weapon being a scalpel. Any crazy could have picked up on the idea."

"And the man was shaved," I said.

"The *man*. That's a big difference."

"True."

"He lost eyelids, not breasts."

I nodded.

"There's also the watch. That could be the Revere killer's signature. Lucas never left us a message."

I hadn't thought of that. "What about the watch, Paulson? You're the one who believes in rigid behavior patterns."

He seemed troubled by the question, but only for a few seconds. "Maybe he'll leave us a message every three murders, or only with male victims, or only in Lexus automobiles," he said. "Those would be rigid patterns. Shall we wait and see which one develops?"

Hancock grabbed the box of Marlboros out of my shirt pocket and lit one. She took a drag and squinted at me as she blew the smoke out the side of her mouth. "If the coroner in Revere is wrong, Lucas could have done this one, too. Time of death is a tricky call. I've seen mistakes hours either way."

Levitsky chuckled to himself. "That's when the police take weeks to find the body."

Hancock ignored him. "What does your gut say, Frank?"

I didn't want to go on my gut. I told her what I knew: Sarah had been Lucas' patient and lover, just like Monique.

"Johnston, too." She shook her head. "That's enough for me." She tilted her glass toward me.

"Did he come close to confessing?" I asked.

"He said he was sorry about my niece. He said he'd *miss* her."
She gulped her champagne. "That got me very angry and . . . well, he didn't say anything after that."

"Perfect," Levitsky said. "Add brutality to wrongful imprisonment."

Hancock glared at him.

"Does the D.A. have enough to indict?" I asked.

"More than enough. The grand jury meets tomorrow morning."

"Who's he got for a lawyer?"

"He's an egomaniac. He says he's representing himself."

"Maybe he'll run for mayor," Levitsky said.

I saw Hancock's nails start working against one another and worried Levitsky might get hurt. I laid a hand on her shoulder. "Let me see Lucas."

"Tonight?"

"Sure."

"Just you? Or you and Dr. Death here?"

"I have work back at the lab," Levitsky said.

"He's rough around the edges," Hancock told me. "I was very upset with him."

"Too rough to talk?"

She shrugged. "He can talk."

"OK, then."

Hancock glanced over at Bennett. "I pay him more than I pay you. And I won't be getting any refund." She stood up. "Give me a few minutes." She walked back to the bar.

"You didn't answer Mayor Hancock's question," Levitsky said.

"What question was that?"

"Your gut feeling."

"I didn't think gut feelings counted with you."

"Yours do," he smiled.

I finished off my champagne. "I don't know why they would. I've been wrong more times than I've been right."

◆　　◆　　◆

Hancock waited in her office while Zangota took me to see Lucas. "How's the kid doing?" I asked as we walked together.

"Registered him for midget football," he said. "My wife thinks he's the next Drew Bledsoe."

"Nice. But I didn't mean *your* kid. I meant the boy from the Highlands—the one who lived under Mercury and Monique's place."

"Right," he grinned. "Enrique. My other two kids are girls."

I stopped walking.

Zangota continued the last few feet to the door of the lockup and shook his ring of keys to find the right one. "I couldn't get what you said off my mind, about foster families being mostly garbage." He looked back at me. "Because it's true. Most of them are in it for the monthly stipend. So I figured, seeing as I lucked out, and good people helped me, it was payback time."

The hair on my arms stood on end. "You took the kid in?"

"Somebody had to." He slid the key into the lock and turned it. "I phoned DSS and told them I was available."

A sense of wonderment filled me.

"It felt good, you know? Full circle." He opened the iron door. "Fourth cell on the left. Need me in there?"

I cleared my throat. "Thanks. I'll be OK." I started down the corridor, then turned around and watched Zangota as he stepped out. Even after he had closed the iron door, I stared after him. Had he given me hints before that he was a hero?

The sound of Lucas' voice snapped me back into the moment. I couldn't make out what he was saying, but he was saying it again and again, in a kind of chant. I hugged the wall as I walked toward him, imagining him pressed against the bars, waiting to grab me. But when I got to his cell, he was seated on the floor, legs crossed, clutching a sheet wrapped around him. His bald head hung near his lap. I still couldn't make out what he was saying—or singing.

"Praying?" I said.

He kept chanting.

"*Lucas.*"

He stopped, took a deep breath and looked up. One of his eyes was swollen shut. The eyebrow was in two pieces, separated by a gash. The white of the other eye was mostly red. A blue-black hematoma distorted the boundary between his nose and upper lip.

I would have made a lousy gladiator. With everything Lucas had done, my hatred for him retreated just enough for me to worry that his internal injuries might be as severe as those on the surface. "You're not vomiting blood, are you?" I asked.

"I'm just fine," he said. "I was dreaming about Kathy."

"Maybe she'll visit you at MCI Concord some time over the next couple decades."

"No doubt she would," he nodded. "She's committed to the men in her life. Too powerfully, I fear." He looked me in the eyes. "You, perhaps, even more than me."

I hadn't expected an olive branch. I stayed silent.

"But I'm not going to prison."

"No? Dropping a dime to Johnnie Cochran?"

"The truth will speak for itself."

"If you have an alibi, now's the time to let the rest of us in on it."

"I have my own sense of timing."

I wondered if Lucas was referring to some ploy that had allowed him to manipulate Wembley's apparent time of death. "I heard. How did you pull it off?"

"What is it you heard?"

I didn't want to contaminate the investigation by feeding Lucas too much information. It still seemed possible he hadn't killed Wembley. "About the Rolex on the dashboard." I studied him for his reaction.

He tilted his head back and closed his eyes. When he looked back at me, he was smiling. "Michael Wembley," he said flatly.

"Your third victim."

"How was he killed?"

I hoped Lucas wasn't trying to concoct an amnesia. And I hoped even more that he didn't really have one. "You hacked off his eyelids and slashed his penis. You left him dead in his Lexus coupé be-fore you turned yourself in. Does that refresh your memory?"

He squinted at me. "He was shaved?"

"You tell me."

"I would think so."

I wanted Lucas to actively claim responsibility for the murders. "Why not tell the truth about what you did?"

"But I haven't done anything."

"Save it for the jury." I started to go.

"Hold on. Think for a moment."

I turned back to him.

He closed his eyes and tilted his head up and to the side, as if he were smelling something he liked. "Why would I kill things that were bringing me joy?" He looked back at me and shrugged. "Take Captain Hancock's niece, for example. I really am going to miss her."

"She never wanted you. She wanted her surgery."

"No," he said. "She *needed* it. She was a wounded person. She believed the surgery could make her whole." He shook his head. "It never does. Underneath, she was more unsure of herself than ever."

"She was sport for you."

"The best kind. Already hobbled."

"Not exactly a worthy opponent."

"I have no interest in a struggle. Immediate surrender suits me."

"Maybe she wanted to back out of the deal, not give you the sex she promised."

"Monique? She was very honorable. I still had twenty-three ses-sions left. And she would have paid. Her roommate was the same way. Very up front, for a transsexual. I'm sure you met Mercury."

"I didn't know you swung both ways."

"Don't be offended. You have a nice build, but I hate ponytails. Pure arrogance."

"What about Sarah?"

"Couldn't get enough of her. She was a very vulnerable soul, yet she had a profound tolerance for pain. That's a very rare combina-tion."

I just stood there, looking down at him. How does a man, I wondered, lose all capacity for empathy?

"A true sadist like me never kills something he can keep tormenting," Lucas smiled. "Sarah and Monique had plenty of misery left in them."

◆   ◆   ◆

Kevin Malloy was with Hancock when I walked into her office. They were looking at a green file folder open on the desk. Two other files lay next to it. "How did it go in there?" Hancock asked me.

"I thought he was about to hand me a confession, then he delivered a lecture on why he wouldn't kill anybody." I started to pace. "I still have a lousy feeling about this."

Malloy chuckled. "We confiscated his socks, in case you're worried about him pulling a Westmoreland."

I stopped. "Teeth fixed?" I asked.

"Like new."

"You get any kind of guarantee—in case they get fucked up again?"

"No cursing," Hancock grinned. She picked up the open folder. "Kevin's done a bit of work to redeem himself." She passed it to me.

The name WEMBLEY, MICHAEL was typed on the folder's tab. A couple sheets of paper were fastened inside. I read the paragraph scrawled on the first page:

Michael Wembley is a 51-year-old white man who looks older than his stated age. He has significant skin duplication under both eyes, as well as skin folds on the upper lids. He states that these imperfections cause him considerable distress and that he wishes to undergo bilateral blepharoplasty.

I knew what I was reading, but I was having trouble believing it could be true. I looked up at Hancock.

"Three for three," she said. "They were all Lucas' patients. Johnston, Monique, Wembley." She nodded at the folder. "Keep going. It gets better."

I read on:

> I have explained the procedure, along with all attendant risks, in-cluding lid lag, nerve damage, infection, allergy to medication or anesthesia, injury to the orbit or eye, chronic pain, paresthesias, blindness and death.
>
> I have informed Mr. Wembley of the fee of $5,750, payable by bank check or cash, 48 hours prior to scheduled OR time. The fee is nonre-fundable. No portion will be returned in the event of a cancellation or no-show.

The note was signed "T. Lucas, M.D." and dated six days ear-lier. A short entry followed, detailing Wembley's vital signs during the procedure and his progress in the recovery room.

"At least the good doctor listed death as a side effect," Hancock said. "Can't say Wembley wasn't warned."

"You always list death as a possibility," I said. "It limits liability."

"Not the patient's," Hancock said.

I turned the page to a sketch of Wembley's eyes, complete with the incisions Lucas planned. At the bottom of the sheet were two-inch, before-and-after Polaroids. In the *after* shot Wembley looked like he was wearing mascara, but I knew the lines were actually rows of stitches. The precise placement of tiny sutures is the hall-mark of a cosmetic surgeon. "How'd we get the chart?" I asked.

"Judge Barton gave us a search warrant for Lucas' office," Mal-loy said. "It was sitting in a pile on his desk." He turned to Han-cock. "What an office. It's all done up like Rome, or something. Columns everywhere. There's even an oil painting in the lobby of Lucas riding a horse. I almost forgot I was in Lynn."

I closed the folder and shook my head.

"What's wrong?" Hancock asked.

"Why would somebody about to kill a man leave his surgical chart lying around on his desk? Why not at least hide it?"

"Maybe he was running out of places," Malloy said. He picked up the other two folders and held them out. "These were jammed behind the top drawer of the main patient file."

I took the folders from him. One was labeled PELETIER, MONIQUE. The other was labeled JOHNSTON, SARAH. I opened the Peletier chart, then paused and looked up at Hancock. I felt uncomfortable stomping around in her niece's life.

Her eyes met mine. "I want you to see it," she said. "She's with the Lord now."

I lowered myself into a chair near Hancock's desk and started to read:

> Monique Peletier is an eighteen-year-old white female who presents for augmentation mammoplasty. Her chest measures 33 inches, and she fills only an A cup. Her torso can accommodate a 36 C/D. Her nipples are adequate, but would require resiting. All risks of the procedure have been reviewed, including, but not limited to: infection, implant rupture, allergy, subjective dissatisfaction, scarring, disfigurement, sexual dysfunction, inability to nurse and death. The patient wishes to proceed. As she cannot afford the $9,500 charge, the standard "sliding" fee scale will be applied.

Sliding fee. I shook my head. Lucas had probably enjoyed the play on words.

"There's a drawing in there, too," Hancock said.

A brief OR note followed Lucas' first entry. I turned the page, expecting a sketch of Monique's breasts, but instead found a diagram of her upper thighs and vagina. The lips were apart, revealing the clitoris, pierced by a tiny ring. Lucas' scrawl in the margin read:

> Placement of decorative ring. Risks, including anorgasmia and pain on intercourse, reviewed. Patient wishes to proceed. Fee to be negotiated.

"He put the ring in," I whispered. I closed the folder and handed all three files back to Malloy.

"The Johnston chart is more of the same," Hancock said. She

fished a pack of Merit cigarettes out of her top drawer, took one out and lighted it. "I think Levitsky's pathologist friend in Revere is wrong. I think the time of death on Wembley is off. My guess is Lucas murdered him, then drove right over here and turned himself in."

"His fingerprints were in the Lexus," Malloy added.

I wasn't surprised anymore that Lucas' prints would turn up around his patients. "He acted like he didn't know the details of the last murder, or didn't remember them," I said. "Part of me believed him."

Hancock squinted at me. "Tell me you're not thinking of injecting him with Amytal."

"It's a quick way to—"

"To lose the case," she interrupted. "Anything he said would be inadmissible, probably even if he kept saying it after he was off that crap."

I nodded.

"So I don't have to worry about you sneaking around here with a syringe. Right?"

"If you say not to, I won't use it."

"OK. *Don't use it*." She glared at her cigarette. "Like sucking air," she said. She broke off the filter and took another drag.

"What about the fact that he doesn't want a lawyer? You don't think that's odd?"

"Like I said, the man's an egomaniac."

"We're talking about someone worth millions, Emma. Why would he just roll over?"

"Because that way he stays on top. We didn't get him. He got himself. It's textbook."

"Maybe. But it doesn't feel good," I said.

Hancock started clicking her nails.

"Something's not right."

"Then try your other hand," Malloy said. "You're just jerking yourself off anyhow. Half of what you—"

"Shut up," Hancock said. She was staring at me, but her words were directed at Malloy. "I want you to forget we've got Lucas. Follow every lead, even if it points in another direction. *Especially* if it points in another direction." She paused. "I hope you're worrying about nothing, Frank. But I'm not taking that chance again."

◆   ◆   ◆

I made it to the Lynx Club in time for last call. Before I opened the door, I could hear Rod Stewart's voice confessing *the attraction was purely physical.*

I went inside. Pulses of purple light greeted me. A black dancer wearing nothing but silver bracelets up her arms was standing in front of a man in denim overalls who was eyeing her crotch and guzzling a beer at the same time. He ran the lip of the bottle up her thigh, then leaned back for another swallow. She knelt down, cradled one of her breasts in the palm of her hand and used the nipple to brush his dollar bill off the railing.

I scanned the room, looking for Rachel, but didn't see her.

"Hey!" a voice barked.

I turned and saw Max behind the bar. He was waddling my way. I walked over and grabbed a seat.

He took a second to catch his breath. "Tiffany—I mean Rachel—ain't here," he said. "She wanted I should tell you, if you stopped in, she's working over at Red Lace Lingerie."

"Who buys lingerie at this hour?"

"Nobody exactly buys it," he coughed. "They pay for it, but they don't take it home."

"Huh?"

"They get to see a girl of their choice model it, you know? Whatever they pick out. In a private room. Fifty bucks."

"Why would someone pay fifty dollars to watch a girl dancing in underwear?"

"They got more than underwear. They got everything from evening gowns to squaw outfits. They put 'em on and they strip. And you're alone with them."

"Even so," I said.

He made a fist and shook it up and down in the air. "You get to beat off while you watch."

"Now I get it."

"I don't. It's not like you can touch 'em or anything. And they don't touch you. At least that's the rule. I hear some of the girls cut side deals. A quick hand job or something." He coughed again.

"Sick?" I asked him.

"I got this asbestos kicking up. Doctor says it's like tiny pins shredding my lungs."

"When were you exposed?"

"*Exposed?* I never got into nothing like that."

"I mean, exposed to asbestos. When were you around it?"

"Oh, I hear you." He nodded. "Navy. I worked the boiler room on a carrier."

"What shit luck. I'm sorry."

"What am I gonna do? Cry over it?" He stared at me.

I felt Max reaching out, even if he didn't realize it himself. My scalp tightened. "Have you?" I asked.

"Have I *what?*"

"Broken down. Cried over it."

"What are you talkin' . . ."

I added an edge to my voice to temper the softness of what I had said. "I mean, who the fuck wouldn't? Right? Fucking lungs torn up? You'd have to be crazy not to lose it."

He looked over at the girl dancing. I looked, too. She was on all fours, moving like she was having sex doggy style.

"Must suck," I said, "being sick."

He kept his eyes on the dancer. "Terrible." His voice broke at the end of the word. He cleared his throat.

I reached into my pocket, took out a ten-dollar bill and laid it on the bar. "Thanks for the message from Rachel."

He glanced at the money. "On the house," he said. He took a deep breath, coughed and turned back to me. "Does she have an ass, or am I a monkey's uncle?"

I wasn't sure whether he meant the dancer, or Rachel. But it didn't matter. It was just his way of regrouping. "She's got a great ass," I said. I got up. "So where's Red Lace?"

"Three blocks down from here, on Broadway, in back of Perky's used-car lot. Look for the red lights in the windows."

I left the bar and headed for Red Lace Lingerie, the top floor of a drab, four-story building. There was no signage visible from the street, and the window shades were drawn, but the red glow Max had mentioned was seeping from behind them. I walked into the building and took the stairs past a hair salon, a tanning studio and, of all things, a chiropractor's office. Those guys turn up in the strangest places.

The shop was arranged like a discount clothing store—a dozen or so circular chrome racks up front, and a counter with a cash register at the back. I didn't see Rachel, so I took my time flipping through the merchandise—hanger after hanger of crotchless panties, rubber vests with steel zippers, thongs, dresses fashioned entirely of chain, a bridal gown, a maid's outfit, even a police uniform. I imagined a customer requesting the fantasy: *You act like you're giving me a speeding ticket, then I whip it out, and you act shocked, but then you like what you see and you decide you want it, so you get in the car and start taking off your clothes.* I chuckled.

"Did you need help with something?" a young woman two racks over asked. She flipped her long, dirty blond hair and smiled.

I was taken by her pale blue eyes. "Yes," I said finally. "I'm looking for Tiffany."

"Tiffany's with a client. She won't be available for ten minutes or so."

"Is it alright if I wait?"

"Of course. Let's get you rung up." She walked toward the counter.

I followed her. An array of sexual aids were displayed under the glass. There were French ticklers, dildos, glow-in-the-dark condoms. I started to wonder whether modeling and the occasional hand job were the only things for sale at Red Lace.

"Have you shopped here before?" the girl asked me.

"First time."

She was filling in blanks on some sort of intake form. "And who recommended us?"

"Max at the Lynx Club."

She wrote the name down. "Will you be paying with a Visa card or cash?"

"Cash."

"That's fifty dollars for three outfits, unless one is a fantasy outfit, which counts as two."

"Fantasy outfit?"

"Like the Nazi helmet or the Girl Scout uniform."

"Naturally." I couldn't help looking at the points her nipples made where they pressed against her cotton T-shirt.

She nodded at the door behind her. "Tiffany could run over a few minutes. Did you want to see me?"

I thought about the idea, but not for long. "Another time," I said.

"Suit yourself. Fifty dollars, please."

I counted out the fifty and gave it to her, then walked back into the racks. I picked out a one-piece black lace body suit and a teddy made of tiny rhinestones.

The girl had been watching me from the counter. "That counts as two," she said.

I held it out toward her and squinted like I was imagining her wearing it. "OK," I said.

"That's cheating." She winked.

The door to the back opened, and a rotund, bald man with horn-rim glasses stepped out. He was wearing a gray suit. He looked like an attorney or a broker. There was a wedding band on his finger. He glanced around the store before walking out. Rachel came through the door after he was gone. She was wearing Levi's and a pink sweatshirt.

I started toward the counter. "Does this really count as two outfits?" I asked. I held up the teddy.

She smiled. "What are you doing here?"

"Shopping. Are you available?"

"Yes, sir."

"Lead the way."

We walked out back to a lobby with several rooms off it. Rachel stopped in front of one of the doors, opened it and took the teddy and body suit from me. "You wait in there while I get changed."

The room was small, around seven by seven. A platform was built into one corner. A love seat filled the opposite wall. I sat down, careful not to step on a box of Kleenex on the floor in front of me. I figured it must be for cleanup.

Rachel walked in a few minutes later, wearing a blue satin robe. She dimmed the lights, then pushed a button next to the switch. "Close the Door" by Teddy Pendergrass started to play.

I watched as she stepped out of the robe and onto the platform. She was wearing the rhinestone teddy, which speckled the walls with reflected light as she started to dance. Her body and the music became one. Her skin was visible as through a jeweled net. Our eyes met, then she lowered her gaze to my groin. Without thinking about it, I had moved my hand there. She closed her eyes, then opened them, like a cat in the sun. I unbuckled my belt, unzipped my jeans and freed myself from my boxers. I began stroking myself, something I had never done in front of a woman. My hand felt rough against my skin. I tightened my grip as Rachel unfastened the snaps between her legs and lowered herself onto the platform. She raised her back off the floor while she ran her fingers over her lips, then between them. I had the impulse to tell her to turn over, so I could watch her, without her watching me. I resisted it. I wanted to see her face when she came, and I wanted her to see mine. In that moment of release, as in the moment of death, there is truth, and I needed to start sharing the truth with someone. I may not have picked Red Lace Lingerie as the place to start, but that's probably because I was still learning that God is not attracted to mountaintops or church steeples. God is drawn to suffering, and the dark places it surfaces, which is why sharing pain freely feels very much like love, and may be the same thing.

Rachel moved her fingers faster, and I matched her pace with my hand. Our breathing became erratic. I heard low groans and couldn't say for certain which belonged to me and which to her. Nor did it seem to matter.

Fourteen

It was after 3 A.M., and we were sitting on the antique church pew Rachel kept in front of the sliding glass doors to her deck. The Boston skyline shimmered in the distance beyond the Tobin Bridge. I took her hand, pushed the sleeve of her leotard over her elbow and lightly scratched the underside of her arm. My nails glided over the four vertical scars where she had cut herself years before.

She looked down at the scars. "You asked me the other night why I'm not shocked by what people do to one another."

I nodded.

"Am I protected by physician-patient confidentiality? Under that oath you took?"

"I think we're as far from a professional relationship as you can get. But you have my word. Whatever you tell me stays between us."

"My uncle sold me to his friends."

Just like that. *My uncle sold me to his friends*. I made an effort to keep my nails moving along her arm.

"I was thirteen. My parents left me with him when they were out of state for two months."

"Why weren't you with them?"

"They didn't want to take me out of school. They were working at the General Electric plant in Lynn and had to go to New Jersey for some sort of training program, or something. I was in the eighth grade, so I guess they thought it would be better not to drag me around."

"But it wasn't better."

"No." She took a deep breath. "The first few weeks were fine, but then my uncle started acting . . . strange. He'd walk into my bedroom while I was getting dressed or open the door to the bathroom while I was in the shower. He always had some lame excuse—that he thought I had called for him or that he didn't know I was in there. But I knew he was lying."

"Were you frightened?"

"Not until later." She ran a fingertip over her scars. "He had poker games at the house for the men he worked with. Four of them came over every Tuesday night."

"What sort of work did they do?"

"I don't remember. Why?"

"No reason, really. You just seem to remember so many other details."

She rubbed her eyes. "It had something to do with construction. Houses, maybe. No. I think it was roads. Or bridges."

I glanced out at the Tobin arching over the Mystic River. The past always dominates the horizon.

"They would drink nonstop when they played, and get loud. I couldn't sleep. So I would read in bed until they left. But one night I had a cold and I was exhausted. It was after midnight. They were laughing and shouting. I walked out to the kitchen to ask my uncle if he could make them quiet down." She squinted into the darkness. "The place was a mess. Beer bottles everywhere. Money all over the table."

I pictured Rachel naked on the Lynx Club runway, surrounded by beer bottles, gathering dollar bills off the floor.

"They stopped talking, one at a time, and stared at me in my nightgown. My uncle asked what was wrong, but I couldn't tell him in front of everyone, so I said I was thirsty. I poured myself a glass of water and went back to bed."

I nodded.

"A few minutes later he opened the door to my bedroom. I could barely see his face in the light coming from the hallway, but he was looking at me differently than he had before. Like he didn't *know* me. Like I was a *thing*, not a person."

"What did he say?"

"He just looked at me that way and left. I thought he was mad because I'd gone out to the kitchen. I couldn't figure out why he would be, though, unless he didn't want my parents to know he drank and gambled. I tried falling asleep. But then the door opened again."

I tightened my hand around hers.

"It was one of the other men. He was fat, with long, black side-burns. He took a few steps toward me. I remember I sat up in bed, and he stopped. He seemed embarrassed." She rolled her eyes. "I thought he had wandered in by mistake, so I told him the bathroom was down the hall."

I stayed silent.

"He stood there, like he hadn't heard me. Then I saw my uncle in the doorway. And he . . . uh . . ."

I moved my fingers along the underside of her arm.

"He said, 'Go ahead, Jimmy, you paid, fair and square.' "

I felt my eyes fill up.

"I tried to get away, but he was huge. So most of the time, I didn't move."

"You couldn't."

"More than one of them came in. They all reeked of beer. By the end, the whole room did."

I knew that smell from the Lynx Club. "Did your uncle force himself on you?" I asked.

"He watched. I still remember him directing everything." She swallowed hard. "One of the men wanted to use his beer bottle on me. My uncle told him it would be ten dollars extra."

"To use—"

"It happened two weeks in a row." She shook her head, then shrugged. "After that, nothing much surprised me."

"Did you tell your parents?"

"I told them a few days after they came home."

"And . . ."

"They didn't believe me. Uncle Paul had already complained that I kept him up, screaming in the middle of the night for no reason at all. He also told them he'd caught me fooling around with one of the boys from school. They figured I was wracked with guilt and looking to blame somebody for my own sins." She touched her scars. "Finally, I did this."

"Did they get you help?"

"They took me to a shrink."

"Did he believe you?"

"He prescribed sleeping medication. But he was mostly worried I might be showing signs of schizophrenia."

My throat felt tight. "I'm sorry," I said. "Didn't anyone listen?"

"I stopped talking about it. The doctor was at the point of hospitalizing me and putting me on Thorazine. Once I shut up, he seemed to think I was improving."

"Where is your uncle now?"

"Orlando. He retired there."

I let my breath out. "The bad things don't seem to happen to the bad people."

"That's because they already did. There's no original evil left in the world. My uncle and those men were recycling pain, not inventing it."

"You feel *sorry* for them?"

"On good days. On bad days I want to track them down and make them pay for what they did. But that's the hardest part of healing."

"What?"

"Realizing there's no one to hate."

"And the dancing? You told me that was part of healing, too."

"Like I said, I'm naked, but no one can touch me. I move as much as I please. The most the men can do—like tonight, at Red Lace—is touch themselves."

"Talk about diving into your fear."

"It beats being afraid. You should try it. You might actually sleep at night." She lifted my hand to her lips and kissed it. "What are you scared of?"

I took a little while to think, and a little while longer to convince myself to share what I was thinking. "I'm scared of the part of me that remembers being humiliated as a child," I said, "the part that can still hear my father's footsteps on the staircase to my room and the sound of that maniac's belt on me."

"You don't look frightened right now. You look angry."

Then it came to me without great drama, as moments of epiphany do. "I think I'm most afraid of the part of me that's still angry enough to kill him."

She seemed to relax. "How?" she said.

"How what?"

"How would you kill him?"

I chuckled a boy's nervous laughter.

"I mean it. You've been around enough killers. How would you murder your father? A knife? A gun?"

"Who knows?" I smirked. "How would you murder your uncle?"

"You don't want to go first. That's OK." She paused. "I'd chain him to the bed and poison him. Then I'd stay with him as he got sicker and sicker. When I picture him, he has vomit on his face and in his hair, and blood seeping from the corners of his eyes. Before he sucked in his last breath, I'd slash his wrists."

"I'd use a belt," I said. "*His* belt." I pictured my father with the leather strap tight around his neck.

She reached over and brushed her fingers across my neck. "Here."

I nodded.

"You'd pull it until your father couldn't breathe."

My pulse quickened.

"Even if he fell to the ground?"

My jaws were set. "It wouldn't matter if he clawed at his skin to get free." I felt light-headed. "I'd drag him around until he was exhausted. Then I'd loosen the belt for him to get air. But only a few breaths. Then I'd pull it tight again."

"You'd keep it tight even if he tried to scream?"

"It wouldn't matter."

"What if he gave up? He sat perfectly still and started to cry?"

"It wouldn't . . ." I had a memory of listening to my father as he sobbed in the bathroom the day Dr. Henry Harris had treated my cracked ribs. I closed my eyes. "I'd . . ."

"Tell me."

"I'd let him go." I felt defeated.

Several seconds went by.

"Me, too."

I looked at her. "Your uncle?"

She nodded.

I couldn't help smiling. "What difference would it make? You already poisoned him."

"That's true," she laughed. "I'd let him call an ambulance. Or I'd give him an antidote."

"Because he cried."

She nodded. "Once you let yourself feel pain, *really* feel it, you can't make someone suffer very long. Only a monster could. I promised myself I wouldn't turn into one." She touched my hair. "Neither will you." She leaned to kiss me.

I moved closer. Our mouths opened for one another. I felt her working my zipper and slipped my hand between her legs, over her thigh and onto her wet lips. I slid my fingers inside her. She sighed and lay back on the bench, with her knees slightly apart. I pushed her skirt over her hips. She spread her legs further. I kneeled in front of the pew and caressed the slightly bowed flesh between her navel and groin. Then I picked her up and carried her to the platform bed. I slowly undressed while she watched. She started to turn over, to give me her ass, but I stopped her. I stroked her hair and traced the curves of her face. Then, looking at each other, into each other, as if for the first time, I took her knees in my hands and pulled us together.

◆   ◆   ◆

"So tell me," Rachel asked later, "why are you in my bed, instead of with your girlfriend?"

I cleared my throat and prepared to defend myself.

She propped herself on one elbow. "You look nervous," she smiled. "I didn't say you're wrong to be with me. I just wondered, with her being a doctor and everything. Don't the two of you have a lot in common?"

My words came effortlessly. "We do. We're not in love with one another." I felt like softening what I'd said, but I knew it was true.

"She wouldn't mind you being here?"

"Oh, she'd mind. She's possessive. Intensely. But I think that's because we've never had a clear commitment to one another. Even living together, we haven't gotten really close."

"Why not?"

"I guess we didn't feel safe enough." I paused. "I don't know how anybody figures out the right time and place to open up. Plenty of patients used to pick my office, but I was never sure why they did."

"They sensed they could trust you."

"Well, they weren't always right."

"Meaning?"

I told her about Billy, especially that final phone call when he'd reached out to me.

"Most doctors would never get that call." She ran her fingers lightly down my face. "He was saying goodbye. He just didn't know how."

My throat tightened.

"Not everyone can be saved."

"You certainly seem to want to try."

"But I always start with myself." She laid her head on my chest. "That's what you need to do. Feel everything you've been trying not to feel."

"The good Dr. Lloyd." I closed my eyes.

"I really should be charging you," she whispered.

I slept until the sun woke me around six. I looked at Rachel, still asleep, and thought I saw the hint of a smile across her lips. Perhaps I invented it. I felt content myself. I knelt down by her side, buried my face in her hair and took deep breaths, as if to make her aura mine. Then I collected my clothes, pulled them on and took a step toward the door.

"Frank," she yawned.

I walked back to the bed and sat on the edge of the mattress. She slipped her hand over the sheet that covered her. I took it.

"Where are you going?" she asked without opening her eyes.

"Lynn."

"It's not over yet?"

"No."

Her hand went limp as she drifted off a few seconds, then her fingers tightened around mine again. "Be careful."

I felt like telling her that I loved her, but I had used the words more than a few times when I hadn't meant them, which had ruined them for me. So I just leaned over and kissed her forehead before heading down to the Rover.

I got in and drove away from Chelsea. I didn't wonder whether I'd see Rachel again. I knew I would. She had become part of me. As exhausted and worried as I was, that fact lifted me. Because it proved that all the beatings I'd suffered, all the cocaine I'd snorted, and all the tragedy I'd listened to and seen hadn't finished me off. I could still let another human being inside the maze of my existence. And that gave me hope of finding my way out.

My euphoria, however, was short-lived. I wasn't a mile over the Revere line into Lynn when I heard a siren behind me. I looked in the rearview mirror and saw Malloy behind the wheel of his cruiser. I pulled over, and he pulled within a couple feet of me. I watched as he jumped out of the car and spit on the ground. He was holding a sheet of bright pink paper in his hand, which I knew was a Section 12, the form used by psychiatrists to order the involuntary hospitalization of patients dangerous to themselves or others. Cops sometimes initiate the commitment process to get some minor offender they think is clearly crazy out of a jail cell and into a locked psych unit. An M.D. has to sign off on the transfer. I figured Malloy was too lazy to track down the psychiatrist on call at Stonehill Hospital. I focused on his pudgy legs carrying him toward my door. I rolled down the window.

"Good morning," he grinned.

"This is twice you've turned up in my rearview mirror. You following me, or what?"

"In a way. You got a box in your car."

"Excuse me?"

"A *box*. The LoJack recovery system. I figured a rig this nice would have the best alarm going. So I ran your vehicle ID number at the Registry. That's all I needed. I can activate the homing device from my cruiser any time. If you're within fifty miles, you light up on a map."

"You're only supposed to track the car if I report it stolen."

"Really? You're kiddin' me."

I glanced at the form in his hand. "I should make you chase the doc-on-call at the ER," I said.

"For this?" He rustled the paper.

"No. Because you and he would make a fabulous couple." I shook my head. "Of *course* for that."

"It's already signed," he deadpanned. "We didn't request this one. It got messengered to the station from a Dr. Pearson. Out of Boston. A few other towns got 'em, too."

"Pearson?" The last piece of paper I'd seen with his signature had been a note from his vacation home on the Cape urging me to get back into therapy. I worried Lucas might be using Pearson and the Impaired Physicians' Program to jump from the criminal justice system to the health care system, paving the way for an insanity plea.

"You'll want to read it." He held the paper up.

I looked at the space for the patient's name, hoping I was wrong. But where I feared I would find Lucas' name, my own had been written in. "What the hell—"

"I'm obviously not the only one in the world who thinks you need help."

A few lines down, Pearson had written the rationale for commitment: *Patient expressing suicidal ideation. Recent suicide attempts. History of illicit drug use. Acute paranoia.*

Malloy folded the pink paper and slipped it into his shirt pocket. "We'll have to leave the Rover here. I can't let you drive. You might decide to barrel into a tree or something."

"I'm not going anywhere with you. Where's Hancock?"

"She's not in today. Monique's funeral is this morning. And it wouldn't matter if she was sitting in my cruiser, because it isn't up to her whether this gets done. It's state law. We get the form, we get you. Period."

I started to roll up the automatic window, but Malloy plopped his hairless arms on the edge of the glass. The motor strained. I took my finger off the button.

"I have to get you to the hospital, any way I need to."

I thought about stepping on the gas, but I knew he was right. He could call as many cruisers as it took to stop me. I didn't see any benefit in a chase scene. "Look," I said, "pretend you never found me. Give me a couple hours to straighten this out. It's either a bad joke, or something worse." I nodded at my cellular phone. "I could probably get in touch with Pearson right now."

"According to the form, you're about to off yourself." He shrugged and looked up and down the road. "Personally, I don't think that's a half-bad idea. For instance, were you to grab my piece and shove it in your mouth, there wouldn't be anything I could do about that." He unsnapped the leather strap over his gun.

"You know something? This isn't the first time you've made me wonder about you. So let me be clear: There's no part of you I want in my mouth. If you like a dick, talk to Monique's roommate. As far as I know, he still has one and he might be interested."

Malloy's face turned crimson. "We're late for your date with a padded cell. C'mon out of there."

"This is another mistake you're making. Emma won't be pleased."

"I'm doing my job. Nobody can say different. And you know what? Whatever she could do to me would be worth seeing you in the looney bin."

I couldn't understand how anyone had convinced Ted Pearson to force me into the emergency room, but I wasn't going to find out sitting by the side of the road with Malloy. I got out of the Rover and walked to the cruiser.

"In back," he said.

"Why?"

"Because that's the way I want it."

I winked. "Exactly," I said. "I just don't understand why you're so damned ashamed of it." I climbed into the back seat and watched as we pulled past the Rover. I knew where we were going, but I couldn't have seen why.

* * *

Nels Clarke, the family physician working the emergency room, saw me come in with Malloy, but looked away as I walked past him, headed for the psychiatric evaluation room behind the nurses' station.

A black health aide named Elijah Randolph opened the steel door for me. He was a big man in his early thirties whose puffy cheeks, half-beard and overalls made him look like the cartoon character Bluto. We'd worked the ER together before. "Cleaned up like the Ritz-Carlton for you, Doc," he grinned. "Ain't often a brother gets to see a white professional man lose his freedom."

"Glad I can even out the scales for you." I paused at the threshold, noticing a set of four-point leather restraints fastened to a gurney against the far wall. I had walked into the room countless times to see patients, but now, knowing the dead bolt would keep *me* inside, I hesitated. For some reason—probably because he was a natural enemy of psychiatry—I looked back at Malloy.

"You've talked your way out of bigger messes," he said, a reluctant hint of kindness in his voice. "You'll talk your way out of this one."

"Thanks. I think." I took a deep breath and walked inside.

Elijah followed me and pulled the door closed. "That pig would best be used for BLTs. I'd fry him up crispy and have myself extra helpings." He sat down on a stainless steel stool.

"For a second there, I sensed a human being lurking inside him." I leaned against the gurney. "What do you know about why I'm here?"

"They say you're crazy."

"I know *that*."

"We all know it. Why else would the maniacs that come through this place quiet down like church mice when they get around you? You ain't quite right. People been saying so for years."

"Who's saying it *now*, for the pink paper?"

He glanced through the observation window at the activity around the nurses' station. A button on the countertop can activate a two-way intercom, in and out of the evaluation room. No one was near it. He stood up and rolled a blood pressure machine over to the gurney. He started to wrap the nylon cuff around my arm. "I'm not one to spread rumor and innuendo."

"The hell you're not."

He jiggled with laughter. "Women been tying men up from the beginning of time. Goes right back to Adam and Eve and that apple pie, if you catch my drift." He put his stethoscope in his ears. "Should be in the Bible that way. *Pie* is the source of all human suffering."

"Which women?"

"Hmm? Speak up." He stuck the bell of the scope in front of my face, like a microphone.

"Why do you say *women*? What do women have to do with me being locked up?" I asked.

He held up a finger, then slipped the bell under the blood pressure cuff. He started pumping the rubber bulb in his hand.

"You gonna tell me?"

"Shhh." He looked down at the blood pressure meter. The silver column of mercury rose. When it reached about 160, he stopped pumping, then turned a valve on the bulb to let the air start flowing out. At 110 he unscrewed it all the way. "A little high. Systolic and diastolic," he said. "Could be that you're tense."

I glared at him.

He checked the window. A nurse was standing over the intercom button. He ripped the cuff off my arm and took the stethoscope out of his ears. Then he fished an electronic thermometer out of his pocket.

"Say, 'Ahhhh.' "

"Christ, do I have to?"

"Ahhhh . . ."

I opened my mouth, and he slid the probe under my tongue.

He turned around long enough to see that the nurse had moved on. "Word is your woman and your mother double-teamed you. Went to court to commit your ass, on account of you being addicted to this or that, you being suicidal and you being generally hopelessly fucked up. The judge called the Impaired Physicians' Program. Then the Section 12 came down." He grabbed the thermometer out of my mouth and read the digital display. "At least one thing about you is normal. Ninety-eight six. On the money."

I had heard what he'd said, but I couldn't quite believe it. "You're telling me Kathy and my mother started all this?"

"I was close by when Nels got the call from some big-shot shrink in town." He paused, checked the nurses' station again, then turned back to me. "They were talking maybe Section 35-ing you from here."

A Section 35 was an involuntary, thirty-day detox, out at Bridgewater State Hospital, which was really more of a prison. "I'm already off the shit," I said. "Tell Nels to run my blood and urine. I'm clean."

"I'm sure he'll be buying that stock on my expert advice," Elijah said. "Let me get him. You can have a go at him yourself." He started toward the door, then turned back to me. "I got to lock you in. Sorry."

I nodded. I watched the door swing shut and heard the bolt slide home. I watched the activity in the ER, focusing now and again on Nels Clarke as he darted between patients. About fifteen minutes passed before I saw him leave one of the curtained cubicles, pull off a pair of latex gloves and walk toward my door. I heard a key in the lock.

"He's all yours, Dr. Clarke," Elijah said. "I'll wait right outside."

Nels walked in. He stayed near the door. "You look very angry," he said.

"Me? Why would I be angry, Nels?"

"I didn't sign the Section 12."

"I know. Ted Pearson did."

"I'd like to help."

"Good. You can start by telling me why the fuck I'm locked up. Who's behind this?"

He nodded. "You feel there's a conspiracy?"

I could see I had my work cut out for me. I took a deep breath. "No. I think everyone is trying to be helpful. I got free transportation here, and the accommodations are spectacular. So you can check off the NO box on the mental status exam under paranoia. The next two boxes are about voices and visions. Why don't you go ahead and ask about those."

He cleared his throat. "This is uncomfortable for both of us."

"For both of us? You gonna make *me* play therapist to *you*, for God's sake? I'm the one who got dragged in here against my will."

"I'm sure Elijah told you everything. He was standing right by the phone when I got the call from Pearson."

"Kathy and my mother." I stared at him.

"The reporting process is confidential. I can't confirm or deny."

"Nels, think about what's going on here. You know Kathy and I are having trouble. She's not an impartial observer of my psyche. As for my mother, she'd go along with caning me were someone to suggest it."

He let out a long sigh. "OK. Just for the sake of discussion, let's pretend they're the ones who got the ball rolling. What are we supposed to do if a close friend and a family member of yours both think you're at grave risk? Ignore them? I mean, c'mon, Frank. Nobody could dismiss what they said without an evaluation." He paused. "And you do have those lacerations on your wrist."

I turned my arm over and pulled up my sleeve. "I told you I did this down at the jail, to get William Westmoreland to stop biting into himself. Didn't I?"

"William . . . Yeah, something like that. I don't know if you went into detail. I pretty much took you at your word."

"You still can. Ask Malloy. He was there. He saw me do it."

"Maybe I will." He looked down at the floor. "They also say you've been using cocaine. A lot of cocaine."

"Was using. *Was*. I'm through with it. You can test me. No booze. No coke. Nothing."

His eyes met mine again. "Pearson was told you jumped out a second-story window."

"Huh?"

"You got high, screamed something about wanting to end it, then hopped right out the window before anyone could stop you. You slammed into the ground on your right side."

"My—"

"Can you pull up your shirt?"

"Nels, this is insane."

His gaze settled on my right side.

"I must have pissed Kathy off even more than I knew. I'm being set up."

"You feel—"

"Jesus Christ, Nels!" I could feel my pulse behind my eyes.

He took a step closer to the door.

I calmed myself down to the extent that I could. "If you want to play analyst, it doesn't mean you have to start every other goddamn sentence with 'You feel.' Mix it up a little bit. Try a few other lines, like 'I think I hear you saying,' or 'I understand.'" I took a few deep breaths. "Look, I'll make this easy for you. To review: I'm not paranoid. I don't hear voices or see visions or smell burning flesh or feel spiders crawling all over my balls. I'm not homicidal or suicidal.

This is Lynn. Stonehill Hospital. It's Thursday. Morning. Bill Clinton is president of the United States. And you're as much of an asshole as you've always been."

"So indulge me. I've got to do a physical exam anyhow. Lift up your shirt."

"Fine." I pulled my jean shirt out of my pants.

Nels winced.

I looked down. A mottled blue, black and yellow bruise ran over the three or four ribs that had broken my fall when I bounced off Trevor Lucas' Ferrari. "Lucas did that," I said. "With his car."

"He's in jail."

"I know. I helped put him there. Before he went, we had a scuffle."

"OK. Listen. Why don't we—"

"There you go again with that let's-not-rattle-the-crazy-person tone of voice. I'm telling you Kathy's paying me back for . . . Well, I'm not sure exactly what she's paying me back for. But she definitely heard about my ribs from Lucas."

"Losing Kathy means a great deal to you."

There are few things more dangerous than misguided empathy. "Nels," I said, trying to control myself. "You should really stick to sore throats. You're wrong to think I'm pining away. Do you know where I just came from?"

"No."

"Good. At least everybody's not dialing up my LoJack number."

"Your . . ."

"Forget it."

He looked even more concerned.

"I was at a beautiful woman's apartment. She's a dancer at the Lynx Club. Perfect ass. Long legs. Gigantic heart. I didn't think of Kathy for one second last night while we were making love. I was too goddamn happy. So believe me, I'm not descending into a psychotic depression. I've never felt better in my life." Before I had finished the last sentence, I knew it might make him worry I was euphoric—as in manic.

"Yeah, well . . . Let's get your physical exam done and that urine and blood tox screen you suggested and wait for Pearson. I can't release you without a psychiatrist approving the discharge, even if I wanted to."

"He's coming? Here?" I was embarrassed to see him with things going so wrong—especially since he had predicted they would.

"The Impaired Physicians' Program requires an on-site eval. Pearson does his own."

"So why am I torturing myself talking to you?" I closed my eyes. "When does he get here?"

"Soon."

My body was examined, and my urine and blood were collected. I tried to sleep on the gurney, but couldn't. Elijah brought me Coffee Cake Juniors and a few *People* magazines. I read a long article about celebrity breakups, like Julia Roberts and Lyle Lovett. An even older issue had a photo of a note from Michael Jackson to the rest of the world in which he asks for understanding from the public because he's been *bleeding a long time*—an obvious reference to Christ. Wouldn't that be something; God coming back as a black pop singer addicted to plastic surgery who likes to hang around with naked kids. And here I was, locked up as crazy, while the Gloved One taped a special for HBO. Go figure.

Fifteen

I watched through the observation window as Ted Pearson checked in at the nurses' station. He hadn't changed in the months since I'd seen him. His silver hair was neatly groomed, and he was, as always, elegantly attired in charcoal slacks, a white-and-gray pinstriped shirt and red bow tie. His deep blue eyes were unblinking as they took in his surroundings. He signed something, flipped through a few sheets of paper on the countertop and headed toward my door. After he'd been let in the room, he bowed almost imperceptibly to Elijah. Then the door closed again.

He looked at the ceiling, around at the walls, nodded to himself, then took a seat on the stainless steel stool. He folded his hands and stared at me. "Well . . ." he said finally.

I felt myself relax, an effect I remembered Pearson having had on me each time we had met. My shoulders dropped, and my hands folded on one another, like his.

He reached up to adjust a hearing aid in his left ear. That was new. "Occupational hazard," he said. "Ears aren't made to listen to as many stories as we do."

"You've been at it a lot longer than I have."

"Forty years. Give or take." He finished tuning his ear. "I don't think I ever told you I worked in this hospital for a short time during the sixties. Back then they called it the Lynn Lying Inn."

"Still plenty of lying going on."

He winked and turned to look out the observation window. "The ER must be four, five times the size it was."

I wasn't in the mood for a walk down memory lane. "You signed my Section 12," I said calmly.

He turned back to me and pursed his lips. "More than that. I issued it."

"Why?"

"Judge Stahl passed along serious concerns a few people in your life shared with him. Then I talked directly with those individuals."

"Then let me clear a few things up. I'm not suicidal. The story about me jumping out a window is ludicrous. And I'm off the drugs. Kathy and my mother apparently misled you."

"Perhaps," he allowed. His eyes locked on mine. "What seemed clear to me is that neither of them has any idea why you might be suffering. I'm sure you'll agree that represents remarkable data." He was silent several seconds. "They want you to survive. They need to have you in their lives, in some very particular way. But they show precisely zero interest in your having a full life yourself."

I took a deep breath and let it out. "How does that add up to me getting picked up?"

"I wasn't sure whether you had any interest in living, either."

"I do."

"I'm encouraged to hear you say so," he nodded. He fiddled with one of his cufflinks, a gold square with an inlaid lapis spiral. "How did you mean to go about it? Cocaine? Freud found it lacking."

"I stopped two days ago. I'm—"

"At the very beginning," he smiled. "At best." Several more seconds passed. His expression grew solemn. "I'm going to do something I don't think I've ever done, Frank."

I was more than a little worried by that. "What? What are you going to do?"

"Breach a patient's confidentiality."

I waited, unsure where he was headed.

"I treated your father in this very place. More than once."

"My father? You saw him?"

"Yes. I did. But more important for our purposes, I see him in you."

I stayed silent.

"He would stumble in, ranting about throwing himself over the tracks at Salem Station. Always drunk. Always the same story."

"My grandfather worked as an engineer for the old Boston and Maine Railroad. Out of Salem Station."

"Ah. Your dad never said a word about that. I wish that he had."

"He wouldn't have opened up. Not even to you. Not to anyone. He never did."

"What a difficult man for you to love."

My throat felt too tight to respond.

"You were with him the night he actually visited those tracks, Frank."

"What? When? I don't remember anything like that."

"You were eight years old. I'm not surprised your mind would put the memory in deep storage."

"What happened?"

"Your father was drunk. Again. He found an isolated platform, hopped over the edge, then lay down between the rails." He paused. "Now that you tell me your grandfather worked for the railroad, I guess your father laid his body on that track partly as a symbol. He'd probably been through hell with the man." He shook his head. "But if it hadn't been the tracks, it would have been somewhere else. Because he wanted to sleep. Forever. His pain had worn him out." He squinted at the floor and nodded to himself, then looked back at me. "And at eight years old, already hating him as you must have, you loved him enough to do a remarkable thing."

I pictured my father passed out on the tracks, but couldn't keep the image focused in my mind longer than a few seconds.

"You climbed down over the edge of that platform and tried to drag him back up. You ripped his shirt trying. You stumbled, skinned your knees and sliced your thumb wide open on a piece of broken glass."

I looked at my left thumb. I'd had a jagged scar from the first knuckle to the heel of my hand my whole life. I'd never known why, or thought to ask.

"And when you couldn't move him, you screamed for help. A janitor working the night shift found the two of you and carried you out of there. Then the police brought you both to this emergency room."

"And you were here?"

"I was. And now we're here again."

My skin turned to gooseflesh.

"I'll tell you the same thing I told your father that night," he said softly. "I can't keep you from destroying yourself. No one can. Ultimately, that choice will always be yours." He stood up and extended his hand.

I took it. It felt soft and warm, and I could have held it a long time. "What happens now?" I asked.

"Good question." He paused. "I'd still be honored to help you answer it."

I watched as Pearson walked over to Nels and conferred with him. People kept crossing in front of them, and my eyes had filled up, so I couldn't get a sense of how the conversation was going. Then the two men shook hands, and Pearson walked out.

A minute later Nels came into my room. "Let me ask you, again. No chance of you doing yourself in?"

"No."

"As in zero percent possibility."

"Zero."

"Fair enough."

"That's it? I can go?"

"You're a free man. According to Pearson, there's no way we can hold you. Your urine and blood are clean, and you say you're safe. So that's that." He reached into his lab coat and pulled out a card. "He said to give you this."

I took the card. It had Ted Pearson's name engraved in simple black letters, with his phone number underneath it. I turned the card over. On the back he had written a quotation from the poet Rilke: *Everything terrible is something that needs our love.*

I slipped the card in my pocket.

"Still angry?" Nels asked.

"A little less every day," I said.

◆　　◆　　◆

I walked out to the waiting area and spotted Elijah sweet-talking the receptionist, a pretty blonde named Jackie. She and I had kept up a harmless flirtation over the years. I started over to them.

"If this don't give me hope we will all be liberated one sweet day," Elijah bellowed.

"Hello, Frank," Jackie said.

"Jax," I nodded.

"Can't seem to stay out of trouble, huh?" She tilted her head slightly.

Elijah looked at her, then at me. "Maybe I should take over the desk and let you two find a call room."

Jackie chuckled.

I laid a hand on Elijah's beefy shoulder. "Thanks for the help in there. I appreciate it."

"No problem."

"One thing, though."

"Fire away."

I reached into my jacket pocket, took out my penknife and clicked it open. "You didn't search me before you locked me up. It didn't matter this time, but the next guy might leave you minus an eye. Or some other piece of vital equipment." I glanced at the bulge in his pants. "A little teaching point for your trouble."

"Thanks. I think."

I playfully poked at his arm with the knife. "Teaching *point.* Get it?"

He squinted at me. "You sure you didn't escape?"

"I know I did."

We shook hands.

"Where you headed?" he asked.

"Upstairs. Ob-Gyn."

He chuckled. "And you're tellin' me to watch *my* back."

◆   ◆   ◆

Kathy wasn't in her office. Kris, her secretary, told me she'd arrived late and had rushed to the delivery suite. I took the department's private elevator up two floors to the doctors' lounge. It was empty, but Kathy's black leather bag was in front of her locker. I pushed through the double doors into the amphitheater over the delivery room. The lights were off, so I used the seats along the center aisle to guide me to the angled wall of glass up front.

The obstetrical team was working on what looked like a difficult case. Usually, the anesthesiologist would be slouched in his chair, barely awake, but he was on his feet, checking gauges. The scrub nurse feverishly arranged surgical instruments on a tray next to the patient. Kathy had been standing between the patient's legs, but now moved to the woman's side.

I looked down at the patient's naked groin, then at Kathy as she doused the woman's abdomen with Betadine. The ruby liquid spread out and ran between the woman's thighs. As a psychotherapist, I had always felt at home coaxing the healing process, waiting out the truth about a patient's life for months or years. The goals of treatment were subjective ones. Recovery could be a matter of opinion. Kathy's work was definitive—*delivering* new life, when it needed to happen, in whatever way it needed to happen. Was that why she felt comfortable invading my life as dramatically as she had?

The anesthesiologist was moving more quickly, his face mask billowing with panicked words.

I thought again about Kathy's sister, lost in the fire that destroyed the family's home. Could any drama mimic that tragedy more closely than the one I was watching? A child was in danger, likely of suffocation. The kid was *inside* and needed to get *outside*. But this time Kathy had the knowledge and the wherewithal to deliver that child to safety.

She took a scalpel off the surgical tray and, with no apparent hesitation, cut an eight-inch, transverse incision below the woman's navel. She sliced through the underlying layers of tissue, set the blade aside, then reached deep into the wound with both hands. A moment later her hands emerged, clutching a screaming infant covered in blood.

I turned around and headed back up the stairs and out of the amphitheater to wait in the doctors' lounge. It was only a matter of minutes before Kathy walked in. She froze when she saw me sitting on the bench in front of her locker.

I stood up and shrugged. "They evaluated me in the emergency room, but I passed for sane."

"Doctors make mistakes all the time."

"How about you?"

"Sure. But not in your case."

"Did Trevor put you up to it?"

"He has bigger things to worry about. He could be locked up for life." She started to walk past me to get her things.

I caught her arm.

"Let go of me!" She struggled to free herself from my grip but couldn't. She took a deep breath and closed her eyes. "You didn't really think I would sit still so you could enjoy your little whore, did you?"

"What?"

"Did you think I was going to let you get away with that crap again? Haven't I been embarrassed enough?"

"You actually did this out of pure jealousy?"

"Humiliation would be more like it."

"And having me committed was your idea of revenge."

She shook her head. "Don't you get it?" she sputtered. "You're out of control. You need to be locked up, for your own good."

"No. I don't get it."

She looked away and shook her head. "It doesn't really matter anymore." She pushed past me to her locker.

I walked over to the elevator and pressed the DOWN button. The door opened. I stepped inside and turned around. Kathy kept her back to me. "You can pick up the rest of your things at the house anytime," I told her. "And leave your key."

• • •

I took a taxi to the Rover, then started the drive home to Marblehead. I needed some quiet time to get focused again. In my private practice I had urged dozens of families to use the courts to force loved ones into detox, and part of me still wanted to believe that Kathy had begun the commitment process out of concern for my well-being, however misguided. But that vision of her motivation didn't square with the morbid jealousy I had seen in her face. I had to take her at her word: She had gone to court in anger, to *control* me.

I reached into the glove compartment, grabbed a Marlboro and lit it. I inhaled deeply and held the smoke as long as I could.

So why did I still hesitate at the thought of packing her things? The answer was the same one I had given to countless patients who puzzled over why they felt bound to toxic relationships: Being controlled, not loved, was what I had known as a child. I was, as a professor of mine used to put it, *lost in a familiar place*. It was no wonder Kathy and my mother had become allies.

Not that I could give myself more credit than I gave either of them. I knew that losing a childhood home and a younger sister could leave a girl terrified at any hint of chaos. I knew a tragedy of that magnitude could kindle intense possessiveness in relationships. Yet I hadn't offered Kathy any real security. And I hadn't dug deeply enough into her past to help her overcome her fears. Far from it; I had held her down during her tantrums, restraining her until her emotions burned themselves out.

The truth was that neither Kathy nor I had done for one another what Rachel had done for me—helped me to embrace the grief and hatred in my heart, thereby lightening it. Why, I wondered, was help of that kind so rare in the world?

I sucked in another half inch of my cigarette and slowed the car as I passed a new billboard at the Lynn line. It read LYNN. LYNN. CITY OF WIN! I smiled. The slogan was part of the Redevelopment Authority's campaign to give the city a facelift. We had all learned the real jingle growing up on its squalid streets: Lynn, Lynn, city of sin. Never come out the way you went in.

I tossed my butt out the window and turned onto Atlantic Avenue. A minute later I took the right onto Preston Beach Road and pulled into my driveway. I sat there a few moments, troubled by something I couldn't quite put my finger on. I shielded my eyes from the sun and squinted at the house. Then I realized what was bothering me.

The door to the house was open a few inches. I hadn't slept home the previous night, and my memory of leaving with Levitsky to find Emma Hancock was sketchy. Maybe I hadn't pulled the door tight. The wind off the ocean had blown it open plenty of times. Still, I felt uneasy. I reached between the seats for the fur handle of my hunting knife, but it wasn't in its usual place. I got out, keeping an eye on the door to the house, and crouched by the side of the car. I ran my hand under the seat. Nothing. I scanned the carpet. No luck. I figured some scavenger had stopped to check out the Rover where I'd left it by the side of the road and had grabbed the only thing that wasn't screwed down. Or maybe Malloy had doubled back to confiscate any "sharps" I could use to kill myself—or him. I stood up. I had my penknife, but that wouldn't do me much good, unless the intruder had a painful hangnail I could help him with.

I walked to the rear of the car, eased open the tailgate, and fished out the tire iron. I started up the flagstone path to my door, intentionally scuffing my boots on the ground with each step. If somebody was in the house ripping off paintings, I wanted to give him every chance to get out. I was insured for theft; I didn't see any reason for one of us to get killed over it. At the threshold I rang the bell several times and shouted, "Hello!" There was no response. I walked inside.

The place was a shambles. The coffee table was overturned, with one leg broken off. Half the curtains had been yanked down. Kathy's collection of colored glass hearts was lying in pieces by the far wall, little dents showing where each had hit the plaster. The oil paintings were still hanging, but the one I liked the best—a scene of the Titanic going down—had been slashed. I took a few more steps and noticed that one of the seat cushions of the couch had been cut open. The phone was on the floor, its cord ripped from the wall. I stood perfectly still, listening for any movement from above, but all I could hear was the distant thunder of waves rolling onto the beach.

I hadn't expected to hear anything else. This wasn't the work of an anonymous intruder. Kathy had obviously spun into a frenzy again—but without me around to stop her. I figured she had come back during the night to talk things over. I pictured her waiting for me, getting more and more furious with every passing hour, until she realized I wasn't coming home at all. Then . . . this.

I laid the tire iron on the couch and started upstairs.

I hoped Kathy had confined her tantrum to the living room, but when I got to the top of the second-floor landing, I saw she hadn't. Vases lay smashed in the hallway. A collage of half-dead flowers and water stains covered the walls and oriental runner.

The bedroom was in even worse shape than the living room. The oak armoire was lying on its side. The dresser mirror had been shattered. Just past the doorway I stooped to pick up a white satin and lace pillow I had given Kathy for Valentine's Day. It smelled of smoke. I turned it over and saw that the embroidered inscription, SWEET DREAMS, I LOVE YOU, had been burned off. Maybe she'd lighted it on fire and tossed it into the room, hoping the whole damn house would go up.

The den seemed to have survived largely intact. The only damage was that Kathy's collection of Trixie Belden books had been swept off the shelf and lay scattered on the floor. I scanned the room. The art deco bar was open, and one of the chrome tumblers was missing. I spotted it on the side table next to the leather wing chair. I walked over and picked it up. It smelled of gin. Kathy almost never drank, so a few long swallows of that might help explain her rage boiling over. I glanced down and saw she had left Volume 1 of her Trixie collection on the seat cushion. The spine was broken, and, as I held the book, the pages parted naturally to Chapter 19. I started to read:

> Trixie rubbed her eyes again. Something white and feathery was seeping up around the roof of the Mansion. As she watched, it disappeared into space, but then, as a puff of wind blew up from the hollow, she could see another pale form take shape on one side of the house. . . .
>
> It looks like ghosts, she thought with a nervous giggle. I guess the moonlight's playing tricks on me, and I must be sleepier than I thought I was. She turned to go back to bed when, with a start of horror, she remembered . . .
>
> "It's not a ghost," she cried out loud, wheeling back to the window. "It's smoke. . . . The Mansion's on fire!"

I shook my head. Between the burnt pillow and Kathy's choice of reading material, I was starting to feel lucky the house was still standing. I wondered where she was at the moment she had exploded. Not *physically* where, but *psychologically*. Was she an adult, a physician, a woman with resources at her disposal, or was she the twelve-year-old who had helplessly watched her sister consumed by flames?

I gathered several of the books off the floor and arranged them on the shelf. I reached for more but stopped, spotting a sheet of crinkled paper near the base of the standing lamp. I picked it up. It was notebook paper, the kind with pink lines that I remembered girls using in grade school. The penmanship looked adolescent, too—big, bowing characters, with hearts dotting every *i* and too many exclamation points. From the yellowed crease, I could tell it had been folded in half a long time ago, maybe to fit inside the cover of one of the books. It read:

> Daddy—
> I thought you loved me! But you love Blaire better! I saw you going into her room tonight. I thought and thought and thought why. Is it because I bleed now?
> I can't help it! It's not my fault!
> Why am I being punished?!?
> I hate her!
> Please give me another chance.
>
> Love,
> Mouse (Remember?)
>
> P.S. Blaire can't keep secrets!

My hand was shaking. I lowered myself into the wing chair, laid the sheet of paper on the side table and stared out the window at nothing.

I hadn't spent more than a dozen hours in the presence of Jack Singleton, Kathy's father. He was a decent-looking man, though slightly underweight, who had made a fortune in textiles—producing the interwoven materials that line coats, waistbands and the collars of some shirts. I remembered joking with him that only in a great country could a man get rich off something no consumer had ever thought about, much less heard of. He had laughed, but tightly, a reaction I was glad for, because he rarely laughed at all. Before I'd met him, Kathy had warned me that he had never recovered from the loss of his younger daughter, something I took to explain his aloofness from Kathy herself. Some parents engulf the surviving child after a sibling dies; others retreat into themselves, as if they believe that declaring their love might tempt a return visit from Death.

I had missed the real drama of closeness and distance between the two of them. Jack Singleton had violated his daughters in the most intimate way possible. Perhaps he wasn't sure whether Kathy remembered the trauma or had suppressed it. And he seemed not at all eager to find out.

I got up and poured myself a scotch, then walked aimlessly from one room to another. I had the impulse to page Kathy, to tell her that I understood, that I felt, strangely, closer to her than I ever had before.

A moment later the phone rang. I have always believed people can take different routes to the same moment and I raced to pick up the extension in the bedroom, hoping she would be on the other end. "Frank," I said.

"Glad I found you," Paulson Levitsky answered. His tone was grave.

"What's wrong?"

"Plenty."

I put my drink down. "Let's hear it."

"Number four came in. About an hour ago."

"God, no." My heart was pounding. "Male or female?"

"Female."

I took a deep breath. "Same MO?"

"Not exactly. The body was badly burned, for one thing. But the breasts are gone. And the groin was shaved."

"We know who she was?"

"Another dancer."

"From the Lynx Club?"

"She worked there. She lived in Chelsea. I got the body because of the ongoing investigation."

My vision blurred. My legs felt short and weighty. "Where in Chelsea?"

"Somewhere on the harbor, I think. The fire department found her when they finally got inside the building. The whole top floor was burning. Our man probably got tired of burying body parts."

I felt as if I was going to pass out. I sat down on the floor, leaning against the bed. "You have a name?"

"Lloyd."

"Rachel."

"Yeah, right, Rachel Lloyd. What, do you know every stripper at the place?"

"I was . . ."

"A big tipper. I'm sure. Now listen, here's another thing: The weapon wasn't the same. This blade was long by comparison."

"Why do you say that?" I managed.

"I don't see any layering of flesh, like I found on the other two females. What I've got are sweeping, five-to-six-inch lacerations. And there doesn't seem to be any fibrotic tissue at the wound margins, although I'm working around a good deal of secondary pathology—liquification from the heat. Still, I'd say if this one had implants, she got them quite recently." He paused. "You there?"

"She didn't have implants."

"Oh. I forgot. You've got that pornographic memory. Was she shaved?"

"Not completely."

"What sort of outfits did she wear?"

"Why?"

"I found a few brittle hairs on the skin near the wounds. Animal hairs. Light brown. Did she wear a fur coat or something?"

I pictured the handle of my hunting knife. "I don't remember."

"I should have known. You only remember what things look like *after* the outfits come off."

"What was Hancock's reaction?"

"Ms. Mayor maintains that this one's unrelated. Too many inconsistencies, she says. The fire. The knife. And Malloy already checked Lucas' files; Lloyd wasn't a patient of his. All of which, of course, fits nicely into Hancock's political plans. The election's not far off, and she can claim she caught the Lynn psycho. She doesn't need votes from Chelsea."

"What do you think?"

"I think it's the same guy. All four bodies are characterized by mutilation of the sex organs. Three were Lucas' patients, and one worked with a prior victim. That's a pretty tightly knit group, if you ask me." He took a deep breath. "It's also possible—*remotely possible*—that Lucas did the first two, and some inspired lunatic picked up from there. That would explain why we're getting variations on the original theme."

"OK."

"OK what?"

I was having trouble focusing. "I'll call you if I find out anything." I heard my words as if someone else was speaking them.

"You don't sound good. Are you alright? You're not back on that shit again, are you? This is no time to cloud your thinking."

"No. No, I'm thinking clearly." I hung up.

I sat there, rocking slowly back and forth. I wanted to cry but couldn't, which made me feel even more empty inside. Dead. This, I thought, is the feeling that drives people to slash their own flesh—to channel a black vacuum of the soul into something that flows thick and red. I walked over to the wet bar, grabbed a chrome bottle and poured a good triple of what turned out to be bourbon down my throat. Then, disgusted with myself for dousing my grief, I hurled the bottle against the wall. That didn't make me feel any better, so I gripped the bar with both hands and threw the whole thing over. The bottles and tumblers crashed to the floor. A half-dozen rivers of booze ran into each other, until they disappeared in the deep hues of my oriental carpet. My gut revolted against the bourbon, and I crouched down and heaved it up. I let myself fall onto my side, my face against wetness that smelled like a foul physic. A curved shard of glass lay within reach. I thought fleetingly of using it, but let the thought go as Rachel's image came involuntarily to me, lying in bed so peacefully just that morning.

I held her in my mind and tried to imagine telling her that I loved her.

Sixteen

Cold sweat, too subtle to feel with my fingers, covered my face and neck. The smell of bourbon and vomit had filled the den. I held the phone to my ear, waiting for Kathy to answer her page at Stonehill Hospital. I knew she could ask the operator for the name of the person on hold, then refuse the call, but my gut told me she wanted to hear from me, *needed* to hear from me. A few minutes later the operator got back on the line.

"She's not answering, Doctor Clevenger, would you like to continue to . . . Oh, there we go. One moment, please."

Real beads of sweat formed on my brow. I wiped the wetness away with my sleeve. My heart was overfilled with grief and hatred and pity. I didn't know if I would be able to speak in measured tones. But I knew that I had to.

"Transferring," the operator sang.

The phone clicked, the line engaged, then . . . silence.

"Kathy?"

"What?" she said flatly.

I couldn't get my breathing under control.

"Do you have anything to say?" She paused only a second. "Goodbye."

"Wait!" I decided to issue a disclaimer on my agitation, rather than risk her interpreting it. I didn't want her to know for sure whether I had heard about Rachel's death. "I'm having a bad time. My hands are shaking. My heart's racing like a bastard."

"Sounds like you sucked up too much coke. Have another drink."

"I haven't touched that crap."

"Maybe it's hopping from bed to bed. You've worn yourself out."

"No. I'm . . . scared."

"That's a new one."

"I can't stand the thought of being without you."

There was no response.

"Kathy?"

"You seemed to manage pretty well last night."

I knew that the quickest route past Kathy's adult defenses would be directly into the primal rage and desire she had felt as a girl. Remembering what she had written in her note to her father, I answered the way she would have hoped *he* would. "I'm done sneaking around in the dark," I said. "I'm asking for another chance. It won't happen again."

"Then tell me: Why did you screw me over? She was younger than me. Was she better than me?"

"She was like a child. She didn't know what she was doing."

"Oh, yes she did. She wasn't a baby. Not any more than the others." Her voice had lost its edge and taken on a pouty, girlish quality. "They were trying to steal from me."

My eyes welled up, but I forced myself to go on. "I don't care about her. The only bed I want to share is yours."

"I ruined the house."

"You weren't thinking clearly."

"I don't even remember some of it. I was so mad." Her voice trailed off. "I've made a mess of everything."

"We'll clean it up together."

"You won't miss her?"

I couldn't tell from Kathy's words or tone whether she was operating entirely in the present or the past, referring to Blaire or Rachel. "No," I said. "I won't miss her."

"I do."

I closed my eyes. "Listen, Kathy. Let's get out of here and head up to Plum Island, to that inn on the beach we stayed at the first night we were together. Walton's Ocean Front. Remember?" I thought I heard her sobbing. "Kathy?"

She cleared her throat. "Huh?"

"Walton's Ocean Front. Meet me there. It'll be like starting over."

"I can't. I have four deliveries. I'll be here all night. I won't get out until the end of the day tomorrow."

"Well, tomorrow, then. Meet me right after work."

"You won't stand me up?" The edge was back in her voice.

"Not a chance."

"Just don't make me sit there alone, like a fool." She hung up.

•   •   •

It took me most of three hours to get the house half organized. I tried not to think of Rachel, but without notice my chest would tighten, nausea would sweep over me, and I would have to sit down with the memory of her.

Just after dark the phone rang again. I ran to answer it. "Clevenger," I breathed.

"The Gestapo have allowed me one last call."

I recognized Trevor Lucas' voice.

"Would you be good enough to come visit with me?"

"For what?"

"So I can tell you the truth."

"Whatever you have to tell me, you can say it right now."

"I think not. You would need to come to see me."

I thought of how much I hadn't been willing to see. "I'll be there," I told him.

He hung up.

I got in the car and drove to the station. Emma Hancock was out, and Tobias Lucey was on duty at the lockup, but my stock had risen with the department, and he gave me no trouble about visiting Lucas.

"Might as well say goodbye. He gets transferred to MCI Concord in the morning," Lucey said. He pulled open the steel door. "The grand jury returned the indictment. Three counts, murder one."

"Who's prosecuting?"

"The new D.A., Red Donovan, is taking it himself. Three murders is a big deal, even these days. Three murders by a *doctor*— well, that's a movie-of-the-week."

"Who'd Lucas end up hiring?"

"He represented himself. Just like he said he would. Didn't call a single witness." He shook his head. "It's like he thinks he's dealing with a fender-bender."

"That, he'd care about," I said.

I started down the corridor toward Lucas. The other cells were empty, and his soft humming reached me before I saw him, sitting cross-legged on the floor again, his eyes closed in meditation. I stood there, surveying his bruised and torn face. His humming grew fainter and fainter, until he sat in silence. Then he opened his eyes and met my stare. "I'm sorry," he said.

"Sorry for what? What are you talking about?"

"Your dancer. The one with red hair and no tits."

My teeth ground against each other.

"The fourth victim," he urged. "In transit from court, I heard a radio report about her cremation in Chelsea." His brow furrowed. "You look awful. I hope you didn't have feelings for her."

"You had three victims," I said weakly. "Maybe you weren't listening to the grand jury."

"No. They weren't listening. I told them I wasn't guilty. I could have proven it. But there's still time."

"If you're innocent, why wait?"

"Why? Because I have been wronged, accused of monstrous acts I did not commit. The gravity of that error must be made plain."

"You think anyone really cares if you meditate in maximum security for six months instead of tucking tummies?"

He chuckled, but tightly. "Of course not. I'm irrelevant. Sport for the tabloids. They'll care about the body count, though. I have dozens of lovers left. You probably have a stable yourself. Kathy might settle on any one of them next."

I went cold. He knew.

"I told you I wasn't your problem. But you wouldn't listen."

My stomach sank. "You can't believe Kathy would kill anyone," I managed.

"I wasn't certain about Sarah. But I knew for sure after you told me about Monique. Or thought I did. So I conducted a bit of an experiment."

"An experiment . . ."

"I called the Kathy monster and confessed that Wembley and I were intimate." He paused. "As it happens, we weren't, but I obviously convinced her. She knows I usually schedule my surgeries to end at 7:30 P.M. Wembley's Rolex on the dash was her attempt to provide me an alibi. I was touched. As I've said before, she really does love me. I'm afraid she started killing off her competition when I told her we were through."

"When was that?"

"Just before Sarah was murdered. Jealousy, it seems, is Kathy's driving passion. Probably some remnant of being seduced by her father. Jack." He smiled. "What a piece of work he must have been, huh? I mean, you have to hand it to the old man. He called her Mouse, you know. 'Be quiet as a mouse,' he used to tell her, just before he sent it home. Is that beautiful, or what?"

"She mentioned you told her about my dancer, too."

"That was your fault. Kathy followed you two to Chelsea. I merely confirmed your attraction for the girl. Judging from what happened to her, Kathy obviously loves you, too."

"You let her go on killing." My gut churned at the horror of it. "You set her up to kill."

"You can't blame me. No one could have resisted. Fucking her, knowing what she'd done, was . . . heaven." He gazed up dreamily, sighed, then looked back at me.

I wanted him dead. Right then and there. It wouldn't take much—a crushing kick to the bridge of his nose. I focused between his eyes.

He tilted his head. "Don't be unfair with me, Frank. We're a lot alike. I bet you enjoyed having her fresh from the kill, too. Even if you didn't know it at the time."

I raised my foot an inch off the floor and tensed my calf. Then I hesitated. A swift death, I thought, would be too kind. Better to let him rot. My lip curled. "No. You're wrong. We're nothing alike."

"How sad. We could have become fast friends when I'm free."

"If." I stepped back.

"Excuse me."

"*If* you're ever free. There's a murder trial between now and then. And there isn't going to be another body to bolster your defense."

He looked at me askance. "I detect a manipulation. Maybe I'll have to tell my story sooner rather than later."

"No one's gonna care about your story, you stupid fuck," I sputtered. "I think you're guilty. So does Emma Hancock, our next mayor. And this new D.A. is out to make a name for himself."

"You wouldn't sit still to see me tried for murder. It would violate your ethics. You're an honest man."

"Honest?" I grabbed the bars, my fists going white around the iron. "I honestly want to see you condemned to life at MCI Concord. I honestly want to visit you there after your sentencing, then again when your appeal fails. I want to be there the day it finally registers in your mind that you're never going to leave that hellhole."

Lucas lost his composure. "Where's Kathy?" he growled.

"Try to focus on yourself. Because who knows? Maybe the parole board will be moved by your growth and let you out in thirty years." I turned and started for the door.

"Frank!" Lucas yelled.

I kept walking.

• • •

Emma Hancock was driving up to the curb as I headed out of the building. She lowered her passenger window. I walked over. "What did he have to say?" she asked.

"He's ranting about being framed. He says we're all in on it. You, me, half a dozen other doctors at Stonehill. He even mentioned Kathy."

She clicked her nails once. "You're not saying he's crazy . . ."

"Not for a second. He knows right from wrong. He chose wrong."

"Well, fine, then. He can say anything he likes between now and the morning. He's shut off. No phone calls. No visitors. Nothing in, nothing out. Red Donovan wants no loose ends. Tomorrow he'll be in maximum security at Concord, and he'll be somebody else's problem."

"Good."

She nodded and smiled a greeting at a cop passing by. "I'm told you had contact with the young lady from Chelsea who was killed."

Contact. "And . . ."

She shrugged. "And that connects you to three dead bodies. Sarah, Monique and this Rachel."

This Rachel. The anonymity of the words wounded me, but I kept my game face. "So I'm connected to dead bodies. Me, and anyone else from Stonehill Hospital who visits the Lynx Club. What are you getting at?"

"I suppose nothing. I just wish you wouldn't put yourself in compromising positions—not to mention immoral." She stared at me. "What's with Levitsky? Why is he still insisting that all four bodies are tied together?"

"He's a statistician. It violates his scientific view of the world to think that four murders within fifteen miles and a few days of each other could be committed by more than one man."

"Another body in Lynn and I'm through."

"With the campaign?"

"The campaign. My job. My badge. The City Council would destroy me. And rightfully so. But you know what? None of that matters. All that matters is that I got the man who killed Monique. They treated me like a hero at the funeral today. If the killer were still—"

"My gut tells me you don't have to worry about another body. And so does yours. It may be the first time we've agreed on anything."

That seemed to calm her, but she told me to stick around in case things went badly. I promised I would. I thought of mentioning my captivity in the emergency room, but decided to let the episode fade—including Kathy's role in it.

"The funeral's tomorrow, at noon."

"Monique's? I thought you just said—"

"Rachel's," she interrupted. "Over at Korff's Funeral Home in Swampscott." She paused. "I didn't know how close the two of you might have gotten."

I cleared my throat. "Thanks, Emma," I said. "Call me if you need me."

•   •   •

I spent a night of broken sleep, parked beside Kathy's Volvo in the Stonehill Hospital garage. I wanted to be sure she didn't try to enhance Lucas' alibi with a fifth body. Then I drove over to Korff's, a monument of a building lost between three shopping malls.

I parked on the opposite side of the street and watched as cars streamed into the parking lot and mourners in black started toward the huge carved doors. I wondered whether Rachel's uncle was in the crowd. My jaws clenched as I fantasized about finding him and dragging him out to the pavement, taking my time bloodying him on the concrete slabs. But then I closed my eyes, realizing Rachel wouldn't have chased him away. She would have welcomed him to make his peace with her, maybe even with himself.

I sat there a minute, then started the Rover. It was only a few miles from Korff's to Salem Station. I drove the whole way telling myself I was silly to go chasing after the past, but never turning around. When I got inside, I walked back and forth along the platforms, looking for something that would jar my memory. I wandered for at least half an hour before I took a seat on a bench opposite Track 4, the far wall of which was decorated with a mosaic of green and white tiles. Those tiles were familiar. A few people were waiting for the train, but they receded from my mind as I focused on the tracks. A mixture of fear and longing gripped me. I wanted to remember the scene as it was, in every detail. But the mind is sometimes wiser than the heart. Only a single image took shape. I saw my father's face, covered by a day's growth of beard, framed by the rails, looking much more at peace than I had ever remembered it. And then what he intended to be his last words echoed in my mind. *I'm sorry. Please forgive me.*

The sound of a train startled me. I opened my eyes and watched it approach the platform. And still, above all the noise, I heard those words again from my father. I waited until the passengers had boarded and watched the train pull away.

Seventeen

I could have made better time driving 95 north, but I wasn't in any rush, so I took 1A, passing by sleepy communities like Topsfield, Rowley and Georgetown. About halfway to Plum Island, I pulled over, slid under the Rover and yanked out the LoJack box; I didn't need Malloy tracking me on any computer screen.

The sun was setting when I crossed the causeway and reached the main building at Walton's, a two-story wooden structure built on the sand. I parked and headed up the front stairs to the office. No one was there, but I had called to reserve our old cabin, and an envelope taped to the door had my name on it. I ripped it open and found the key to Cottage 6.

The cabin was as I had remembered it—small and rustic, with unfinished pine paneling covering the walls and ceiling. An efficiency kitchen was tucked in an alcove, and a folding screen separated the bed from a sitting area that ended in sliding glass doors onto the beach. I watched the waves pound the sand, the last of their white froth petering out just a half-dozen yards from me. A flock of birds flew in formation overhead. It was a place full of peace, which only made me more aware of my anxiety. I checked my watch. It was 6:25 P.M.

I reached into my jacket pocket for the hypodermic syringe and vials of liquid Haldol and Ativan I had brought with me. I drew up 3 cc of each, the dose I had used as a psychiatry resident to sedate violent patients in the emergency room. I walked over to the bed, knelt down and laid the syringe on the floor under the headboard.

I needed to rest, but I didn't want to risk falling asleep, so I sat down on the couch and turned on the evening news. I was too wound up to follow the stories, but the anchor and correspondents provided enough white noise to keep my mind from turning in on itself.

Not ten minutes later I heard knocking—soft at first, then louder. I clicked off the television and walked to the front door. I took a deep breath and opened it.

Kathy was standing there, clutching her black leather overnight bag.

I stared at her, as if I might see into the madness behind her. Part of me wanted to grab a handful of her hair, drag her inside and make her feel some of the pain she had inflicted on others. On *me*. But I doubted that I could make her feel anything. Her own suffering had deadened her.

"Here I am," she said. She bit her lower lip and looked down at the light pink dress she was wearing. It was a takeoff on a man's shirt, with fake pearls where buttons would be. She had opened it low enough at the neck to expose the gentle sloping of her breasts. "I stopped at Ann Taylor for something new so I could look pretty for you." She shrugged and scuffed a shoe on the ground.

I noticed that the shoes were new, too—black patent leather penny loafers. "You look perfect," I said.

"So I can come in?"

I held out a hand. She took it. I suppose I had expected to sense something chilling in her flesh, but I didn't. Her hand felt warm and familiar, and I marveled at how normal it felt to draw her into the cabin and into my arms. But why be surprised? She was the same woman, after all, who I had made love to hundreds of times. Her perfume still soothed me, and her caresses on my neck made me groan with real pleasure. It was not until we kissed, opening our mouths for one another, that revulsion surged in me. I stepped back.

"Shy, all of a sudden?" she whispered.

My jaw was set. I took one side of her collar in each of my fists and ripped her dress open to the thighs. I looked at her. She was naked and freshly shaved and every bit as magnificent as the first time I had had her.

She smiled and caught her lip in her teeth again. "Be as rough as you want. I deserve it."

I watched as she slipped off her dress and stepped out of her shoes. My anger and excitement, close cousins before, became one thing. I grabbed her shoulders and forced her onto the bed, facedown. She struggled against me only weakly as I whipped off my belt and bound her wrists. I knotted the leather strap around one bedpost. Then I kneeled behind her. Her blond hair was fanned over her back, and the cheeks of her ass quivered slightly. I could hear my pulse in my ears. I pulled her hips up off the mattress and yanked her head back by her hair. I wanted to and I would have rammed myself inside her had I not been restrained by a memory. It was Trevor's loaded question the night we had met at the Lynx Club: *Why does she scream "Daddy!" when I put it in her ass?*

I let go of her and ground the heels of my hands into my eyes.

Kathy flipped onto her back. "What's wrong?" she asked. She spread her legs. "You want me this way?"

"I was thinking of your father."

"You were *what*?"

"Your father. I was thinking how he hurt you."

"My father would never hurt me." She closed her legs. "He loved me."

I sat on the edge of the bed. "I found the note about Blaire. The one you wrote when you saw him visiting her at night."

"Why the fuck are we talking about this? Untie me."

"Tell me how she died."

"You're insane!" She pulled against the leather strap, trying to loosen it.

"Did you see the fire start? I want to know. I need to know."

Her eyes thinned with rage. "You're such a dummy," she said in a child's voice. She pulled harder on the strap, but the knots only tightened. "You don't need to ask where I was when Blairey got punished." Her voice returned to normal. "You already know."

"Punished?"

The child's voice again: "For being a sneak."

I was almost certain Kathy was flipping back and forth between mature and immature parts of her psyche. In psychiatric lingo, she was *dissociating*. "Did you start the fire?" I asked.

"Blaire made me, by taking Daddy," she whined. "I didn't want to use the matches. I tried other stuff first."

"Like?"

"Cutting off my hair . . . down there. Daddy said he didn't like ape girls."

"But that didn't work."

"Did, too." She bit her lower lip and blushed. "For a while. Until the bleeding."

"And then?" I got up and walked to the end of the bed, where Kathy had dropped her black leather overnight bag. I picked it up.

"Then it didn't. So a fire started under Blaire's bed, while she was sleeping."

My eyes filled up. I had to fight to keep my hands steady enough to unzip the bag. Kathy's scrubs were balled up inside. A length of pipe lay between them, the fur handle of my hunting knife protruding from it. I drew out the knife. The blade was caked with dried blood. "What about the others? Like Sarah and Monique."

Kathy's lip curled. "They were cunts," she said. "Humiliating me."

"And the man? Michael?"

"Disgusting." She pulled so hard on the strap that it ripped her skin. For a moment she seemed calm, watching a trickle of blood start down her arm. Then she fought against the leather even more fiercely. The trickle ran faster and thicker. "You missed one, Frank. I mean, as long as you're getting off hearing about what you and Trevor forced me to do. You know who. Rrrr . . ."

"Kathy, don't. Please."

"Rrrr. Rrrrayyyy. Rachel."

I was sweating. My temples ached. I tightened my grip on the knife and walked to the bed.

"Your little whore dancer."

I straddled Kathy's waist. She kicked wildly, to no avail. I pictured plunging the knife under her sternum and severing the aorta. Or, better yet, I could make her watch me take her breasts. I ran the blade lightly under one nipple, imagining the flesh giving way. Then Rachel's words echoed in my mind: *There's no original evil left in the world.*

I stopped and closed my eyes, remembering Rachel teaching me what no professor of psychiatry had ever managed to get through my head—that the brightest light greets those brave enough to open their eyes to darkness.

I got off Kathy and knelt by the side of the bed. I reached under the headboard for the syringe.

She saw me bring it out. "Don't you dare put anything in me," she sputtered.

I reached into my pocket, took out a tourniquet and knotted it above her elbow.

"Get away from me!" she yelled.

I pictured Rachel pleading for her life. I felt light-headed. I uncapped the needle. I tried holding Kathy steady, but she was jerking back and forth, and the needle scraped bloody lines across her arm. I noticed she didn't grimace at all. On my third attempt I managed to bury the tip in her biceps. I put all my weight on her to keep her from dislodging the needle and slowly pushed the plunger down.

She stared at the empty syringe in my hand. "You fucking bastard. I'll *kill* you!" She kicked and twisted some more, but her strength was already being drained by the Haldol and Ativan. She turned her face away from me and started to sob. I got off of her, sat on the edge of the mattress and waited. Her breathing slowed and deepened. Not a minute later she lay perfectly still.

◆   ◆   ◆

I injected Kathy with another dose of Ativan to make sure she stayed deep while I went for the Rover. Without turning on my headlights, I drove onto the beach and parked in front of the sliding glass doors to the cabin. I took a blanket from the back seat and went inside.

Kathy hadn't moved. She was lying on her side, her legs drawn up near her stomach, her hands still tied above her head. She looked as if she were praying. I reached down and touched her furrowed brow. Then I draped the blanket over her and tucked it around her shoulders and knees.

I leaned over, untied the belt binding her wrists to the headboard and picked her up in my arms. Her head fell against my neck. I could feel her warm breath. I carried her out to the car and laid her across the back seat. Then I knotted the belt around her wrists again.

I got in the driver's seat and headed off the beach, across the causeway and onto 1A south, back toward Rowley. It took me only twenty minutes to reach the center of town, but at least as long to snake my way through the back roads, into pristine woods that sheltered the Austin Grate Clinic, a hundred-year-old psychiatric hospital owned by its medical director, Matt Hollander.

Hollander and I had met when I was an intern at Tufts. He was finishing his last year of residency and had volunteered to mentor a new trainee. I was taken with him immediately. He was bald and overweight to the point of being very nearly round. He looked like Humpty Dumpty. Every movement taxed him. But his mind idled at speeds that made mine overheat.

"I'd get in shape, but it'd ruin me," he told me, gobbling fries one day in the hospital cafeteria. "Something in the fat greases the wheels upstairs. I know it's true, even if I can't prove it, which I probably could if I had the time." More fries. "But why go to the trouble? We all know it. That's why Santa's fat, and the Grinch is thin. Reverse it, the legend falls on its face. Of its own weight, if you will." A gulp of vanilla shake. "Think about Churchill versus Hitler. The Buddha. Minnesota *Fats*. Ben Franklin. Pavarotti." Oreos. "I defy you to remember the last time you saw a fat bum. Whereas, your killers, derelicts, thieves—nearly every one of them, thin as a rail."

Since I'd finished residency, Hollander and I had stayed close. While I opened and closed my practice, he used his family fortune to acquire a half-dozen first-rate psychiatric facilities. He'd asked me more than once if I would run the Secure Care Program at Austin Grate, a twenty-five-bed locked unit for dangerous patients. He'd even baited me with one of two majestic homes on the hospital grounds as my private residence. But I'd never taken him up on the offer.

"Not enough grit in Rowley for you," he concluded after one of my refusals. "You like walking mean streets."

"I'd make a lousy monk," I said.

He shook his head. "You make a damned fine monk. You just picked a different church. They're graced to have you."

I hadn't quite believed him then. And I believed him less now.

I cut my headlights as I pulled into his circular drive. I left the car running and walked up the stairs to his door. Before I could drop the bulbous brass knocker, the porch light went on. Then the door swung open.

Hollander filled the doorway. He was wearing a white button-down that could have doubled as a spinnaker. He clapped his hands. "Clevenger!" he bellowed. "A friend at my door!"

I couldn't keep myself in control. My chin quivered, and my eyes filled up.

"What the fuck? What happened to you?" He engulfed me, stroking my head as I wept.

He must have been able to see into the Rover, because moments later he gently backed away and lumbered down the stairs. I watched his shoulders rise and fall with labored breaths as he peered through the passenger window. Then, with uncharacteristic grace, he twirled around and pointed at me. "Get her inside."

He turned off the porch light, and I carried Kathy into the living room and laid her on the couch. Hollander poured himself into a huge, tapestried armchair. "Start," he puffed. "Omit no detail."

I paced the room, hemorrhaging my story. I told him what Kathy had done to Sarah and Monique and Michael. I told him she'd taken Rachel from me. I told him about Blaire and about Kathy's father and about Lucas. And I confessed that I'd been blind to Kathy's pain, powerful enough to spawn murderous rage and envy.

"You loved this dancer. Rachel," he said, his eyes tracking me as I walked back and forth in front of him.

"Yes. I loved her."

He nodded at Kathy. "The panic button on the wall over there will bring a cop to my front door in under two minutes." He paused. "Unless, of course, you were planning to dig a hole in my woods."

I stopped pacing. "If I turn her over to the police, she won't stand a chance. Nobody in this state can remember when an insanity defense worked."

"Nineteen eighty-one. *Commonwealth* v. *Barker.*"

"Sixteen years ago." I shook my head.

"Barker's the one that got away, if you ask the governor. They wanted to electrocute him."

"Kathy didn't *choose* to be a monster, Matt. She wasn't *born* a killer."

"In the eyes of the law, it doesn't much matter."

"I want her treated," I said.

"Is that what your Rachel would have wanted? To see her killer healed?"

"I think so," I said. "I don't think I would have wanted it myself before I met her."

"She must have been extraordinary."

My throat tightened, but I forced my words through it. "I need Kathy admitted to Secure Care."

"No chance. No jury will let it happen."

"We could make it happen. Right now."

"Oh . . . I see. I thought we might be headed that way." He folded his hands over his girth. "You know, Frank, you got real *balls*." He breathed like a bellows. "You're talking about several rather serious offenses. There's kidnapping, from her perspective; harboring a fugitive, from the Commonwealth's. And those are just the appetizers."

I looked at him. His face was set with a mixture of contempt and resolve. I worried he might turn Kathy in himself. "I'm sorry, Matt," I said. "I didn't know where else to go. I had no business asking you to . . . I'll figure something." I walked toward Kathy and knelt to pick her up.

"So we sure as hell couldn't use her real name," he went on.

I stopped and turned to him.

"I don't want the long arm of the law clawing at my rectum. I'd have to admit her under a pseudonym to my private service. Make up a compelling clinical history. No access to mail or phones. No visitors." He paused. "Not even you."

I nodded. Then the gravity of the conspiracy settled on me. "You're right, you know. We could both end up wearing stripes. Obstruction of justice, contempt of—"

"Contempt?" He leaned slightly forward. "No court could guess the depth of my contempt for this miserable civilization. I'd happily devour a judge if I could find a tender one."

I couldn't help smiling.

"Won't anyone miss her? Here today, gone tomorrow?"

"Party line: We broke up. She took off. I've got somebody who can dummy up a one-way airline booking out of the country, canceled ticket and all."

"This Lucas character will make an issue of her."

"Absolutely. He'll probably make her the mainstay of his defense. The state doesn't have a perfect case, anyhow. I wouldn't be surprised if he walks." I looked down and shook my head.

"What?"

"I'm not sure I could bring myself to try to help a man like him."

"That's why it's Christ on the cross, not you. Some people can only go to God to be healed. You and I are human. We have limits. That's why we need God, too."

I was too stressed to dwell on Hollander's comment just then, but it was something that would come back to me again and again over the years, whenever I felt powerless and needed to forgive myself.

Hollander sighed. "You know, if you press that panic button, some crackerjack attorney might be able to get Kathy off on a technicality. Best shysters in the world, right here in Boston. This way, she'll be locked up indefinitely. Years. Maybe decades. Might eventually have to spirit her off to my facility in the Virgin Islands. Or Puerto Rico. Who knows? Not to mention the problem of what to do with her when and if she gets well." He stared at me. "You sure you're comfortable playing judge and jury?"

I thought about that. "Why the hell not?" I said. "They seem to be."

*　　*　　*

We gave Kathy enough sedatives to keep her under until morning. I slept next to her, in a towering four-poster bed in one of Hollander's guest rooms. When I drifted off, I was on my back, rigid, as far to the edge of the mattress as I could get without tumbling off. But when I woke with the sun, just after six, I was on my side spooned against her. For a moment I forgot where we were and what had happened. I reached to touch her hand, and the feel of leather binding her wrists reminded me. And yet, cradled there with her, I felt on balance more sadness than horror, as much pity as rage, and even stole a few deep breaths at the nape of her neck.

She turned her face toward mine. "Where are we?" she asked.

"Someplace safe," I said.

She closed her eyes and put her head back down on the pillow.

"Sorry it couldn't have been safer, sooner," I whispered.

*　　*　　*

Hollander woke me so I could leave before his attendants came for Kathy. We agreed I wouldn't contact him for at least a month.

I drove home, but sat in the driveway, feeling like home was the wrong place to be. I wanted to be closer to memories of Rachel.

I headed to Revere, pulled into the Lynx Club lot and went inside.

The Lynx Club by day is darker than by night. The runway lights are dormant. Music flows from two, not ten, speakers. The girls are a little older and not quite as pretty, and the drinks are stronger.

I walked past two men in suits, wolfing the breakfast special, to a seat in the corner of the room. Elton John's "Candle in the Wind" had started to play, and a brunette in a thong had appeared on stage. When the waitress came by, I ordered a screwdriver, but sipped it just once.

A contorted man in a wheelchair was the only customer on Perverts' Row. He took out his wallet as the dancer began her routine and floated a dollar bill toward her. She lifted her long, slender leg by curved toes, like a ballerina, and pulled aside the cloth triangle over her crotch. Then he sighed and smiled and looked over at me, and I smiled back.

We are, all of us, crippled and twisted. Most of us strive desperately to keep our grotesqueries out of sight and mind. Our suffering is transformed by an alchemy of the soul into addiction, ulcers, strokes, hatred, even war. But a very few people, who we may as well call angels, appear unpredictably in our lives and help us stop running from ourselves. Sitting there at the Lynx Club, raw and alone, I at least knew that I had been lucky enough to find one.

DYING ON PRINCIPLE

Judith Cutler

From the acclaimed author of *Dying Fall* and *Dying to Write*, *Dying on Principle* is Judith Cutler's gritty new Birmingham mystery. It looks as if lecturer Sophie Rivers has fallen on her feet at George Muntz College. Her new employer offers pleasant, even lavish, facilities and state-of-the-art equipment; in fact the College seems to lack only one thing – students. Perhaps all is not as it seems, as Melina, a computer technician, may have been about to explain. For once Sophie doesn't have time to listen – and Melina ends up dead.

There's no shortage of suspects, from the elusive Principal to the dead girl's erratic colleague. Not to mention Richard Fairfax, the property tycoon who enters Sophie's life. There's certainly more to George Muntz College than meets the eye. And Sophie can't resist a mystery . . .

0 7499 3023 3   £5.99

now available in paperback . . .

DANGEROUS GAMES

Jodie Sinclair

Sometimes the past won't stay buried...

There were five of them, Oxford's brightest, an exclusive group until they allowed Jenny into their close-knit circle. Then the games began to get out of hand – and one of them ended up dead. No one ever suspected: no one even knew there had been a crime until the body turned up after six years, stripped of flesh and clues...

Then journalist Kathryn Brooks, in pursuit of a story, begins to dig around in Oxford. She unwittingly stirs up memories which a certain group of people would prefer to forget. And someone will stop at nothing to make sure Kathryn leaves the past undisturbed...

0 7499 3043 8 £5.99

The very best of Piatkus fiction is now available in paperback as well as hardcover. Piatkus paperbacks, where *every* book is special.